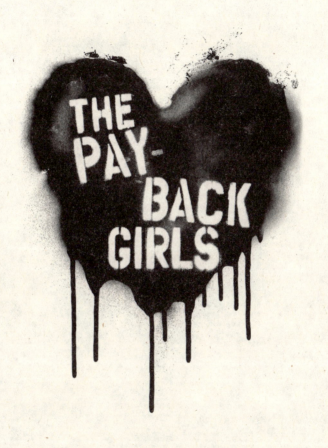

# THE PAYBACK GIRLS

## ALEX TRAVIS

Copyright © 2025 by Alex Travis
Cover and internal design © 2025 by Sourcebooks
Cover design by Aarushi Menon
Cover images © Tomekbudujedomek/Getty Images, Steve Collender/Shutterstock, andrey_l/Shutterstock, Doctor Letters/Shutterstock, maradon 333/Shutterstock, kittipong053/Shutterstock
Internal design by Laura Boren/Sourcebooks
Internal image © Budi yanto/Getty images

Sourcebooks and the colophon are registered trademarks of Sourcebooks.

All rights reserved. No part of this book may be reproduced in any form or by any electronic or mechanical means, including information storage and retrieval systems—except in the case of brief quotations embodied in critical articles or reviews—without permission in writing from its publisher, Sourcebooks.

No part of this book may be used or reproduced in any manner for the purpose of training artificial intelligence technologies or systems.

The characters and events portrayed in this book are fictitious or are used fictitiously. Any similarity to real persons, living or dead, is purely coincidental and not intended by the author.

Published by Sourcebooks Fire, an imprint of Sourcebooks
P.O. Box 4410, Naperville, Illinois 60567-4410
(630) 961-3900
sourcebooks.com

Cataloging-in-Publication Data is on file with the Library of Congress.

Printed and bound in the United States of America.
MA 10 9 8 7 6 5 4 3 2 1

*To all the Black and Brown girls who have been labeled too much or too intense, I see you, and these three girls are for you.*

# 1

**THEY SPRAY-PAINTED MY LOCKER. I'M ALWAYS HERE** forty minutes before the first bell, so they must have snuck in overnight. Or maybe they stayed late after the basketball game, waiting for me to leave. My boyfriend's friends are so certain I'm going to ruin him, and they made sure to let everyone know.

I stab at my cafeteria salad, forcing a bite into my mouth with a fake smile in their direction. The salad tastes like stale tap water and sour tomatoes, and my boyfriend's friends make everything seem more bitter. They're not the first bullies I've had, but this group I'm pretty sure I hate. They're sitting barely ten feet away from Nate and me, glaring at me because I'm the wrong Black girl.

Two freshman girls walk past our bench, whispering to each other. They flutter their eyelashes at Nate, who spares them a small smile.

I elbow Nate. "Don't give them any more ammunition, please."

"I can't ignore everyone who looks at me, Meghan," he replies.

"Everyone is already staring at us. Can you just . . ." I rub my temples.

I spent the entire morning in the front office, demanding to see the security camera footage. But somehow, the cameras didn't capture the vandalism. That's what the assistant principal told me with a completely straight face.

His son, Andy, is on the basketball team with Nate. Andy's a member of the art club, which is the explanation I was given for why his fingers are stained with spray paint.

"They'll come around," Nate says. He rubs my back, tracing circles across my spine with his fingertips.

He's always saying things like that. He even got me a promise ring last week to prove to me that he's serious, now that we've almost hit the three-month mark. It's my birthstone, peridot, and I love it even though it's half a size too small. Not that it matters. I'm not supposed to wear it in public until the season's over, since his parents don't want him dating during playoffs.

"*Black widow.* That's what they think of me. I've been my *absolute nicest* to them for three months, and I'm still a poisonous bitch? How can you defend that?" I reply.

"Give them a little more time. They'll love you as much as I do. Don't overthink it, please. We don't know the spray paint was them," he says.

"You haven't even looked at it."

"I had to run to calculus, and you cleaned it off before second period."

I watch as one of Nate's friends gives the freshmen a thumbs-up. He makes eye contact with me afterward and shrugs. They're really willing to do anything to take me out of the picture.

I had real friends, once upon a time. The kind of friends who steal the YOUNG, GIFTED, AND BLACK pin off of your crush's backpack so you can use it as a talisman as you manifest earning their love. The kind of friends who will let you rant about that teacher you're so certain hates you and stay up all night planning your postgraduation lives together. The kind of friends who show you how to put in a tampon for the first time in the five minutes between classes. I had everything, I thought. But then they turned on me.

The last three months of junior year were completely unbearable. My so-called friends abandoned me after "the incident." So when I had the opportunity to switch schools for senior year, I jumped at the chance, even though it was only two weeks before classes started. I thought that maybe I could make real friends here at Burke High. Instead, two weeks into November, I have vague acquaintances who have never given me a chance.

"Sure. I'm overthinking," I reply.

Overthinking is what I do best. It's either this or the Early Decision results, which are still six weeks away.

"Stressed about Brown?" he asks.

"Always."

I feel a headache coming on, and I don't know if it's because I have three early action applications to finish by tomorrow night or because I'm imagining his friends filling my locker with real black widow spiders.

"That application could not be more perfect, just like you," Nate says. "*Nous êtes très belle.*"

I take a deep breath. We met when he needed a French tutor at the end of summer school. He's never been great at learning languages, and even with me in his corner, he's barely treading water. He just told me that *we* are beautiful and used the wrong verb conjugation.

"Well, if your friends keep pulling this sh—stuff, then I'm going to have to reveal the skeletons in my closet," I say.

I keep my tone light, as if I'm joking. Nate can't keep a secret to save his life, and I can't let anyone see me crack. My humor trends toward the dark side, but Nate doesn't know that yet. I laugh at all his dad jokes, even though not a single one has been funny; I gush over how clever he is. That's what a girlfriend is supposed to do. His last two girlfriends were perfect in other ways, but neither of them is considered particularly nice. If the whispers I've heard in the girls' locker room is any indication, I'm considered much nicer than them, but for some reason, I still can't break in. The worst part of my brain reminds me that we haven't dated as long as he dated Robin or been as publicly over the top as he was with Bria, and his friends loved, or at least respected, them. Every day with him is like walking a tightrope in my head, waiting for him to agree with his friends and push me off.

"The only skeleton in your closet is from Halloween," Nate replies.

"Meg Skellington in a little cheerleading skirt makes your heart race, no?" I ask.

Nate snorts, and my heart flutters up into my neck. Making him laugh always feels like an accomplishment. His laugh when he saw Meg Skellington on my porch, decked out in a Catwoman costume, replays in my head all the time. He thinks I'm funny, and no one's ever seen me that way before.

"I'd rather see *you* in said little cheerleading skirt, but if you need your emotional support skeleton, I'm game," he replies. "Is that really all that's on your mind?"

I'm always thinking about how other people or colleges perceive me. I'm obsessed with looking like the perfect daughter, student, girlfriend. But I know that's not what he wants to hear.

"Well, I'm thinking of you, of course. How we're going to be the most powerful Black couple since Barack and Michelle," I reply. "How you're going to win your game tonight."

He sucks in his cheeks and takes a deep breath. Despite being the first one to say, "I love you," he's sometimes still a little skittish when I mention our future in public. I mean, technically, it's only been a few months, but he told me he knew I was the one from the first moment he saw me at the senior kickoff carnival in August, even before I started tutoring him. We went on our first date a week later, on the second day of school. But even if it's only November, they say when you know, you know. And he'd better know.

"Babe, you know I identify as biracial," he says. "If we're going to keep this going into playoffs, you're going to have to get the talking points right."

I swallow. Here I go, breaching the sacred guidelines of being Nate's girlfriend. I may meet the initial requirements—perfect GPA, Black but not *too* Black, and independently ambitious—but I'm terrible at following his unspoken rules. We have to pretend that racism doesn't exist here because Nate, a local celebrity, thinks that being an activist will alienate his supporters. Whether those supporters are the neighbors who have called the police on his Black father three times in the past year "by accident" or his white maternal grandparents who "haven't seen color" since the invention of HDTV remains unclear to me.

"Of course," I reply. "I'm sorry."

I'm always the one to say sorry. And I usually am sorry. I really do love him, but my heart is torn between butterflies and frustration. When I'm his whole world, it's incredible. When I'm reminded that we're isolated because Nate's friends me for reasons I don't understand, it's horrible. It's the kind of whiplash I thought I was used to after my last relationship, but I'm clearly not.

"No, it's fine. I get it. It's just . . . You know my mom gets offended when you bring it up. Don't want you to slip again at dinner tomorrow night."

I never slip. Anytime I've referenced race in his parents' house, it's been strategic to see where they, and subsequently I, stand. I'm not an idiot. I need to know what I'm getting into. So far, I've learned that his mother and I completely disagree about our local school board elections, whether book banning is a form of discrimination, and if voting is even important. What's important is that *I've* learned these things. Mrs. Walker hasn't.

"Your mom didn't seem too upset. She was *so* happy to share. She told me that she felt I aligned with your family's values better than Rob—your past girlfriends."

Nate's parents haven't actually heard me express a real opinion. Just like I've never heard Nate make a definitive statement on any issue outside of our narrow school environment.

Nate silently concedes, taking another bite of his burger. My mouth waters. I haven't had a burger since his teammates gave me the side-eye at their last cookout.

"I don't want you to come across as some sort of . . . you know . . . Like, you know I'm down with the cause—" he says.

"I'm only trying to prepare you." I have to cut him off before he says something I can't bite my tongue about. "A lot of universities have had racial discussions recently, and as a prominent Black—biracial—athlete and future merit scholar, you're going to be asked to comment, or join the Black Student Union, or something else that your mother might not be the most comfortable with," I say.

He sighs. "I know. But for now, can we put a pin in it? At least until after the game? I've got to focus."

Nothing comes between Nate and basketball—not me, not his mother, and certainly not reality. He really is incredible to watch on the court. His dad taught him to dribble before he learned to walk and before he started traveling so much for work. Nathaniel Walker Sr. is almost never home except when Nate makes the playoffs. I've learned many things about Nate since we started dating, but this is one of two secrets we share. The public nature of Nate's basketball trajectory sometimes makes the sport feel more like a prison than the safe haven it used to be. It's how he's earned love from his father, his friends, the school, but not from me. I would love him no matter what.

"Of course. Do you want to meditate together?" I ask.

He nods, and I take his hands.

We started practicing meditation to help keep him calm before French exams. The first time I showed him my favorite breathing technique, he asked me to be his girlfriend. That was about two weeks after we met. Out of the corner of my eye, I can see Nate's friends staring at us with increasing levels of disdain. They're the obstacles to my success, and I want them gone.

Nate's other girlfriends, the exes, they're different. They're the flashy and exciting Black girls from families who own at least four luxury SUVs and maybe even a private yacht. They're familiar to Nate's friends, whereas my carefully curated Goodwill wardrobe is a little too last-season, and there are nasty rumors that I'm from the "wrong side of the tracks." It's not my fault that Nate spends less time with his friends now that he's dating me. Maybe if they hated me less, he'd be more receptive to hanging out.

As Nate and I work to get our breaths in sync, I think about our biggest moments to center myself. I went from Nate's tutor to his girlfriend in two weeks, and he introduced me to his mother three days after our first date. When he says my name, he gets these crinkles in the corners of his eyes, and his smile flashes so bright it's like a strobe light.

Nate squeezes my hands tighter, and I tap my thumb on the

outside of his hand, trying to bring him back to the rhythm of our breathing.

Someone clears their throat above us. It's Nate's friend Andy, who looks like he wants to throw up.

"Strategy meeting before the pep rally," he tells Nate.

"In a minute. Let me finish up lunch with Meg," Nate replies.

"No can do. It's an emergency."

I force my mouth into the faintest smile.

"It's fine, babe. Team comes first," I say.

"Good girl," Andy replies. Then he leans in so I can smell the onions on his breath. "Jess says your nose contour is a little obvious."

Nate raises his eyebrows. "Instead of gossiping, maybe concentrate on your game, since you've airballed four times in the last two games."

"She just wants to help. Can't have Nate Walker's girl looking a mess at the pep rally, right? Locker room in five."

I imagine a basketball hitting this guy in the face over and over in front of the whole school. He'd be splayed out on the floor, blood pouring out of his nose, maybe even his mouth. His cruel green eyes would be swollen shut with nasty purple bruises that no makeup could cover. Maybe he'd even get a concussion and be benched for the rest of his senior season. His college offers would be revoked, and he'd be forced to stay in town, living like an invalid in his parents' house until he recovered.

"I'm sorry. You know how they are. Their girlfriends are all friends with . . . you know," Nate says.

"The rumors . . . about your past relationships." I have to choose my words carefully. "They don't bother me. And of course I don't believe them. Like, why would you cheat on either of them?"

His face turns serious. "Then why bring them up?"

Technically, he brought them up. He always brings them up, like they sit on the tip of his tongue, at the center of his brain. Where I should be. Where I have the nagging feeling that I'm still not.

"I don't understand why they're all starting up again. Is it because of the big game? Or the pep rally later? It's cruel, don't you think? For people to lie about you, about us?"

God, I sound insecure, and not in the endearing way. My voice is higher than usual, dangerously close to being squeaky. But the thing is, I am insecure. When you put me next to his exes, I stand out, but not for the reasons I want to. Next year, in college, that's where I can reinvent myself hundreds of miles from home instead of just twenty. Or better yet, be myself without getting expelled. But right now? I need to survive, and at Burke High, I need Nate to do that.

"Baby, you know I don't care about them. You're the one for me. Even my mom thinks so. She loves you," Nate says.

Rest assured, Mrs. Walker does not love me. Whatever Nate is hearing, it's all in his head. But I'm not going to tell him that. He can delude himself into thinking his mom likes me as long as it keeps us together. As long as he keeps looking at me like I'm the best thing that's ever happened to him.

"Your friends barely speak to me and *maybe* vandalized my locker. I know they wish I were Robin or Bria. I'm just . . . I'm scared it will be like before, at my old school. I really want to fit in here for real," I say.

"You will. I know you will. The pep rally is your moment. We'll make it yours," he replies.

"Um, all-state basketball star, I think it's *your* moment." I squeeze his hand.

Jess slithers over to us, waving a contour stick in one hand and her iced mocha in the other. The other basketball girlfriends snicker behind their French tips.

"Jess, not now," Nate says. "I'll meet the team in a minute."

"You're always keeping our girl away from us! How can we ever get to know Megs if she's attached to your hip?" Jess asks.

Technically, she could get to know me in the stands of any basketball practice or game, in our mutual study hall, during lunch, or at the weekly postgame parties. But that would be too convenient, too logical.

"I'm sure she'd love to sit with you all at the pep rally next period," Nate says. "Right, sweets?"

I swallow the lump of rage in my throat. "So much."

"Amazing!" Jess does a little dance.

It almost happens in slow motion. She shimmies, and the top of her cup shifts. Her finger nudges the lid so it slips even farther.

I see it coming, but I don't have time to get out of the way. I'm resigned to my fate.

Nate jumps up as the coffee splashes down my white shirt.

Jess's hand flies up to her mouth as if it was an accident. Her eyes twinkle, daring me to react.

"Clumsy!" I say, forcing my voice up an octave. *I wish I could melt the skin off your face and laugh over the ashes of your cheap lash extensions* is what I wish I could scream at her.

Jess's jaw twitches. "Oh my God, I'm *so* sorry."

"I know you are," I reply. "It's okay. I'll go clean up and meet you in the bleachers."

She doesn't even bother to hand me a napkin. She slides back in with the rest of the basketball girlfriends, barely concealing her smile.

Nate hands me one of his gently used napkins. He closes his eyes for a few seconds. "Why don't you wear my jersey? That way you can cover the stain and match the other girlfriends," he says.

According to their Instagrams, Bria never wore his jersey, and even Robin only did it once or twice. Robin couldn't come to most of his games, since their seasons overlapped, and he and Bria were never serious enough to warrant it. This is it. This is my way into the inner circle of popular kids. The circle who will root for me, root for Nate and me. Wearing a star athlete's jersey is the biggest sign of commitment there is. At least, that's what Jess and her friends have loudly whispered behind my back during homeroom.

He digs the jersey out of his backpack. It smells a little stale, like sweat has seeped into the fabric and settled there for good. It's a symbol, though, of his feelings for me, of my eventual acceptance here.

This won't be like before. This is real. We're real. I know it now.

"See you in an hour," Nate says, planting a kiss on my lips. "Cheer super loud for me, okay?"

"Always," I reply. "I've got you."

"Nothing's going to ruin this for us. We are about to become the 'it' couple of the fall season," Nate says.

I've never enjoyed pep rallies, but I'm looking forward to this one. Cheering on my boyfriend from the sidelines, wearing his jersey. I know they'll all be seething. I'm about make them all realize I'm not going away.

**ROBIN ELLISON HAS NEVER MISSED A SHOT. BE IT HER** swing or her stance, when she makes contact with a ball, it is game over. This is perfect for her role as star forward of the Burke High School field hockey team. It is decidedly less perfect when it happens before a pep rally and the ball is the student government president, Bria Kelly's, head.

Sitting in the stands, wearing Nate's jersey, I am sick to my stomach. The cold metal bleacher is digging into my butt, even on this unseasonably warm November day, and I'm catching whispers of Nate's two exes getting into a fight in the tunnel leading to the basketball court. Could it really be true though?

Both Robin and Bria are incredibly image conscious. Bria, especially, has a knack for making sure things are seen the way she wants them to be. If Robin is the queen, then Bria is the kingmaker and destroyer of the crown, wrapped in a five-foot-two package of more ice than fire. Her extra-long acrylics are sharpened into stilettos. I fully believe she'd slit a throat, probably mine, given how she looks at me in calculus.

Someone in the row in front of me cheers as Robin jogs out onto the court, holding her field hockey stick up in the air. The cheerleaders follow her out, barely waving their pom-poms. They're all trying to move as far to Robin's left as possible. Oh my God, did they actually see the fight?

"I hear he rotates, one girl each night. Each has their own special place, so they never overlap," someone says. "Nate Walker's hoe-tation, except none of them know about the others. Until now."

The band's tuba player comes in too early on the "Stars and Stripes" march, and the noise booms out of the tunnel before the first drummer can even make it out onto the court. It almost drowns out the sound of a walkie-talkie screeching with feedback. The band pauses.

"Keep them on the court, I'm on the way with security," a voice echoes from the tunnel. Someone, I assume the band teacher, has their walkie way too close to their microphone.

Robin grits her teeth, leaning forward like she's going to lunge back into the tunnel. Bria holds up her hands as she exits the tunnel behind the band like she's trying to negotiate with a raging bull. Unfortunately for her, she *is* wearing red, and I'm almost certain red is all Robin sees. Every time Robin moves, the microphone pinned to her lapel rustles.

From what I understand, Bria, as president, is supposed to present Robin with an award, since the field hockey team raised the most money for the annual town charity auction. Robin even auctioned off one of her field hockey sticks from her state win, scoring ten thousand dollars for the local food bank.

"Robin, be serious," Bria says. "We're in *public* now."

"Since when have you ever cared about that, B?" Robin seethes.

The vice principal sprints through the gym doors, nearly tripping over the foot of the field hockey cocaptain as he steps onto the other side of the court. He's followed by the school resource officer, who's gripping his utility belt. Oh shit, did Robin *actually* hit Bria in the tunnel?

I squint, trying to spot Nate in the crowd of basketball players forming around the vice principal. A few guys are still behind the banner planted in the middle of the court. Did Nate see what happened? Is he going to break them up before it happens again? Is anyone going to break up this fight?

"Ms. Ellison, that's enough!" the vice principal shouts, charging to the center of the court.

Robin's field hockey teammates, who are standing just out of the line of fire, have an IMAX-level view of the conflict. None of them look particularly surprised. So either Robin has a history of using her field hockey stick for alternative purposes, or they knew something was going on with Bria.

"I didn't do anything! Ask *her* what happened," Robin says, pointing at Bria.

"Didn't he cheat on Robin with Bria? What is this, last year?" someone in the row above me says.

I recognize the voice. It's Jess. She and the rest of the basketball girlfriends didn't save me a seat, but of course they want me to overhear their commentary.

"Only actual couples can cochair the charity dinner. So shouldn't it be Meg? Or is she too new?" another girl asks.

"Well, *I* heard that Nate and Robin never even broke up," Jess says. "So he's cheating with Bria *and* the other one."

I accidentally lock eyes with Robin, who is glaring into the crowd as if she's looking for someone. But who?

"I don't *care* who her parents are. Are you going to discipline her or not?" Bria snaps as the vice principal freezes a few feet shy of Robin.

Robin is still staring at me. She clocks Nate's jersey almost immediately, and her mouth tightens. Robin never misses. And now she's swinging at me too.

Bria's gaze follows Robin's. She rolls her eyes and gives me the finger.

I feel my eyes filling with tears. I force them back.

Robin's face scrunches in fury, and she pulls back her stick while everyone gasps in unison.

The vice principal takes a step away from her, gesturing to the school resource officer.

Robin swings as if she's going to hit Bria's perfectly symmetrical and meticulously highlighted face. She drives her stick into a patch of weeds, sending dandelions flying inches away.

Robin smirks as Bria flinches.

The school resource officer reaches toward Robin.

I imagine this is what spectators felt like in the Colosseum. It's exhilarating and horrible. I've never liked Bria, but she looks truly terrified, like she really thought Robin was going to hit her. Potentially for the second time today.

"Touch me, and my family will sue the school," Robin says to the officer.

Her father is a state senator, and her mother is one of the most well-respected civil rights lawyers in the country. I fully believe she'd sue and win, particularly given that relations between the Black students and this particular SRO are already tense.

The SRO pulls his hand back and shrugs at the vice principal. This vice principal has barely been on the job for three weeks, and he's already lost control of the situation. Our previous one would have dragged Robin and Bria to his office before they even made it onto the court.

The assistant boys' basketball coach, Coach McGregor, nods at the vice principal and grabs Robin around the waist while one of the football coaches grabs Robin's wrist. One of her teammates pries the field hockey stick out of her hand.

Noah Walker, photographer for the school newspaper, is intently taking pictures from the sidelines. I can only imagine what that headline will be on Monday.

Noah is only eighteen months younger than us, but everyone knows him as Nate Walker's baby brother. He and I have made small talk, but he's so painfully shy that it's apparent he'd rather be anywhere his brother isn't. Nate draws attention. But Noah seems to be holding his own up front.

"Are you kidding me, Noah?" Robin says, loud enough that her voice floats into the stands. "Maybe if the coaches had their eyes checked, they would have seen what actually happened before lying on the walkies." She tries to wiggle out of the coaches' grasp.

Noah shrugs and takes a few steps back, shielding the lens of his camera, as if she can reach him while being restrained.

I look back to the banner. Nate is peeking around the side, watching the show.

Bria catches him, and she covers the mic pinned to her lapel while she says something.

Robin's face falls. Coach McGregor drops her, and Robin staggers forward on the linoleum, trying to get her footing. She holds up her empty hands, as if that means she's less likely to lunge again.

"Ms. Ellison, you'd better start walking to my office before someone carries you there," the vice principal yells.

His threats ring hollow, now that he's let this go on for what feels like forty-five minutes. I check my watch. It's barely been five.

"This isn't how it was supposed to go. And why would you drag Meghan into it?" Robin asks, pointing at Nate.

I hear my name echo, like a thousand Robins are repeating "Meghan." My ears begin ringing. If I cry here, the crowd might enjoy it. If I were just a spectator, I might find it fun too. It really is incredible drama when you're not at the center of it.

Nate reaches out and covers her microphone. He says something that the rest of us can't hear.

Bria marches over to the banner, leaning into her handheld

microphone. "And I'll never forgive you. You could die, and I wouldn't give a flying f—"

The field hockey coach blows her whistle, drowning out the rest of Bria's sentiment. Funny how they react faster to foul language than a fight.

"Over a *guy*?" the field hockey coach says to Robin. "Seriously?" She motions for Robin and Bria to follow her.

The rest of the field hockey team glares at Robin. If she gets suspended, their chance of winning the playoffs will be in jeopardy.

"*I'm* the victim here," Bria says into her mic as they walk. "I should be allowed to give my speech, then decide whether I plan to press charges for what happened in the tunnel."

Robin's head turns so that she's facing Bria. "For *what*? I *didn't fucking hit you*."

"You just told him it wasn't supposed to be like this. So you knew. You knew he was screwing me over again," Bria replies. "So don't underestimate what I *would* do."

?? I text Nate. Tell me they're lying.

The way my stomach turns, I know they aren't. He cheated. He cheated on all of us.

"See, I told you they were violent," I hear someone say.

"Take the girl out of the hood, but you can't take the hood out of the girl," Jess adds, loudly enough for everyone in the stands to hear.

No one in a ten-mile radius of this school has even driven past what could be considered the hood. Assume, assume, assume. That's all anyone does about any of us Black girls. Even I'm guilty of it. I have all sorts of assumptions about Robin and Bria that I'd never dare say to their faces.

Robin and Bria are whispering to each other as the field hockey coaches finally lead them into the building. Robin gestures to Nate back on the court and me in the stands. It's then that I realize my hands are still frozen, shielding my face from what's happening, not the sun. And now the entire senior class is staring at me.

I fix my face. My hands drop to my sides, and I smile out at the crowd. Time to practice large-scale diplomacy in a war zone. I'm covered in glitter that will take two hours to scrub off; I can't possibly embarrass myself further.

"Brutal," the girl next to me says.

"Hmm?"

"You really didn't know that you were one of many?" she asks.

Nate finally walks out, his eyes trained on his shoes. He doesn't look at any of us, not even Robin and Bria being led away. The vice principal follows them. He shakes his head when the basketball coach whispers something to him, glancing toward Nate. My heartbeat thuds up into my throat. Is he really going to pretend that none of us exist? This is just business as usual, apparently.

"Whatever Nate has done in his past isn't relevant to our relationship now," I reply. Classic politician's wife response. I'm not looking the other way; I'm just focused on the road ahead. Hopefully it's not paved with the blood of the most popular girls in school.

Nate stands at the podium, staring down at what I assume is his speech. The band half-heartedly starts playing the national anthem.

Coach McGregor slides over to Nate and says something into his ear.

Nate shakes his head and points to the podium, before remembering to put his hand over his heart. The hand that's holding his brand-new iPhone.

The speech is on his phone. The phone he could have used to text me back.

"You're lucky you aren't the one who got clocked," the girl replies.

I swallow hard. Today is a test of how nice I can really be. At least outwardly. Inwardly, I would *almost* sacrifice my chance at a full merit scholarship to roundhouse-kick out this girl's teeth.

I'll give Nate one chance to explain. He has to have a side of the story. A reason he watched two girls fight over him in front of the entire school, never intervened, and now won't make eye contact with his girlfriend even though I'm easy to spot, up front and wearing his jersey. He could have texted me back. And if he's saying nothing, after telling me I was his everything, then I have been completely wrong about him.

"I really appreciate your concern," I tell the girl next to me. "Whatever's going on up there has nothing to do with me. I'm always rooting for other girls, and I'm sure Robin will come out of this unscathed. She's an absolute queen."

"And Bria?" she asks.

"She loves a scarlet letter," I reply. "And it looks like she's wearing it proudly."

My phone buzzes. It's a reminder, not Nate. I have a yearbook committee party after school. The committee always gathers at the editor's house after a pep rally with boxed wine, cheap liquor, and the worst yearbook photos so far. I've been the designated driver since I joined, and there is sure to be increased police presence at the school and in the surrounding neighborhoods because of the home game, especially since there's been an altercation.

Nate can clean up his own mess. I've got to get out of here.

I scoop up my eco-conscious tote. I'm going to say something much, much worse if I sit here any longer with my sister wives glaring at me on their way out of the gym.

I slide off Nate's jersey and drop it in the nearest trash can. Only one of us is allowed to be a heartbreaker, and I won't let it be him.

# 3

**WALKING INTO THE YEARBOOK COMMITTEE PARTY, I** know I've made a colossal mistake. I don't have friends. I have people who tolerate me and my fake sunny disposition because they want to be close to my boyfriend. Sorry, *our* boyfriend. I can't believe I have to get used to that.

I'm a sideshow attraction, and everyone wants to know what I knew. Did Nate tell me about Robin and Bria? What was the timeline? Are we still together? Is it a polyamory situation? Am I going to murder them all with my AP European History textbook?

The yearbook editor, Lily, slides over to me, her wine sloshing precariously in her hand. She pushes a sheet of paper over to me, barely containing her smile.

"Anything you want to add?" she asks.

She's printed a proposed yearbook page dedicated to Nate. It's supposed to be a tribute to his success as an All-American athlete, only the second in Burke's history. That's what we all agreed on last week with our faculty and parent liaisons. Except, instead of charting his basketball career, it's a collage of photos. The first two rows are Instagram-perfect photos of Nate and Robin. Nate and Robin at homecoming three years in a row. Nate and Robin kissing after he won state. Nate and Robin kissing after *she* won state. Nate and Robin both holding trophies. Nate and Robin, Nate and Robin.

The next two rows are either social media or faux yearbook paparazzi photos of Nate and Bria. Nate and Bria canoodling in the hallway. A selfie of Bria from Instagram where you can see Nate's state championship ring on her finger. Nate holding a *Bria for Pres!* poster. Nate and Bria wearing matching *A Vote for Bria Is a Vote for Feminism* T-shirts.

Then, finally, there's me. I've been relegated to a corner of the page, a single photo. It's of Nate and me at last week's basketball game. I'm hugging him from behind, and he's looking off at something—or someone—else. Can I disappear now?

"I think it's great," I say. "Always a good idea to play into the idea of accomplished girls fighting over some dude. Makes you look *so* progressive to reduce all of us to our connections to Nate."

I've heard plenty of rumors about Nate having unfinished business with Robin and Bria. People even love to throw out that they saw Nate in a hidden corner of the school with a girl who clearly wasn't me. But there's never been any proof. There were just rumors. But something has changed. It's only been an hour since the pep rally, so unless Lily had a glue stick and a murder board of pictures of us with Nate in her backpack, the three of us were truly the last to know. But how? And why does this girl who I've barely been able to get face time with since joining the yearbook now have a vendetta against me?

"Big change from the girl who called Bria Kelly a whore, what, an hour ago?" Lily says.

That's a harsh interpretation. I wasn't direct about it, but perhaps I was a little rude in my wording. And anyway, maybe I deserve a bit of slack. I'm being held to some invisible standard that clearly doesn't apply all around.

"I did no such thing!"

Lily clears her throat and throws her voice up half an octave. "'She loves a scarlet letter. And it looks like she's wearing it proudly.'"

Well. I did say that. But I didn't mean it in a derogatory way. Okay, I did. But I didn't think anyone else had actually read our AP Lit assignment. Do I really have to be defined by my meanest moment? I'm sure nothing I've ever said about Bria compares to what she's said about me.

"I respect both Robin and Bria. And I'm sorry this all had to get so messy for them."

"I thought Bria was the politician," she replies.

I want to roll my eyes, but I know it'd be rude, especially since I want to at least be a featured section editor in this year's book.

"We're all a little more complicated than you'd think," I say. "Maybe I'll tell you more about it sometime."

I step away as her drink starts to spill over the side of her cup and onto the kitchen floor. She slides a bit in the puddle it creates before grabbing on to the kitchen island. Apparently, I wasn't invited to the pregame. Not that I've ever partaken in pregames at Burke. When you're on scholarship, you aren't afforded the same opportunities to mess up. And today is already the biggest possible screwup.

The student government yearbook liaison bumps into my shoulder in what feels like an intentional shove. He leans into my ear, and I feel flecks of his spit hit my cheek.

"Someone left an envelope in the yearbook office with the pictures and a note," he whispers. "What Lily did really sucked."

Before I can ask him who, he disappears back into the crowd.

And he doesn't say anything to anyone else. He didn't speak up when Lily made the comment. No one did. They silently let me take it. Like Nate with my locker.

It's been a long time since I've felt this kind of anger rising in my stomach.

My phone buzzes and I glance down. A text from Nate. Took him long enough. It's been two whole hours since Robin and Bria reenacted a *Housewives* episode in front of the entire school. At least they have friends to check on them. I just have—had—Nate.

I open the text, and it's three heart emojis. Two hours later. He hasn't said anything to me for two hours except this. If he wants me to believe that he didn't cheat, this isn't really selling the story. It's way too casual for the situation. This is a guy who's gotten away with it before, and he thinks I'm just going to look away. Or I'll forgive him, the way Robin must have last year.

Did he send anything to them? An apology? Another heart emoji? Are theirs red like mine? I don't know if they have special colors. Or couples' songs. Or special places.

Another text pops up. Je t'aime bien. He likes me. Like I'm a crush and not his jilted girlfriend. He likes me, but I love him. I love him, and right now, I don't particularly like him.

Does he even know what he's saying? Has he been paying attention during our tutoring sessions? I'm so certain that I covered the difference between *like* and *love*.

And I wore his freaking jersey. The jersey that I slid off and dropped in the nearest trash can on my way out of the stands.

The moment I was supposed to have was ruined. Nate ruined everything.

Another text buzzes on my phone, this time from an unlisted number. I'm outside. Let's talk.

I blink again before trying to peek out of the nearest window. Whoever it is doesn't want to be seen.

I stuff the phone into my purse and shuffle outside with my head down. Everyone is still looking at me, whispering about me. Laughing at me. I fold my arms across my chest, trying to pretend it doesn't register. They all thought I was lucky to be with him anyway. Lucky to be accepted as the new girl. Lucky to land someone they didn't think I deserved. Every senior has to complete a community service or charity obligation to graduate. They acted like I was Nate's.

When I close the door behind me, I hear a throat clear from behind the nearest bush. I look to see if there's anyone else around in case this is some kind of setup. If we're going to have a *Carrie* situation, I'd rather no one watch.

Robin Ellison is crouched behind the bush, her face still puffy from crying. She hasn't changed out of her uniform, which is now wrinkled and riding up in the back, revealing the firmest leg muscles I've ever seen. Her knees are caked with dirt from the yard.

"I took three years of martial arts," I warn. "In case you're planning anything."

"Do you really think I'd hit you? What do you think this is, a reality show?"

I mean, she did maybe *literally* hit the other girl involved, so it's not far-fetched. Though she and Bria have a longer history than she and I do.

"At this point, it might be the best outcome for all of us. If this was faked. You know, to keep everyone relevant for the rest of the season?" I say.

To Robin Ellison, I'm a lost puppy, kicked when she's down. I can see it in her eyes. She thinks she knows something I don't.

"Nate never broke up with me. We've been together for the past three years," Robin says.

"No," I reply. "He's been with me for three months."

"You were supposed to be a decoy."

"Excuse me?"

A decoy for *what*? We've gone out to dinner, breakfast, the movies. We've been seen all over town. I've been getting dirty looks from Robin's best friends and teammates for weeks. Someone scratched *whore* onto my locker. And Queen Robin let all that happen when she knew the entire time? She let Nate use me for months?

Anger bubbles in my chest and begins to heat up my neck. Was she responsible for the locker too? And the pictures for the yearbook?

"When everything happened with Bria, my reputation tanked. Nate insisted nothing had happened and that they were just friends. But the rumor mill said otherwise, and I looked like a dumbass. So we pretended to break up, and he found someone new to take the heat off of me while we're getting media attention before college," she says.

"That makes no sense."

"You're new. You're cute, inoffensive. A good public face for Nate's redemption, before I very kindly forgave him publicly and we got back together. You were supposed to be in on it, and hopefully it would help you find your Nate."

Oh, how benevolent of her. She didn't want Nate to use me; she wanted us to use each other on her behalf. Screw this.

"Well, apparently I found yours," I reply. "Let me guess, you had parameters about how far he could go with me?"

Her mouth tightens, and I know I've hit the right nerve. Whatever agreement they had, unless Robin is more progressive than I think she is, it was broken.

"So, I'm just really stupid. Right? That's what you think?" Robin asks.

"Why do you care what I think? You were perfectly content to let me take the heat off you. Your friends have spread rumor after rumor about what kind of girl I am to steal Nate from you. So yeah, you probably are stupid. We both are for believing in him. And I am for thinking you were so much cooler and prettier than me," I reply.

Robin smiles for a moment before seeming to remember why she's here.

"I shouldn't be surprised. You're everything someone could want. Every time he talked about you, I was like, *Damn, how could he* not *fall for her?*" she says. "He was supposed to break up with you so I could cochair the charity dinner and we could stage our public reunion."

Where do I fit in here? And how much do Nate's friends know? Has this all been a game, a sadistic extracurricular for the popular kids at Burke? If I'm just the picture in the corner, can I please fade further into the background until graduation?

"So why are you here? Besides to tell me I've been a pawn in whatever weird chess game you two have been using to keep the spark alive?" I ask.

Robin chuckles softly. "I always knew you couldn't be as sweet as you seemed. Which is actually why I'm here."

I've already been the popular girl who gets completely humiliated before. I just didn't have the same options as Robin. Her parents can donate a new library or field house, and the administration will conveniently forget that she basically committed assault.

It isn't that easy for me. And now, here I am, being used again in someone else's story. I won't be.

"How long was he supposed to use me for?" I ask.

Robin reaches out to touch my shoulder, and I jerk back out of her grasp. Her nails are painted the Burke colors. Green and gold. Perfect for all these shallow, power-hungry future venture capitalists.

"It was supposed to end three days ago," she tells me. "And he didn't do it. Then I found out about him and Bria, and I knew that he was using me too. He was using all of us."

"Yet you were willing to swing at Bria. And let me get played. Girl power?" I set my jaw.

"I absolutely screwed up, but I barely grazed her in the tunnel. I want to make it right with both of you. We're all victims here. So let's take back the narrative?"

I assume she thinks I'll be easier to crack than Bria, who is probably entertaining a social media war against both the basketball and field hockey teams.

"How?"

"I want to take Nate down. Get revenge for how he treats girls. For how he treated all three of us. And I want you to help me."

I roll my eyes. "And what's the plan? He's untouchable. Also, why should I even trust you?"

This whole scandal could torpedo our senior years, but it will never impact Nate. He gets woke points for dating the only three Black girls in the grade, even though he's half Black himself, and he has guaranteed Ivy League admission for maintaining a 3.5 GPA and a thirty-point average per game so far this basketball season. Even though I wrote his essay. That's great ammo, but I can't use it yet. Nate knows exactly what happened at my last school, and if I fire early, so will he. Mutually assured reputation destruction, but only one of us will actually get our heart broken in the process.

"What do I have to lose at this point?" Robin asks. "They're seriously considering suspending me over Bria, even though my parents basically fund the athletic department, and half the school would have done the same thing. Do you think Princeton typically admits perceived thugs?"

I mean, it's Jersey, but who knows? A Black girl with sister locs threatening another Black girl with a field hockey stick probably isn't the image the Ivy League is going for. Plus, getting suspended right before the game against our biggest rivals? The entire team would fully turn on her too. It already seemed like they were ready for it.

"I'm listening. What are you thinking?" I ask.

"Well, you're critical to the plan. Are you in?"

"Before having the plan? Knowing you and Bria? Hell no."

"Well, Bria said no, but she'll come around. So you just have to trust me," she says.

Trust her? Why on earth would I ever trust this girl? She's the architect of my heartbreak.

"Why would you trust me?" I ask.

"Because I understand my role with you and how hurt you must be hearing all of this. Bria and I . . . there's history there, and I hold her to a different standard. At least I did when I thought we could be friends. But she's incapable of being a girls' girl. Since there are only three of us Black girls, she sees us as competition instead of allies. It's just you and me."

I pause. "So how am I integral to this plan of yours?"

"I need you to keep dating Nate."

I throw my hands in the air. *Is she kidding? How can I even stomach being in the same room as him after this?*

"Absolutely not."

"Think of it as doing the same thing to him that he did to you. Make him feel safe, like you've forgiven him, while we figure out how to ruin his life. I know he crushes Adderall into his protein shakes, which is technically performance-enhancing at a small dose. What if we added a little extra? Enough to make him play badly and maybe get drug tested?" she suggests.

"You want a Black guy to get in trouble for drugs? Are you out of your mind?"

Plus, we don't know what other meds Nate is on. Changing his Adderall dosage could cause blood pressure increases, tachycardia, and who knows what else depending on what else he takes. Don't ask me how I know.

"*Actually*, he's biracial, don't you know?" she says, deadpan.

A laugh escapes before I can pull it back. I guess he's used that line on all of us. I wonder how they reacted.

Robin sighs and pulls a small notebook out of her bra. As she's flipping through, I catch a combination of field hockey plays and random facts. A complicated quadrangle formation is drawn alongside *NW: no celery in green smoothie*.

"We could steal his clothes from the locker room so he has to roam the halls to find them," she says.

"Yeah, I'm guessing we've both seen what that would look

like, and it's not going to have the negative impact you want. Do you seriously have a notebook of Nate facts? That's... obsessive."

"It's for general ideas," she replies. "We could try and trip him outside the gym, make it look like an accident, so he can't play the rest of the season?"

I sigh. These ideas couldn't be worse. If we really want to get a little revenge, we have to keep it aboveboard. No one can know we're involved. If I've learned anything in the last year, it's to put distance between yourself and the guy you want revenge on.

"He has to maintain a three point five to play. His French grade depends on his next two papers. He asks me... Sometimes I help. A lot. So, if I deliberately *skew* that help, he will drop below the threshold," I reply. "How's that?"

Robin claps her hands together. "A fantastic start! See? We make a good team."

"Yeah, this is really feeling like an independent project right now," I tell her.

Am I really going to tank Nate's French grade as revenge? Work with Robin, the girl who set me up? Robin is also somehow bringing out the real me. At least, I think this is the real me. Someone who's a little bitter and very hurt. Someone who has now lost two people she loved over things she still can't wrap her head around.

Plus, no one can ever really take Nate down. He'll somehow eke out the right grade to pass, either through actually being decent at French or backdoor negotiations between Madame and his coach. At least this way he'll feel a twinge of the betrayal I do right now. Nate Walker can't be tamed, and his ascent can never be stopped. Not while he's still breathing.

"Woman up," Robin says. "We've got this."

"I'm fine," I reply. "I'll handle my part."

"Can I give you some advice?" She doesn't wait for my answer. "Don't let them see you sweat. Stop being the designated driver for people awaiting your downfall. Take a couple of shots and pick up your car in the morning."

The old Meghan would have loved to do that. But private school Meghan? She can't.

"I'll think about it," I say. "I'd better go back inside. In case people think I couldn't stand it in there."

"We shouldn't have to," Robin says. "We shouldn't have to stand it in any of their spaces. We should be welcome without a guy like Nate. For being us."

"Yeah, well, I'm going to take the Baldwin route and flee to Paris as soon as I can."

"Baldwin came back," she points out. "Maybe you will too."

Robin disappears back into the darkness, and I feel a twinge in my chest. Of course she's the one he really loves.

Maybe she was right. A couple of shots would do me good. The stronger, the better.

I push past two sophomores lingering by the front door smoking cigarettes. I glare at them. "You know those give you and your close contacts cancer, right?"

They roll their eyes, and one of them blows a puff of smoke into my face. I snatch the cup out of her hand and down it in a single gulp. I'm relatively sure this is the sting of cheap vodka shooting down my throat, which means I might regret this in the morning. I burst into the foyer and march over to the liquor table.

Tequila shots? Why not. Truly, what's the worst that could happen? Is that cognac? Rich kids really are a different breed, but it goes down a little smoother.

The last thing I truly remember is texting Nate.

> Baby, you really hurt me. Can we meet up? I have some things I need to get off my chest.

He responds almost instantly. Picking up Noah from Bulletin meeting. Meet at our bench?

Noah's a few months away from getting his license. Nate picks him up most nights and ends up waiting outside while Noah locks up the office. Lately, I've been joining him, mostly to make googly eyes at him while he half completes his verb conjugation worksheets.

> Our bench is perfect. Promise I won't bring my boxing gloves.
> Please. We both know you'd bring your heaviest encyclopedia if you really wanted to do me in.

I snort. That would be the perfect cliché. Faux sweetheart bookworm uses her favorite tome as a murder weapon. Eh. Not punchy enough to make headlines.

My body's axis feels tilted, and the party has a light fuzz surrounding it. Someone hands me another drink and I take it.

Screw being the designated driver. I don't want to remember a single detail of tonight.

**I WAKE UP THE NEXT MORNING TUCKED INTO A BED THAT** isn't mine. As my eyes adjust, my first thought goes to Nate. Did I seriously end up back here with him? After everything I told myself yesterday?

I'm disgusted with myself. Really, I've got to figure out some self-respect. I push the covers off of me. I freeze. Nate's bed wouldn't be draped in kente cloth.

Oh my God, who did I sleep with? I roll over, and my face smacks into something hard. I lean back, holding my nose, which is pulsating.

"Good morning to you too," Robin says, sitting up.

The hard thing I rolled into just now was her back muscles. I'm in Robin's bed. With Robin. How much did I drink? I have a vague memory of the two of us agreeing to take Nate down and making plans via text? No, it was DMs. Or handwritten notes? Did we even make plans?

My head throbs, and I have a killer case of dry mouth. I don't actually know if it's because of the hangover or because I just remembered that the girl I'm in bed with "grazed" Bria Kelly yesterday. Could be worse, I suppose. At least I'm not nauseated.

Robin hands me her water bottle and an aspirin. The trash can is already by my side of the bed. Robin is taking better care of me this morning than anyone ever has before.

"Did we . . . ?" I ask.

"You drank too much and called me from the school after meeting up with Nate. I couldn't figure out your address, so I brought you back here. Your mom called you like forty-five times, but I told her that we were working on college apps and having a sleepover. I'm your new best friend that you've never mentioned, by the way."

I feel a rush of emotion I can't quite place.

"Ugh. Thank you. I owe you one."

"We're even. Rumor has it you gave Nate quite the tongue-lashing in the courtyard." She hands me my phone, which is overflowing with texts from people I don't remember giving my number to. The entire yearbook committee, several members of the theater department, and the French club?

"Well, apparently I'm the most popular girl in school." I open the first text.

The texts give me a vague idea of what I allegedly said to Nate. But not one of these texts is from him.

"People love a spectacle," she says.

"Have you—"

"No, I haven't heard from him either. You're the only one he texted last night . At least, between the two of us," she replies.

"Well, I messed that up too. So much for our plan," I say.

Did you seriously insult his mother? Savage.

You called his hairline uneven?? Harsh but true.

Okay good girl, you're actually a badass.

You're a huge bitch, why would you say that to him?

Racist, antiwhite, jealous, bitter, ugly slut.

Robin, who has been reading over my shoulder, snatches my phone and slips it in her bedside table.

"They're full of shit," she says. "You don't need to read any of those."

"I can take it."

"But you shouldn't have to. What Nate did to you isn't okay. What I did to you isn't okay, and I am so sorry I dragged you into this," she says.

She sounds so genuine that it makes me pause. Pause being angry with her, pause being sad about Nate, pause being embarrassed about all of it. I can't remember the last time someone apologized to me.

"I smell like a distillery. I should go home and shower," I say.

"There are clean towels in the bathroom, and you can borrow some of my clothes. I'll get you a toothbrush too."

"Do your parents know I'm here?"

"Oh, they're in another state. Not that they'd care anyway. I have girls over all the time." She adds, "They're not big micromanagers."

Lucky. In addition to needing a scholarship, I'm also supposed to set a perfect example for my siblings. Especially after last year.

"Thanks for letting me stay over," I say.

"Anytime. We're in this together, right?"

"Together. Yeah."

Robin takes my hand for a second and nods.

It's the simplest gesture, but it means so much. I don't know why she's being so nice to me. She's the one person from this school I don't hate right now.

Robin's bathroom is the size of an entire floor of my house. She has a beauty supply store's worth of hair products, which explains how hers is always impeccable. Her caps and wraps are hung around the room, each with its own place in the ecosystem. Well, at least if I want what she has, it's warranted this time. She has enough conditioning products to keep my hair looking flawless for thirty years.

The water pressure in her shower is heaven, though it feels like I have some scratches on my back, and all of her soaps have names like Bergamot Lime and Desert Rose. Even the tile looks like it was flown in from a remote village in Greece. Her bath mat is cork, and I just know it's from a trip to Portugal.

Her towel feels like I'm being wrapped in a cloud made of only the finest plush. I think I want to live here.

Robin has left a pair of underwear and an evergreen tracksuit folded on one of the sinks for me. It fits me almost perfectly.

Green is my favorite color.

When I step back into her bedroom, Robin is wearing a red crop top and baggy jeans. God, I'm obsessed with how effortlessly cool she is. Gone are the puffy eyes from yesterday. She looks like she's never even heard the name Nate Walker, and for a second I'm right there with her.

Meanwhile, my silk press is in disarray, even though Robin mercifully must have tried to wrap my hair last night. I did the best I could without using too many of her hair products, but strands are still poking out of my ponytail and into my face.

"I might have to let you keep that tracksuit," Robin says. "Looks better on you than me."

"Don't lie to me. Again," I reply.

She rolls her eyes, and I find myself smiling back at her. She reaches out to tuck a rogue strand of hair behind my ear.

I hold my breath, but her hand stops before she can touch me.

Someone is ringing her doorbell quite insistently, over and over.

"Do you think it's Nate?" I ask.

"No, he texts when he's outside," Robin says. "Probably one of the field hockey girls looking for the inside scoop." She hands me my phone, with my notifications somehow deleted, and motions for me to come with her.

I stand out of sight of the doorway, sheltered by the drawn blinds. Why am I still here? If one of her field hockey friends catches me here, it will only raise more questions. Our supposed-to-be-secret team-up will definitely get out. And I'm wearing her clothes. What does *that* say?

Robin takes a deep breath and looks through the peephole. She gasps and takes a step back.

Whoever is on the other side of the door starts ramming what I assume is a Hulk-size fist against the door.

Robin swears under her breath and opens the door.

Bria Kelly spills inside mid-knock but steadies herself as she turns on her heel to Robin.

"It's fucking November, and there's frost on the ground. I could have gotten hypothermia in your yard; how would that have landed in your prom queen bid?" Bria says.

"Really well, actually. I'd pretend we were still friends and nail the sympathy vote," Robin replies.

As Robin closes the door, Bria's gaze lands on me. "Oh, you have *got* to be kidding me. *Her?* You're teaming up with Pollyanna, queen of cheer, who stole our boyfriend?"

"Well, I asked you, and you weren't interested," Robin says. "Meghan has actually been very enlightening."

So am I just backup for Bria saying no? Did Robin ever want me here? I got too comfortable and believed that maybe something here was real. That maybe, in a really messed-up way, I'd started to make a friend.

"Don't tell me you're falling for this innocent act too," Bria says. "She got kicked out of *public* school. Do you know who's allowed in public school?"

"Literally everyone, hence the word *public*." Robin rolls her eyes. "Do you want to take a breath, Bria?"

Bria huffs out what I imagine she wishes was fire in my direction. Every time she moves, the beads on the ends of her braids clack together. The soundtrack to her disdain for me is collision.

"What is she even doing here? And is that your. …? Oh my god. How incestuous can you two be? It's been, like, fourteen hours since all of us found out we're technically single."

"Meghan had a bit too much to drink last night, and I thought it'd be best if she slept it off here," Robin says. "Does this mean you're ready to join us?"

"Join you, maybe. But I don't associate with juvenile delinquents." Bria adds, "Bad for the campaign, bad for the image."

"You're not campaigning now, and you don't know anything about my old school," I tell her. "And optics-wise, I'd reconsider calling one-third of the Black senior class a criminal."

Bria looks me up and down, her eyes narrowing. She appears to concede internally. Maybe she's realizing that since there are only three of us and we're all up against the same obstacle, we've got to work together for survival.

"Noted. But I have my eye on you," she replies. "Don't question what I know; I'm excellent at opposition research."

I hold her stare. "Why am I your opposition? Nate told me he was never even in a relationship with you. You hooked up a few times, and he cut it off when you wanted more."

Bria snorts. "What a coincidence. That's what he told me

about *you*. You were a rebound after Robin, and you got clingy, so he dumped you after three weeks."

"I was literally wearing his jersey yesterday. We're not broken up," I fume.

Unless one of us ended it last night, which I can't remember. He hasn't texted me since arranging our meetup. I'm not Bria. How mean could I have even gotten?

Bria chews on the inside of her cheek. "Well, looks like we're all suckers, huh? He was literally crying on my shoulder last night when you texted him. He told me he was going to tell you to screw off forever. But apparently, that's what you told him."

"I don't think I told him that."

"You don't *think*?" she repeats.

"I don't remember everything that happened last night," I say.

If I close my eyes, I think I can see Nate in his letterman jacket, standing by our bench with open arms. He may have called me sweetness. I don't think I ran to him. I probably wasn't doing too much running, given the alcohol. Which means he must have seen me stumbling over the curb and walked over to me. Yes, that's it. I can see him walking toward me and telling me, "Sweetness, you smell like a distillery. Let me take you home." His hand squeezed my arm tightly enough to make me wince.

No... he wouldn't have said *distillery*. I think he told me that I smelled like a frat party. I don't remember him saying it in the nicest way...

Bria snaps her fingers in front of my face. "E.T. phone home?"

"Shut up, Bria," Robin says. "Meghan, you okay? You kind of zoned out there."

"Yeah, just trying to piece together last night," I tell her.

How did I even get to the school? I never would have driven. I don't care how blackout I was; I know that. Plus, my car keys aren't with the rest of my stuff at Robin's house. I pull out my phone to check the GPS tracker.

Thank God. My car is still parked down the street from the yearbook editor's house. I didn't drive it after the party. A small victory. The only law I broke was underage drinking. Though that doesn't explain how I got to the school. I doubt I walked. The house is two miles away. It's not out of the question, but it's not likely.

Someone must have driven me, but who? And why? I don't have any real friends at this school. Robin had already left. If Robin's my friend. The local taxis aren't out that late, and the driver would have reported me for being drunk.

No Uber charges either, and my Fitbit didn't record any more steps than usual. I didn't walk, and I didn't pay for a ride.

"You're not going to find whatever happened last night in your phone," Bria says. "Unless you open Instagram. Or TikTok. Maybe it will go viral."

"I'm not a big yeller," I say.

Bria looks towards Robin. "Um ... there were a lot of people around. There was even a Snapchat video of you insulting his mother," she says.

"I can't imagine actually saying anything bad about her." *To his face.*

I'm not going to pretend that I love June Walker. I'm not even going to pretend that I like her. I tolerate her as an extension of Nate, and I hold my tongue when she makes those little biting comments. Nate has told me a lot of lies, many that I probably don't know about. Telling me that June Walker loves me may take the cake.

Mrs. Walker has never met my mom because she refused to. She assumed I didn't have goals or ambition because I wasn't what she expected of Nate's partner.

"If you did, I wouldn't fault you," Bria says. "I hate that woman."

Robin chews on a hangnail. "She's not that bad."

"She hates all of us," Bria corrects. "I overheard her begging Nate to bring home someone a little less urban three days ago."

"I live on a cul-de-sac," I say.

"Yeah, so do we all," Robin says. "She really is the worst."

Robin's foot bounces against the floor, as if it has a mind of its own. In reality, I think Robin and I may be more alike than I realized. Right now, she's nervous. She wants us to like her as much as I want her to like me. But why do I want her to like me?

"Should I make breakfast?" Robin asks. "We can discuss next steps over coffee and pancakes."

"I'll take coffee, but only if it's from a French press," Bria replies.

"I'll never turn down pancakes," I say.

Robin smiles at me again, and something in my chest loosens.

We're about to leave for the kitchen when there's another

knock on the door. It's less insistent than Bria's but more authoritative. Whoever's knocking really feels like they have a right to be here.

"Police, open up!" a voice says on the other side.

Our eyes widen. Why are the police here? And at the one Black house in the neighborhood? Did someone report us for gathering? Do they know we were drinking last night?

Did I accidentally spill the beans to Nate about our revenge plan? Or did he report me for everything I told him about my last school?

This is Robin's house, though. They're not looking for me. It's probably a scam that Bria orchestrated, pretending to be ready for a team-up before pressing assault charges.

Robin opens the door. She looks so much calmer than I do, and I'm weirdly jealous of it. "Hello, Officers, how may I help you?"

Six officers step inside, glaring at us one by one. They sent six officers to arrest one girl? Robin's strong but not that strong. These don't look like the police for Robin's neighborhood either. Those cops spend more time in the local donut shop than they do making arrests. Nothing ever happens here. These cops? They look like they've seen some shit. They look like they were sent here on a mission by some higher power.

"Robin Ellison?" one officer asks.

"Yes, this is my house. What is this in regard to?" She keeps her voice steady, though she must be terrified.

I'm terrified too.

Bria hits a couple of buttons on her phone out of view of the officers. God, I hope she's calling for backup. I hope she's got a secret army waiting in the wings somewhere.

Another officer looks at Bria, then me. "Bria Kelly? Meghan Landry?"

"Yes," Bria says, jamming her phone into her pocket. "What seems to be the issue? Are our parents worried?"

Yes, our parents. Assuming that at least two of us never made it home last night, this is probably a safety call, even if it is hostile.

"You're wanted for questioning."

That party definitely got busted up after I left. I can't believe the yearbook people are so sloppy. The people who are supposed to keep our records, share our stories, are out making the news for all the wrong reasons.

"Oh, she didn't actually hit me. We only exchanged words," Bria says. "So this is all a misunderstanding. Robin and I are good, and Meghan is irrelevant."

Still had to get her shot in, of course. I don't know why she hates me more than Robin. It's not like she's innocent in all of this. But why would I be asked about their fight? The entire school was there.

"All three of you are wanted for questioning in the case of Nate Walker."

*The case of him cheating on us? Or the case of me maybe allegedly yelling at him in public? What kind of case could Nate be building?*

"The case of him screwing over all three of us?" Bria asks.

"The case of his attempted murder late last night in your school."

Bria, Robin, and I all exchange panicked glances. Nate's *what*? He was fine. We all just saw him. He and I texted; we talked...

I don't remember last night, and now I really have to. Nate wouldn't have been at the school much longer after we spoke, which means I might have seen whoever attacked him. If I can make myself remember, I can clear all of this up.

"Oh my God, is he okay?" I ask, my voice sounding tight.

Bria elbows me, and I can't tell if it's because I spoke up or because my first thought wasn't to deny everything.

Robin doesn't miss a beat. "None of us would do that. What evidence do you have? I want my lawyer. She'll represent all three of us."

My phone buzzes with a picture from my second-youngest sister.

It's a picture of a field hockey stick, a trophy, and my copy of *Anna Karenina* next to sports equipment and shards of glass. Her text comes in a second later. Nate found unconscious in storage closet with Robin Ellison's stick, Bria Kelly's trophy, and your book.

Bria and Robin are staring slack-jawed at their phones too.

I look at my two allies. One of them must have tried to kill Nate. I just have to remember who.

# 5

**THE OFFICERS SEPARATE US, CONSIGNING EACH OF US** to our very own police car. Real VIP treatment. For a second, they seem to entertain the idea of handcuffing us, but then Robin calls her mother on speaker while calmly explaining her record of contesting wrongful arrests. Mrs. Ellison says that she'll meet us at the station and reminds us not to say anything without her. So, that's how I end up being chauffeured to the local precinct by Officer Hernandez, who by the looks of it is on one of his first shifts, and his partner. He's shaking a bit, like he's trapped in the car with a serial killer.

Once again, I'm left to wonder what they suspect we've done. Nate's alive, as far as we know, but he was attacked. I don't know how hurt he is, and while I'm trying to convince myself that he's okay, the words *attempted murder* keep ringing in my head. Why would anyone want to kill Nate?

Well, I guess I can come up with a few reasons.

I have moments where the fury I felt last night zaps back into me, but even with that anger, I can't imagine anything worse than this. Nate might be really hurt, and I don't know if or when I'll be able to see him again. Does he think I did this? I don't care how upset I was or how drunk, I'd never physically hurt him, or anyone, despite what people seem to believe.

But Robin would. So would Bria. They have already fought over him. What if one of them took it a step too far last night? Not that I think either of them would actually try to kill him. Maybe rough him up a bit. But attempted murder makes it sound like whoever hurt him never intended for Nate to make it out of the school.

I'm eternally grateful that Robin's mother is on her way, until I realize, trapped in the back of a police car that smells of male body odor and acrid metal, that Robin told me her parents were out of state. What are the odds that her mother just made it back into town? And why would Robin lie to me about something so seemingly insignificant?

The officer flips on the lights as we leave Robin's driveway, and some of her neighbors are gathered outside, watching. I duck my head. Could this be any more embarrassing? Not only am I potentially being arrested, but I'm in a line of police cars with the two girls my boyfriend was cheating on me with. I'm never getting past those black widow allegations.

I feel like my heart is being twisted into a series of ever-complicated knots as my brain begins inventing images of Nate in the hospital, ranging from him with a broken leg to him on a ventilator. If someone really tried to kill him, they could come back. Is someone protecting his hospital room? Is he really safe if the police are wasting time and resources on me?

"Can you tell me if he's okay? Please?" I struggle to get the words out of my dehydrated throat.

The officer in the passenger seat glances back at me in the rearview mirror and shakes his head.

We continue the ride in silence.

Someone tried to kill Nate. And they left a shrine of our belongings behind, as if we had something to do with it. Maybe one of us did, though it certainly wasn't me. I'd immediately suspect Bria, given that she seems the angriest of all of us, but if Bria is anything, it's effective. Nate would be dead if she wanted him to be.

Robin was with me all night, so she couldn't have done it, right? But I don't know if she was with me. The night is a complete black hole. Whoever did it had access to several locked areas of the school. There's no way Robin would have gotten her field hockey stick back after the pep rally, so I assume it was locked in someone's office. Bria's trophy has been front and center in a glass case since last year. *Anna Karenina* was in my locker, and no one knows the combination.

Well, Nate does. So God forbid, if he wrote it down somewhere, anyone could have gotten it.

Of the three of us, Bria could have a key to the school since she's class president. But then again, so could Robin. As field hockey captain, she at least has access to the locker room, which has a back entrance and coaches' offices. Which one of them would be better at picking a lock? Bria seems like she'd have watched too many episodes of *The Americans* or *Killing Eve* as research, but Robin definitely has secrets and resources. Rumor has it, the Ellisons have some kind of deal with the principal by virtue of being among the top donors, making it next to impossible for Robin to ever get in trouble. Would that cover her in this case, as long as Nate doesn't actually die?

Officer Hernandez slams on the brakes, and I catch myself against the glass partition in front of me. As my head is jolted back, I have a sense memory of spitting in Nate's face. I hold my hand to my cheek, trying to force myself to remember if that really happened.

I decide that he'll be okay. He has to be. He's Nate Walker. Nothing truly bad can happen to him. I bet we'll laugh about this in a few days. Attempted murder is probably too strong a charge. This is all procedural. It's assault, likely relatively uncomplicated. Or it was an accident and someone set out our personal items as a joke.

*Nate is okay. Nate is okay.* That's my mantra.

Officer Hernandez doesn't apologize for almost concussing me. He and his buzz cut put the car in park, then fling my door open and pull me out by my forearms. VIP treatment over, I guess. I'm just like any other perceived common criminal.

I fight the urge to wriggle out of his grasp. He's hurting me, but I know how quickly that narrative can shift. One wrong move, and I'm the aggressor. One twitch, and I could be in the hospital next to Nate. Or the morgue. An image of Nate's body lying frozen in the morgue flickers in my mind.

*Inhale two-three-four, exhale six-seven-eight. Inhale two-three-four, exhale six-seven-eight.* I can't have a panic attack. I have to keep my wits about me. It's too late, though. I'm starting to sweat despite the cool breeze outside, and it feels as though a vise is constricting my throat. Once the lightheadedness starts, I'm fucked.

I let myself be dragged through the parking lot, trying to count my steps to distract from my rapidly increasing heart rate. I get up to fifty-four before I hear someone shouting my name. The surprise of her voice jolts me back to reality, and for a moment, I don't care if she tried to kill Nate, I'm simply glad she's here.

Robin is walking beside an officer who is glaring at her. Beads of sweat pool above her upper lip. But *she* gets to walk inside independently with a modicum of dignity. Can they smell the class difference on us, or am I the number-one suspect?

"I'm going to get you out of this," Robin says as she passes me. "I know you wouldn't do this."

Technically, she doesn't know what I would or wouldn't do. She doesn't actually know me. Plenty of people would believe I could do this, whether it's true or not.

I nod at her as her officer motions for her to stop talking. The sentiment is appreciated, but the wording isn't. *Getting me out of it* sounds like I'm involved. Who knows who else they've pulled into this? Nate probably has girlfriends all over the state. It's not like I've made his Instagram grid, only stories. It would be so easy for him to pretend that I'm out of the picture. *Maybe he's the one out of the picture.* I'm losing my fucking head. I haven't done anything wrong, and Nate is going to be fine. We're both okay.

My phone has been buzzing against my thigh since we got into the car. I've been too afraid to check it in front of Officer Hernandez, but I'm pretty confident that the police have been to my family's house. And if they have, my mom is panicking worse than I am. I was supposed to "watch" my younger teenage siblings while she was at work this morning, and if they actually arrest me, there's no world where she can make bail.

My mom would probably come to the police station, but she wouldn't have any idea what to do. When everything blew up last year, I basically handled it myself. This is, unfortunately, a game I've learned how to play. Sitting in the cold metal chairs of an interrogation room last year prepared me for the bleachers of Burke.

Everyone stares at me as I walk into the station. I can feel the hostility radiating from the officers. But what evidence do they have beyond a few personal items? Unless . . . Bria said someone took videos of the fight between Nate and me. Probably multiple people, from a variety of angles. Maybe the footage has a clue as to who else was around him or, at the very least, how bad this looks for me as a suspect.

Robin is already sitting in a chair outside the interrogation room. Her foot is vibrating, and she keeps tapping the arm of the chair in increments of three. She offers me a weak smile as Officer Hernandez walks me to the other side of the station. I pretend not to see. She could have set me up again.

Bria stalks into the station, holding her arm out of her officer's reach. "I'll be on the six o'clock news, *trust*, and I've memorized every single one of your badge numbers," she says. She sits down next to Robin, and no one seems to have the courage to tell her otherwise. She rolls her eyes when she sees me sitting so far away.

Sometimes I admire Bria, or at least her gumption. It's almost as if no one can stop her. It's Bria's world, and we're all just living in it. She lives her life as if she's a privileged white man who has never been told no, and I envy that she can exist like that. I can't imagine being that uninhibited.

The door to the interrogation room behind us swings open, and Nathaniel Walker Sr. walks out, his hand on Noah's shoulder. Noah is a perfect mix of both of his parents, but Nate is the spitting image of his father. They're all too handsome for their own good, and ours.

Bria's officer pulls at her arm to move her to another part of the station. For a second, I think she's going to fight him on it, but she doesn't. I think her eyes may be glistening with tears.

Mr. Walker speaks low in Noah's ear before noticing the three of us. He purses his lips, though his eyes soften when he sees Robin. Looks like he and I have something in common. And I guess, so do he and Nate. God, that's a disgusting thought.

Robin lifts her hand but pauses before she can wave. Then, Mr. Walker seems to remember why he, and we, are here. He tries to steer Noah away from us, a flash of protectiveness in his eyes.

Noah is wearing the same clothes as he was last night. I remember because the red and blue vertical stripes made him look like an off-center hanging flag. I have a sudden flash of him outside with Nate and me. It's blurry, but he was there. Did he intervene? Can I even trust my memory of last night? I need to check my phone. I'm sure someone has either sent me the video or posted it on Instagram for anyone to see.

I pull away from my officer. "Please tell me he's okay." I look more at Noah than Nate's father.

Noah knows me. Admittedly, we have more in common than Nate and I do. More of the same interests, more of the same top songs on Spotify. He's the only Walker I've heard actually make a political statement. In a world where I wasn't enmeshed with his brother, I think we'd be good friends. He's said as much too when we were both waiting for Nate outside of practice.

I have to know. This can't be the way our relationship ends. Mine and Nate's, or mine and Noah's. None of us deserve that.

"Come on, Noah," Mr. Walker says, trying to steer him toward the door.

"Please, Noah. Is he okay?" I beg.

Noah won't make eye contact with me. He can't believe I would hurt his brother, no matter what happened last night. He knows me better than that. I know he does. He has to.

I take a step toward him, and Mr. Walker drags him away from me. Out of the corner of my eye, I see officers starting toward us.

I hold up my hands and look desperately at Noah. *Just a word, anything*, I silently plead.

Noah's mouth twitches.

"Ms. Landry, sit down before we place you under arrest for disobeying an officer," one of the officers says.

Noah shrugs off his father and takes a couple of tentative

steps toward me. He stops, his eyes shining with tears. He quickly brushes one away.

I hold my hand out, and he squeezes it. Another tear falls. Oh God. It's bad. One of the cardinal rules of the Walker men is to never cry. It's part of their family motto, unofficially, but heavily implied given the family crest. Nathaniel Walker Sr. created a family crest featuring two stars, a basketball, and a puma and gave a special signet ring to each member of the family. Mrs. Walker's features a star, Nate's features the basketball, and Noah's features the second star.

Noah being the second star is actually a pretty apt metaphor for the Walker family dynamics.

"He's in a coma." Noah's voice wavers. "They don't know if he's going to wake up."

My hand slips from his as I sink to the floor. I hear someone gasp behind me, and I can't tell if it's Robin or Bria.

"Let's go," Mr. Walker says.

Noah steps closer and puts his hand on my shoulder. After a few breaths, I stand and hug him. He sinks into me.

*It's real. This is really happening. Nate isn't okay. Nate is in a coma, and he may never wake up.* My heart is pounding against Noah's chest.

"It wasn't me," I whisper. I need him to know. I need everyone to know that I would never do this. But that nagging thought sits in the back of my mind: I don't *actually* remember where I was last night. That's the most terrifying thing of all.

"I know," he murmurs. "Don't trust the others. You're different."

Before I can ask him what he means, he walks back to his father and shuffles toward the door.

How can he drop that bomb on me and leave? Robin and Bria are the only two people who could possibly understand what I'm going through right now. We're in the same boat, and I'm not supposed to trust them even a little?

Officer Hernandez's boots clomp across the linoleum, and he directs me into the interrogation room like it's business as usual. My head is swimming, and if anyone touches me, I might banshee scream.

Nate might be gone. Not dead, but gone in every way that counts. We're the suspects, and now this *man* wants to come near me in my moment of grief. Hell no. No. No. *No*.

Although it's possible that one of us had something to do with this, it's not the only conclusion. Are they even looking into all potential angles? I know that one of the girlfriends doing it would be a great story, but if they're only looking at us, then Nate isn't safe. They need to exhaust other options too.

My mind spins and goes blank as I sit down at the table, Robin's mother sliding into the seat next to me.

I feel like I blink and Officer Hernandez is telling me I can go. "But stay in town. We'll be calling you back in, I'm sure, with your parents for further questioning."

I've got to get out of here at soon as possible. I'll implode if I stay in this precinct any longer.

The police think they know where I was last night, and they're letting me go. That must mean they don't have enough to link me to the crime. At least not yet. There's still time for me to figure out who did this before the police do, to shape the narrative if needed. I have to watch what my sister wives do next—and piece together what I've done.

**AS I WALK FROM THE POLICE STATION BACK TO WHERE** I left my car at the yearbook party, the increasing number of texts exploding on my phone reveal three key details about last night.

First, there are at least seven separate student accounts of me leaving the school after my confrontation with Nate. There are photographs of me getting into, or out of, a car that isn't mine, and the driver isn't identifiable. Apparently, the game had ended when I came back to yell at Nate, so there were plenty of people around to capture visual evidence that should exonerate me from having been at school at the time of the attack.

Second, Bria was working the concessions stand, so she was seen at the school both during and after the game, potentially overlapping with when Nate was attacked. However, she was rarely alone, leaving an extremely narrow window when she could have snuck away and committed attempted murder.

Third, Robin, who typically attends every game when she doesn't have her own, wasn't seen at all. Besides our encounter outside of the yearbook party, which no one else knows about, no one saw her last night, except for a couple of moments around my confrontation with Nate. No wonder she kept trying to make eye contact with me at the police station. I'm her alibi.

For some reason, the Robin part sticks with me the most. How much of last night was a coincidence? Was I part of her master plan to get rid of Nate? I don't get to dwell on it too much before my phone begins vibrating with yet another call from my mother.

I sigh. "Hi, Mom, I'm on my way. Sorry."

"Meghan, tell me it's not—"

I cut her off. "Way to have faith in me, Mom. Or check in on me. *Hey, Megs, how are you? Were the police nice to you?*"

"I've been on the overnight shift. Lot of traumas coming through. This looks really bad for you," she says. "What are we going to do?"

Mom's an ER nurse who honed her skills in several Level One trauma centers across the East Coast before settling at the teaching hospital a few miles from our apartment. She's often on overnights, and according to the doctors she most frequently partners with, she's almost pathologically unfazed by anything she sees. Her saying, "A lot of traumas coming through" is code for her not coming home for at least another six hours.

"Yeah. I know how bad it looks." The background noise on Mom's end gets louder, and I end the call. She's busy.

She's always like this. It's always about what I've done or haven't done, my alleged transgressions. She's barely had a caring word to say to me these last few years. It's my fault when a guy chooses to act a fool in pursuit of me or when someone else does something violent involving me, however tangentially. It's never *their* fault. You'd think as a trauma nurse, she'd know that guys can often—and easily—end up in stupid or foolish situations without my assistance. She holds me to a higher standard than anyone. My youngest sister once punched a guy at recess, and I swear Mom scolded me for not knowing that she was being bullied, even though we were at different schools.

My legs are burning by the time I make it the two and a half miles to my car. I'm going to have to wash Robin's outfit before I give it back to her. My face flushes hot at the thought. Part of me wants to avoid her, avoid both of them, until this blows over. The other part of me is tantalized by the thought of throwing myself in Robin's path, even if she had something to do with what happened to Nate.

God, Nate. He really might not wake up. I shake my head, trying to push the thought as far away as I can. Of course he'll wake up. And when he does, I can't wait to give him a piece of my mind. At least, once my apps are submitted. *As long as I had nothing to do with him being in a coma.*

A woman leans on my car, tapping her acrylics against my hood. This cul-de-sac doesn't usually have loiterers, hence why I parked here. But there are a few people milling around, and several have their phones out.

"Can I help you?" I try to force my voice into a sweet, vaguely Midwestern tone.

She straightens, her hands dropping to her sides. "Meghan Landry?"

"Yes, why?" I ask.

I bet she's a journalist, already swooping in on what probably is a killer story. Pun intended. I should probably lock down my social media more than it already is if the local news circuit is going to start this early. My phone keeps buzzing with texts and social media alerts. I make the mistake of looking down at the screen while waiting for the woman to respond and see that someone has tagged me in a photo of my car from several hours ago.

She hands me an envelope. "You've been served."

I almost drop it like a hot potato, but a crowd is already forming around us with their phones out. I smile tersely and dig my nails into the paper. Could this get any freaking worse? *Served*. Legal papers. Will this go on my record? Can people find out about this? Oh God. Brown. Is Brown over?

Someone snaps a picture. Which social media platform is about to make me a star? *No.* I won't allow this to happen. I can't give them a reaction; I have to keep it classy, the way I have since yesterday. Minus the drinking part. And given my continued dry mouth and nausea, I'm not really looking to drink again anytime soon.

I climb into my car, my heart pounding. Everyone is still watching me, and my hands are shaking too much to drive. *You have to drive, Meghan. Hit the gas and find someplace safe and empty to calm down.* Does my inner voice sound like me, or does it sound like Nate? Or Robin? *Damn it damn it damn it.* I'm panicking. I can't be panicking *again*.

Inside the envelope is a restraining order. I'm forbidden to come within fifty feet of Nate's hospital room, short of me being put in the hospital with him. Even if he were to wake up right now, I wouldn't be allowed to talk to him. I'm not supposed to talk to his family either, with the exception of Noah, but only if it's required for an unavoidable school event.

I can't even make sure Nate's okay. How will I find out if he wakes up? I'm screwed in the court of public opinion. This looks bad, but it'll look really bad if I don't visit him. I wonder if Robin and Bria got restraining orders too, or if they're going to take back their romantic heroine narratives.

I take out my phone to text Robin but reconsider when I see the crowd watching my every move.

I've got to get out of here.

My car takes three tries to start, and at least four random people are recording my struggle with their phones. It's probably too much to hope that someone will start a GoFundMe for my legal and car travails. Everyone already wanted me to fail, to falter in some way with Nate. And now I've hit the biggest roadblock possible, along with two of the most formidable co-leads.

I hit the gas a little too hard and almost clip the sidewalk as I try to turn left. Great, now I look like a terrible driver too. It's barely noon, and this day is already one of the worst of my life.

One more mildly terrible thing and it'll overtake my number one. Here's hoping the shitstorm stops here. I speed away, over to the area of town where I live. Yet another difference between my classmates and me. They can smell the scholarship student status on me, and at a school that literally invites underprivileged students to tour and attend a day of classes, that is basically a death sentence for your popularity.

Our apartment is seventeen minutes away, seventeen minutes that feel like a lifetime when it feels like everyone is watching your every move. At every red light, I wonder if I'm seeing the glint of a phone screen in the car next to me. Or if the buzzes from my cell are logging new sightings of my car. Am I being followed?

The paranoia gets so bad that I pull over into the nearest shopping plaza, park near the back, and glance around. It's a Saturday morning, so it is abuzz with brunch-goers. I scroll through my phone. Several people who live in the cul-de-sac are students at Burke, and they photographed my parked car while I was at the police station, but there are no new posts after that. I'm safe here.

I meander into the nearest store, a bagel shop that's sold out of everything except cinnamon raisin and three plains. I buy what I can as a peace offering for my sisters. If I'm going to show up late to my loosely defined babysitting shift, I've got to at least feed them.

When my car sputters into our apartment building's parking lot ten minutes later, my three sisters are standing in my spot, waiting. They're standing in oldest-to-youngest order, leaving a space at the head of the line for me. Mila and I are practically Irish twins, born almost exactly a year apart. Mariana has started her freshman year and is *way* too online. Molly is in seventh grade and barely wants to talk to any of us. Her being here is the biggest shock.

Mila's jaw is practically locked with tension as she guides Mariana and Molly to the sidewalk. She looks at me as though I might choose to run all of them over at any moment. This is why we don't always get along. She's more like Mom than I am. Whereas Mom is no-nonsense and a silent provider, I'm constantly striving for the next step up, the thing that will make me prominent and respected. I can be a provider too, but I'm much more inclined to remind everyone of what I've done for them.

"I stopped for bagels," I say as I step out of the car, holding up the hastily ordered dozen.

Mariana holds up her phone and scrolls through several tweets. "You getting served is going minimally viral."

What even is "minimally viral"? Ten people? Twenty? People Mariana follows? She may only be three years younger than me, but sometimes it feels like she's speaking a completely different language.

"Did you at least get scallion cream cheese?" Molly doesn't look up from the TikTok video she's watching at full volume.

"We might still have some," Mila says. "Get inside. You're bringing so much *attention*."

Good to know that I can continue to embarrass the family name by simply existing. There are two other people outside, and I don't think they're looking at us.

Mila double-bolts the door as soon as we're all inside. She'd for sure be the final girl in a horror movie, but only because she'd never allow herself into a horrifying situation in the first place.

"What are you *wearing*?" Molly asks. "Isn't that from, like, the nineties?"

"Late twenty-tens at best, nice try," I reply. "It's Ro—A friend let me borrow it."

Mariana shoves her phone in my face. "Robin Ellison? Here she is on her Insta wearing it six months ago."

Jesus Christ, how fast do this girl's fingers work? How has she already dug up what Robin was wearing six months ago? The police should contract her expeditiously. I bet she'd figure out what happened to Nate based on social media snippets by the end of the day. These cops mainly deal with petty fraud and traffic crime. There haven't been more than five violent crimes in this area within the last decade, and one of them was technically out of this precinct's jurisdiction. However, I am going to need Mariana's particular set of skills if I'm going to figure out where I was at every point last night, especially if the police already seem to know. I may not have been at the scene of the crime, but I can't stand to have missing gaps.

"Why are you wearing *Robin Ellison's* tracksuit? Where are *your* clothes? You were wearing my shirt yesterday," Mila says.

Sisters. There's no one like them. As if Mila hasn't made a sport out of stealing from my side of the closet. Having sisters is basically like living in a consignment shop, only it doesn't usually benefit me because I'm the oldest. And I don't benefit from

Mom's wardrobe since she exists exclusively in scrubs and the occasional pair of exceedingly high-waisted jeans.

I roll my eyes.

"Is it because of blood?" Molly asks. "From your boyfriend? We can keep a secret."

"No! Jesus, do you all think I'd do something to Nate?"

"Your boyfriends have a bad habit of turning up incapacitated," Mila replies. "And Mom can only clean up the messes so many times."

"This is only the second time," I say. "And Mom doesn't clean up anything for me."

Mila throws her hands up. She snatches the bagel bag from me and starts furiously throwing them into a Ziploc bag that's lying on the kitchen table. She is clearly seething, but at which of us is unclear which of us has pissed her off. She thinks that Mom working at the hospital has helped me in some way. The only thing it did was teach me how to take care of my own injuries. She could literally be treating Nate himself right now, and I'd never know. She holds her work close to the belt, either because of what she sees or because she doesn't trust me.

"It's not looking great for you, image-wise," Mariana says. "But your socials are blowing up. You've gained like a hundred followers, all Burke students, since last night. Plus, you're a hashtag. Hashtag MadMeghan. The videos are incredible."

"Someone stitched a video of you getting served with one of a woman who cut her husband's penis off," Molly adds casually.

"Molly! Don't talk about that," Mila says.

"Penis!" Molly shouts.

"I meant the violence," Mila replies.

Thank God Mom isn't home. I can barely deal with the three of them, and they're showing me more sympathy than Mom ever will even if Molly shows me Lorena Bobbitt x MadMeghan videos for the rest of the weekend.

Last year, when everything went down, Mom kept reminding me how difficult things were at the hospital for *her*. Did I know that people were asking her about it? Did I know that the other parents from my school were spreading rumors to her superiors?

She never asked if what they were saying about me was true. She only cared about her job, which to some degree I understand, since she provides for all of us on her own. But sometimes I want to feel like I have a mom, not a detached caretaker.

"Did they charge you with assault? Do you have to go to court?" Mila asks.

"No, it was a restraining order, which I'm sure is standard procedure in these cases," I tell her.

"You'd know," Mila mutters.

"I yelled at Nate in front of witnesses. I didn't hurt him. Thanks for believing in me, sis." I turn away from her.

I'm sure Mila will go running to Mom later, telling her how mean I am. And Mom will take her side, like she always does. I try to present the perfect image at school, but Mila succeeds in it at home; hence she's Mom's favorite. It doesn't make me jealous. It's just annoying. Mom has already texted that the police have been to the hospital to interview her and several other members of the hospital's staff. Like, why is that even relevant?

Mariana starts going through each of my social media accounts and showing me my follower counts. She's trying to spin #MadMeghan as a good thing, as if selected clips of me calling Nate "an asshat who doesn't deserve to even look at me," is going to help my potential criminal case.

Considering that there are five of us in a three-bedroom apartment, I don't have my own bedroom to seek solace in. I share with Mila, and Mariana shares with Molly. Mom's room is barely a regulation bedroom; it's a converted closet and only counts as a room because there's the tiniest window.

I bet Robin and Bria don't have this problem. Hell, I know Robin doesn't. They can probably retreat, turn off their phones, and luxuriate with bath salts in their jacuzzi tubs without a care in the world. Without a single sister to bother them.

My cell phone rings, and I answer it without glancing at the caller ID. I'd rather talk to anyone besides my family right now.

"Hello?"

"Meghan Landry?"

"Speaking."

"This is Helen Reyes from WJDC, your local television station."

I hang up without another word. Nope. Absolutely not happening. I'm staying as far out of the media as I can and lying low until someone figures out who really did this. Maybe then I can get on with my life and concentrate on Brown.

I look down and see that I have four texts from Robin. I delete the thread. Nothing good can come from fraternizing with the other girls. I've got to distance myself from all of this as much as possible. I'm the only one of us a scholarship to lose, and I don't intend to lose anything.

# 7

**I MANAGE TO PUSH THE EVENTS OF THE WEEKEND OUT OF** my mind until Monday comes along and ruins everything. I try to get to school early so I can sneak into homeroom without running into my classmates gathering in the halls. What I didn't count on, especially given that I'm not a part of the basketball girlfriends' group chat, is that the entire boys' basketball team, girls' field hockey team, and student government would be having a joint meeting before school. As I walk in, they're all exiting the auditorium, led by Chad Hess, Bria's vice president. Notably, Robin and Bria are missing from the crowd.

As the boys' basketball team passes by, Andy slams his shoulder into mine. I bet he's thrilled about what happened to Nate since he gets to take Nate's position in the starting lineup. He's been the most consistent bench rider all season, thanks to Nate's historic scoring record and the strong power forwards.

"What the fuck, dude?" I try to keep my voice steady.

"I know you did it, you poisonous bitch."

"Andy, I swear I didn't." I hold my now throbbing shoulder and try not to remember the last time this happened to me. "And Nate certainly wouldn't appreciate you assaulting me regardless of what happened."

I wonder if Bria and Robin are going to get the same treatment or if this particular batch of cruelty is reserved for me. The black widow who supposedly took it a step too far this time. The black widow who finally proved them all right. Now I have to prove them wrong. I wish I knew how to do that.

One of the other basketball players shoves me into the nearest bank of lockers, and I fall to the ground. He walks away without saying anything. No one stops to help me up. No one says a word to him. He earns a couple of high fives, along with Andy. Oh, they're *so* happy about this turn of events. They all wanted to see me knocked down a peg, and here I am—fully knocked down. God, I hate them all.

Robin's field hockey cocaptain, Liv Forrest, reaches out. We've been at a few of the same parties but have never really interacted. There's nothing she can say I've ever done to her. For a moment, I think she's actually going to help me up. Then she pulls her hand back and slides it over her hair.

I roll my eyes. This is all so immature. She's not friends with Robin either. The word on the street is that they haven't gotten along in more than a year due to team politics.

Liv smirks and kicks me full force in the stomach.

My breakfast surges up my throat, and I try to hold it in. Throwing up would probably bring her satisfaction. I almost kick back to take her out at the shins, but I know how that would end. I'd be the one in the principal's office, and she'd be on the field tonight. I look up at one of the security cameras to remind the administration that I know they're watching. I'm on excellent terms with the security guards. One of them even goes to the same church my mom used to take us to. The security guard was willing to roll the footage of my locker being vandalized, but the vice principal put the kibosh on it. Maybe now someone will come and help me.

I squeeze my eyes and lips closed against the nausea. Then I hear an unrepeatable insult, followed by a metallic thump. There's no way that's the typically mild-mannered security guard by day, church deacon by Sunday who watches the cameras. As I force myself to swallow what came up, I shift to see Robin pinning Liv to the wall.

"The fuck is wrong with you?" Robin asks. "Leave her alone."

"You're next," Liv tells her.

"Try it. See how that goes for you," Robin snaps. "Touch her again, *any of you*, and I'll show you what I could have done in that tunnel."

Then she shoots the crowd a look that makes them all retreat. A warm tingle shoots through my chest. She looks up into the camera too, as if daring someone to come after her. As if anyone would.

She waits a beat before turning around to me. Her hand extends and grabs mine. She pulls me up with an ease I didn't think was possible, and I try not to swoon. Swooning might exacerbate the throbbing in my stomach.

I clear my throat. "Thanks."

"Anytime. I'm not going to let them mess with you. I know you didn't do it," she says.

"How? You don't really know me." *You don't know my past.*

"I don't have to. I just know."

She stares so deeply into my eyes that I wonder if she's having some kind of dissociative episode. I don't know what she sees, and I'm not sure I want to. Who knows what secrets my eyes reveal? Maybe that's why everyone here except her seems to hate me. They all see what she doesn't.

"Did you *just know* about the meeting this morning?" I ask.

Robin swallows. "No. One of the girls texted me."

"Oh good, so not all of your teammates are like *her*," I reply.

"Well..."

"Well?"

"I was hooking up a bit with the student government secretary, and she let it slip," Robin admits.

The student government secretary? Robin does have connections everywhere. And they were hooking up. God, am I sweating? She said *she*. Not *he*. Robin was hooking up with a girl.

I raise my eyebrows. "You managed to hook up with someone *after* being accused of attempted murder yesterday?"

She chuckles. "I did what Nate would do if it were one of us." She's smiling, but her eyes look sad.

I turn my laugh into a cough as a group of theater kids walks by us, whispering. As the rest of them dissipate, one stays behind. The lone Black girl in the Burke High School Fall Shakespeare Festival. She's looking right at us. For some reason, she's dressed like *The Crucible* by Hot Topic.

Robin bites the inside of her cheek, trying to avoid this girl's gaze.

*Damn, did she hook up with theater girl too? How does she find the time?* Theater girl looks familiar. Is she in one of my classes?

"I don't think we've met," theater girl says, moving her gaze to me. "Janet Kelly."

*Kelly... as in...*

Ugh, there's more than one? Bria seems like the type to have killed her siblings in the womb to absorb their power and nutrients, leaving it uninhabitable for anyone else.

"Meghan Landry."

"Yeah, I know," she says. "Obviously."

Okay... I was trying to be polite, but I should have known better. Looks like no one in Bria's family is open to kindness and diplomacy.

"What do you want, Janet?" Robin asks with an edge to her voice.

I know Robin and Bria used to be friends pre-Nate, but the clear tension between her and Janet leads me to think there's something deeper there. What happened between them? And who all is involved?

"The lighting booth in the auditorium is empty right now," Janet says in a conspiratorial tone, like she's a gender-bent James Bond. "If you sit on the floor, you're completely out of view."

I don't care about the lighting booth in the auditorium unless Nate's assault weapon is stashed there. And even then, I'd prefer not to get involved. There's enough drama as it is.

Robin nods at Janet. "I see."

*She sees? She sees what? What on earth is this coded language they've concocted, and why do I have to be involved?* I gape at them, but it doesn't seem to help.

After dropping that completely incomprehensible set of statements, Janet struts down the hall toward her locker, looking quite pleased with herself.

Robin takes my hand again, and a lightning bolt flashes in my chest. She pulls me through the set of doors across from us. I'm way more receptive to Robin's brand of conspiring than Janet's.

I try to ignore the pain in my shoulder, which pulsates down my arm. I don't bruise easily, inside or out, but this one is going to stick. It's not the first time I've been thrown against a locker, and I think my injury from last year is flaring up.

Robin swooping in like my white knight is the only thing distracting my brain from the fact that I was assaulted in school, *again*. And no authority came to help me, *again*. Instead, my classmates made it worse. But this time, someone *did* defend me, and she maybe cares? Hell, Robin has defended me more in the past twenty-four hours than Nate did in months of dating.

Robin gently pushes me against the nearest wall so that we're shielded from the view of the stage. Two of the theater kids linger, running lines in front of one of teaching aides. Robin covers my mouth with her hand, and I'm alternately tempted to bite it and press my lips to her palm. What kind of hormonal reaction is that? What are these contradictory and confusing urges I'm having around the most popular girl in school?

Robin leans against the wall beside me, then leads me around the corner while the aide gives feedback. She quietly pushes open the door to the lighting booth and ducks down, motioning for me to do the same. What's next, a barrel roll?

I don't know why I'm even going along with this. Not that I have much of a choice; at this point Robin is basically running the show. Plus, I'm blinded by a healthy mix of my bruised shoulder and stomach, confusion, and a heaping lack of motivation to be around any of our other classmates.

We shuffle onto the floor, our hips pressed together. Robin turns to me, and our noses practically touch.

A light shines in our faces. I jump and almost hit my head on the underside of the table. Great, after all that sneaking around and we're still caught? No one's getting an FBI summer internship in this group, for sure.

As my eyes start to adjust, I see that the light is coming from a phone flashlight held by Bria.

She's wearing a burnt-orange jumpsuit with a *Bria4Feminism* campaign button prominently affixed to her lapel. You've got to love her boldness. Maybe I should let her control my social media instead of Mariana. If anyone is going to assemble this narrative as she wants it to be, it's Bria.

"So which one of you crazies tried to off our boyfriend?" Bria demands, moving the flashlight from Robin's face to mine.

Robin pushes the phone down so the light is shining at the floor.

"How do we know it wasn't you?" I ask.

"Because I'd have succeeded," Bria replies. Her eyes are defiant, but I notice her lip quiver.

"Doing one kickboxing event in the school gym as part of your campaign doesn't make you strong enough to take out a six-five, two-hundred-pound basketball star," Robin says.

"Well, obviously if it were any of us, we'd have needed the element of surprise, probably coming from behind," I offer.

Bria snorts. "Spoken like a fucking murderer."

"He's not dead," Robin says. "And anyway, she's right. Even I couldn't take Nate alone."

Why were we summoned here? Is Bria playing investigator? Or is she trying to shift the blame? If we're spotted together, especially in a hidden place, this is all going to look worse than it already does. Plus, a murderer would totally pretend they were looking into the case. I've read enough Agatha Christie to know that.

"So assuming that none of us attacked Nate, which I'm skeptical of"—Bria narrows her eyes at me again—"we need to figure out who did. I have a contact with the police—"

"How?" I interrupt.

"I know a lot of people," Bria replies.

Robin rolls her eyes. "She sneaks Principal Turner's secretary homemade Portuguese butter tarts three times a week. The secretary shares them with her sister, who's an administrative assistant at the police station."

"You're a *class president*, why do you need contacts with the local *police*?" I ask.

Bria shrugs. "I like to know who I'm dealing with. Maybe someday I'll share what I know about *you*, lovie."

My heart pounds. What can she possibly know? It's a different police station. How much information do they share if the investigation is closed? That doesn't even matter right now. What matters is when exactly Bria is going to play her card to inflict maximum damage. As if my reputation could get any worse.

"I doubt Meghan has gotten so much as a parking ticket," Robin says, playfully elbowing me.

"Well, she was served with a restraining order, courtesy of the Walkers," Bria says.

"So was I," Robin says.

"Well, I wasn't," Bria replies.

My jaw drops. We're supposed to be three suspects, not two. The Walkers are already pulling us apart, deciding who is the more likely killer. Now I really shouldn't be seen with Robin. We both have motive, and probably the brains and brawn to pull off an attack.

"Maybe that means you're the one going to jail," Robin offers.

"Hardly," Bria replies. "And I intend to keep it that way."

"Why are we here, Bria? Are you planning to set us on fire and see if we burn?"

This interrogation is annoying. And it's not fair. *Don't send your sister to fetch us to play murder mystery party. This isn't a damn joke.*

"We're *here* because we need to pool our mental resources and social connections to figure out who really did this. We're easy targets. They're going to try to screw us over as Black girls, especially if Nate doesn't wake up in two or three weeks to tell them what happened. I refuse to allow that, and I expect that you'll join me," Bria says.

"Why two or three weeks?" I ask.

Bria rolls her eyes at me. "Because most people wake up from comas within the first few weeks, if they're going to. The police haven't had to investigate an actual crime in this area in years; they have no idea what they're doing. With all the pressure from the Walkers, they'll want to have answers sooner than later, regardless of the truth."

"Do you have something to offer us, B?" Robin asks. "Why should we team up with you?"

"Connections, brains, and an extensive knowledge of true-crime podcasts," Bria rattles off.

I suppress a laugh, earning a glare from Bria.

"Listening to *My Favorite Murder* doesn't make you a detective," I say.

"Neither does reading Nancy Drew and copying her pencil skirts," Bria replies.

Touché.

The intercom above us crackles, and I nearly hit my head again. God, I'm jumpy today, worse than usual. This little chat with the girls isn't helping. Neither did getting jumped in the hallway.

"If we're going to work together, then you two need to stop taking shots at each other. We all do," Robin says.

"Eh, I can multitask," Bria replies.

The intercom sputters to life. "Robin Ellison, Bria Kelly, and Meghan Landry to the principal's office immediately."

Of course. I'm surprised it took this long, honestly. What are the odds we'll be suspended for a few days "for our own protection"? To keep us from distracting the masses? It'd be a precaution that ends up on our permanent records. There are already local news articles circulating. A suspension will keep me out of college for sure. Brown may be the crunchy-granola Ivy, but I doubt they're into admitting violent offenders. And if Nate dies... what if it really was me?

Bria's pointed nails *tip-tap-tap* across her phone screen. She lets out a huff of air.

"Janet's causing a distraction and got those theater nerds out of the auditorium. I'll leave through the main entrance; you two each go out of opposite sides. Stagger it. Keep your heads down," Bria says. "Morning announcements should start any minute." She smiles and cocks her head to the side. Bria tapes morning announcements every morning before first bell, then sends them to the principal.

We swing out of the booth one at a time. Bria motions to us when she determines that the coast is clear. She points to opposite doors and practically pushes me toward her left. I get that she doesn't like me, but that push felt like there was vitriol behind it. Though I can't say the feeling isn't mutual.

I stumble toward the door behind the stage, my heart pounding. I've only been called to the principal's office one other time in my life, and that didn't end well for me. My shoulder continues to throb, and my stomach lurches uncomfortably again. Would puking in the principal's office be a strike for or against me? Should I call him sir or simply keep my mouth shut? I haven't met the man yet. Maybe I should introduce myself.

There is not an Emily Post section on this.

I push past the surprisingly dusty, thick red velvet curtains on the stage and into what I assume is one of the dressing rooms. It's bare, with the exception of one sad playbill from last year's musical taped to the mirror. After at least seven sneezes in a row, I find the door leading back into the hallway.

I stagger into the fluorescent lighting of the hallway. Here comes a stress migraine. Of course I'm stressed, possibly as much as I have been in my life, but could this be worse timing? Having a migraine is never convenient, but this might be my most awkward one. Plus, with all that dust I just inhaled, my head might explode. The combination of congestion and pain is a special form of physical torture.

The cold surface of the nearest bank of lockers calls to me, and I lean my head against one, trying to moderate my breathing. If I can get this under control, maybe I can keep it together in the principal's office. I can't look as suspicious as I'm starting to feel.

"Meghan Landry to the principal's office!" The intercom noise rattles my skull. God, is it right in my ear? Now my ears are ringing.

Someone might be trying to speak to me, but there's no way to know. Dark spots have taken over my field of vision. I'm passing out. I know it's happening, and there's no way to stop it.

I don't know whether I hit the ground before I throw up or after. What I do know is that I still end up in Principal Turner's office, propped up on a couch, with the nurse peering down at me and the school resource officer standing in the corner.

My hand wanders up to the cold compress on my forehead. As my eyes adjust, I notice that at least Principal Turner has closed the blinds and dimmed the overhead lights. The smallest of kindnesses. The faint smell of vomit clings to me, but as far as I can tell, there's none actually on me, even though I can still taste it.

"Nice of you to join us, Ms. Landry," Principal Turner says. His mostly salt, minimally pepper hair is pushed to the side just so to conceal the ever-growing bald spot fighting for dominance on his Q-tip-shaped head.

I push my strained voice up an octave to its "customer service" decibel. "Sorry, sir, I—"

"You know, you were a last-minute scholarship awardee. We passed over many qualified applicants to let you into this school," he says.

He glares at me, an extra reminder of how many white people at Burke tacitly think I don't belong here. I'm the first person to be admitted from my previous school district, despite the fact that we had two National Merit Scholars. I refuse to believe that I am anything other than extraordinary.

"I'm very grateful for this opportunity," I say.

"You don't act like it," Principal Turner replies, leaning back in his chair.

I'm supposed to display a certain level of appreciation to be treated like somewhat of a human at school. As if I'm not nearly at the top of the senior class despite not having the advantage of attending the prestigious classes at Burke for my entire educational history. I'm simply the scholarship kid, the charity case who should be on her hands and knees thanking every single person for the privilege of existing near them.

"Excuse me?" I ask.

"As someone whose departure from her old school was less than ideal, you wasted no time getting involved in drama. And now you have the police and the media calling me incessantly because you can't stay focused on what's actually important: your academics. Officer Nichols, who is usually stationed at the *public* high school, is now on tap to be here three days a week and is authorized to pull any of you for questioning at any time."

I swallow the increasingly inflammatory language that threatens to slip out of my mouth. I'm a better student than almost every person here. I'm certainly a better student than both Robin and Bria, who I doubt got this same spiel, given their pedigrees.

"With all due respect, sir, I'm a straight-A student and nearly at the top of the class. I am indubitably focused on academics, and I was asked by one of your most acclaimed teachers to tutor your star athlete in the first weeks of school. Just because I've been dragged into drama that I didn't create does not mean I am not a serious candidate or less worthy of being here, and I seriously question whether you'd make these implications if I had a different pigmentation or bank account," I respond.

Principal Turner's mouth twitches. "Are you insinuating—"

"No, I'm saying it outright. Or questioning it. I'll leave it to you to confirm."

My voice has dropped down to its normal timbre, and I realize that I've straightened up so I'm eye to eye with Principal Turner. Emily Post be damned, I'm not about to be polite.

"Get the other girls in here," Principal Turner says to the nurse. "*Now.*"

Bria and Robin walk in, each looking at me cautiously. Robin's face is streaked with tears, and Bria is stone-faced.

*Are you okay?* Robin mouths to me.

I turn my head so that I'm staring at the window shades. If I look too friendly with her, I know Principal Turner will retaliate.

"All three of you are in serious trouble if this isn't resolved soon. Ms. Kelly, you are hereby stripped of your class president title until we have more information on what happened Friday night," Principal Turner says.

Before Bria can protest, he continues, "Ms. Landry, you are on academic probation, regardless of your current grades. If this isn't resolved by the Common Application submission date, it will be included in your regular admissions applications."

*Shit. This is really bad.* How can a letter of recommendation from a respected guidance counselor mean anything to elite colleges if it's accompanied by a warning that their star athlete might die when I'm around?

"Ms. Ellison, you will be removed from the field hockey team until you prove you weren't on campus Friday after the game with Mr. Walker."

Bria raises her hand. When Principal Turner tries to ignore her, she waves it in the air and leans forward so her acrylics are inches from his eyeballs.

"Why is it that Robin has the option to prove her innocence, but both Meghan and I are definitively punished? Seems inequitable, like perhaps her status as a donor's child and star athlete are being taken into account as opposed to our academic and leadership contributions." Bria says.

"It would be disruptive at this point in the season—"

"It would be disruptive to disavow the votes of my constituents, the students whose parents pay your salary, to alter the results of a democratically valid election," Bria replies. "Are you hearing this, Officer?"

Bria certainly has the chutzpah to get herself into an actual office before she earns her law degree.

Principal Turner sighs. "Ms. Kelly, this isn't a democracy."

"Can I get that on the record? The editor in chief of the student paper, my childhood neighbor, would love to put that quote on the front page of this week's issue," Bria says.

"All of you, get out," Principal Turner snaps. "I don't want to hear a single word about any of you until Nate Walker wakes up."

Bria smiles and whips out a legal pad from her backpack. Her red ballpoint pen dances across the paper in strokes as smooth as an Olympic figure skater's double axel. Her handwriting looks like it came from a typewriter.

When Bria holds up the paper, Robin can barely hold back a laugh.

*I'm keeping my position. —President Bria Kelly*

Bria pretends to lock her mouth and throw away the key as she turns on her heel to leave. God, she's quick-witted. What I wouldn't give to come in sharp like that. Maybe I wouldn't be in this position.

Well, I guess Bria is still in the same position as me, so that's not even true. I hate this.

Principal Turner shoots me a look, and I know that I don't have the same option. I'm screwed until I can clear my name.

But first, I need to brush my teeth and find the strongest headache medicine I have in my bag. I can't go home. I'm going to ride out this day until I physically cannot. They will not win.

## 8

**I SPEND THE REST OF THE DAY TOUGHING IT OUT, TRYING** to avoid Bria, Robin, and anyone associated with them. The feeling seems to be mutual, and I don't know if it's because of Principal Turner's threat or because I still smell like vomit. Luckily, I always keep a bottle of Chanel No. 5 in my locker.

My thoughts drift back to Robin. Why is she getting off easier than Bria and me? Is it because her parents are well-known donors to the school? Because the field hockey team is ranked number one in the state? Is she more valuable than us? At least to Burke, it seems like she is. Robin is a wild card though. I still don't know how I ended up back at her place. Where she found me. What she could have done in the interim. What we could have done together.

No. Robin wouldn't . . . Actually, I don't know what Robin would do. I don't know her. I only have an exquisite idea of her. That seems to be the mutual situation between us.

When the final bell rings, I sprint to my locker, hoping to grab my calculus textbook and make it out to my car in record time. But the moment I slip the book into my bag, my peace is shattered.

My phone won't stop vibrating in my pocket, and I make the mistake of looking at it in case it's one of my sisters.

People keep DMing me a post on Instagram. When I open it, I see that it's from a new account with only one post. As someone who's been trolled before, I think that I know what's coming.

But I can't see the post because the account is private. Ugh. I roll my eyes but still request to follow. I have to know what the trolls are saying if I'm going to combat them. Plus, the court of public opinion is increasingly valuable here at Burke.

Every single person in the hallway seems to be on their phone. I'm quickly approved and followed back. I finally look at the name of the account.

NWTruther.

Fuck.

The bio says quite simply: Seeking #JusticeforNate. The profile picture is Nate's photo from the school athletics website. My heart drops.

The sole post is a picture of Nate in the hospital, hooked up to a ventilator, with an IV drip and heart monitor visible at the edge of the frame. And there's a poll for which of us is responsible.

What the hell? Who would post this? How did they even get this picture? I'm sure the Walkers aren't sharing photos with random students. Did someone visit him in the hospital and then start this ghoulish account?

I'm tagged in three comments as I ponder this. Jesus Christ. I know that my fellow students are obsessed with Nate to the point of cruelty, but this is another level. Robin and Bria have been tagged too, but I've by far been @-ed the most.

When I look up, my eyes are filled with tears and everyone in the hall is staring at me.

I go to close the app, but I drop the phone, and it clatters on the floor. He's really not okay. And from what I know about being on a ventilator . . . god, it must be so awful.

A milky-brown hand wearing a signet ring hands me my phone. The yellow-gold star gleams at me.

"Noah . . ." I burst into sobs.

"I can't be seen with you," he says. "Especially not after you're the leading candidate on NWTruther's post about who did this to my brother."

Why is he talking about this account as though it's some kind of authority? Just because it's the first of its kind doesn't mean it's relevant. But to get a current photo of Nate, they must have an in somehow. Could it be someone Noah knows? Someone the family would allow in?

"*What*? Are you kidding me?"

"Plus you're the person everyone thinks started the account," he says.

Why would I make an Instagram account speculating about who tried to kill my boyfriend when I'm a suspect? I'm not stupid.

And I'm certainly not a gossip hound who'd violate the Walkers' privacy like this.

Noah slips a piece of paper into my hand, hidden by my phone. He raises his eyebrows at me, then scurries down the hallway, his camera swinging at his side. God, that thing is always with him. Up close, it's covered in scratches and dings, like it's been dropped at games.

I turn back toward my locker, trying to ignore the looks from my classmates. Opening the piece of paper out of view, I see that Noah has slipped me a phone number. I grab my things and leave.

I have to shove past the entire boys' soccer team to get through the front door of the school. They grab at my arms, trying to pull at me. The boys' basketball team is behind them, waiting for the soccer team to throw me into their flames.

One of the midfielders snags my wrist, and my heart starts to race. My body begins to tense. I take a deep breath, close my eyes, and swing my leg as powerfully as I can. My foot connects with something hard that crunches. As I force my eyes open, I wonder if I actually broke one of these dudes' shins.

Nope. Probably a bruise at best, given that the player is wincing, but I caught him when he was already wearing shin guards. Is it wrong that I'm a little sad that the crunch was plastic and not bone?

I squeeze my fists, my nails digging into the palms of my hands, and channel my inner Bria. Every part of me yearns to panic, but I can't. When I panicked, he won.

"Touch me again, any of you, and I will make sure that you're expelled. Or arrested. My father's a lawyer, and my aunt's a cop. That clean record you don't deserve? Over. College? Fucked. I will end you," I say. "Plus, Nate is going to wake up, and we're still together. He doesn't take kindly to people messing with his girl."

All of it's a lie. I don't have a father, never have, and my aunt sells craft jewelry at the farmer's market. The police probably wouldn't believe me, and Principal Turner couldn't care less about me. After seeing that photo, I don't know if Nate will wake up. I don't even know if we're still together, since I can't remember our last conversation. I'm going to have to protect myself and myself alone.

"Well, how could he possibly keep track of all his girls?" one of the soccer guys asks.

"He doesn't have to. I'm number one on that list. Don't believe the rumors," I reply.

I turn on my heel and power walk, trying not to shake in front of them. I hate them. I hate them all. They're dead. To me. Dead *to* me, not because of me.

When I'm safely in my car with the doors locked, I lay the piece of paper flat against the steering wheel.

My fingers are practically vibrating with excitement, fear, and curiosity as I dial the number. I press the phone to my ear.

One ring, two rings, three rings, four...

"One moment," the voice on the other end says. It's a woman's voice, but not one that I recognize. "All right, you're on."

"I'm on?"

"Nate Walker's direct line. You can talk to him for however

long you want. The phone will cut off if another call comes in for him on the switchboard or if his vitals change. He can hear you through an earpiece we give him whenever he doesn't have visitors. Hearing the voices of loved ones can be a critical part of recovery for patients. May I ask who's calling?"

Oh my God. I can talk to him. Alone, without anyone listening in. He can't respond, but... maybe that's better right now.

"Um..." Shit. A name, any name that isn't my own. "Liv Forrest. I'm a friend." Why I've picked Robin's cocaptain, the one who assaulted me, I don't know. It will have to do for now.

"Okay. Go ahead, Liv. I'll disconnect my line."

"Thank you."

I sit in silence, the phone pressed against my ear, until I hear the click of the other line. Then I hear a beep. Then another. Nate's heart monitor.

"Hi. Oh my God, hi. Nate. Baby. I-I can't believe I can talk to you. I'm so happy I can talk to you. It's been awful. And I'm sure it has been for you too. I'm so sorry. I miss you. I love you. They're all so mean, and I know how it looks, trust me, *I know*. But I would never hurt you, you have to know that. I said some less-than-kind things in the parking lot, which I swear I don't even remember, but I was upset. Please wake up. Set this all straight. Be okay. Please be okay."

Is it me, or are the beeps coming faster? Is his heart rate rising? Does he recognize my voice? Oh my God. Could talking to him really make him wake up?

I hear someone clear their throat. "Hi, Liv. Sorry to interrupt, but Nate's mom is on the line to talk to him, so I'm going to have to cut you off."

"Of course." I pause. "Can I call back? Whenever?"

"Yes. Someone will be at the switchboard twenty-four seven, courtesy of the family."

"Okay. Thank you."

The phone call ends, and I heave sobs into my steering wheel. He was there. I felt him. He was there, and I can talk to him again. Thank goodness. I am so grateful Noah shared this with me.

When I get home twenty minutes later, Mariana is sitting on the sidewalk by my parking spot. She's squinting at her phone but jumps up as I put the car into park. No sooner do I close my car door than Mariana runs up beside me, her phone in my face.

"Megs, what is this? How could you let this happen? This narrative is *bad*."

It's NWTruther's Instagram account, which has added another post. It's a collage of photos of the three of us with Nate. A red question mark is superimposed over the center of the image. The caption keeps it simple: Choose your murderer. Oh, come on. Really? That's so trite.

"I know." But if people are engaging with this stupid fearmongering account, what can I really do? This isn't a logical situation. As long as it stays within Burke and my sisters don't accidentally spill the beans to anyone at their much larger public schools, I should be able to contain it.

"I told you that we need to get ahead of this. Let me manage your socials," Mariana says.

"Mari, I love you, but what do you really think you can do here?" I ask.

Molly trips as she walks out of the apartment, her head buried in a TikTok video she's playing at full volume. I hear the sound of a crash against a locker. Is that . . . ? No . . . Ugh.

*Damn it. Of course someone was taping.* Someone is always taping—that's the number-one lesson I should take from all of this. Or at least number two, behind *stop dating athletes with a fair number of enemies and a predilection for cheating.*

Someone has put a video of me being shoved into the locker and kicked in the stomach earlier today on a loop with the song "Lyin' Ass Bitch" playing over it. The caption is what really sells it, though: Fight Club ft. #MadMeghan. As if I'm a willing participant. As if I even fought back.

"You're hurting our cred," Molly says. "You could have at least kicked."

What cred? None of us has even played a sport since, like, third grade. We may be poorer than my current classmates, but we're basically middle class and live in the suburbs, albeit in a middling apartment complex.

"Well, would you like to see me *kicked* out of school?" I ask.

"You survived last time," Molly replies. "And what's this?" She holds up a ring, the green center reflecting the sunlight.

Mariana gasps. "Is that an *emerald?* Did Nate give that to you? Oh my God. You're engaged!"

I snatch the ring out of Molly's hand. "Where did you get this?"

Having sisters is sometimes fun, like when we can experiment with each other's hair or go treasure hunting at the local Goodwill. It's less fun when you have three people who routinely go through your closet like it's their personal shopping mall. Retail theft from your older sister's closet is basically the most accepted crime in the world.

"How could you not have told us? This changes everything!" Mariana exclaims.

"We're not engaged. It's just a promise ring—and it's peridot, my birthstone," I explain.

"Put it on," Mariana demands.

"Where's your rose-gold sweater?" Molly asks. "We're dressing like millennials tomorrow." She holds up another TikTok of me getting slammed into the locker stitched with a video of Robin swinging her field hockey stick at the pep rally. This one is tagged #ThelmaandLouise and #WomenWhoKill along with the seemingly ubiquitous #MadMeghan and a new one, #RagingRobin.

I wonder what Bria's hashtag will be. Knowing her, she's already planning to make one go viral that sounds less incriminating. She's a beast at social media.

"*Putthefreakingringon*," Mariana growls.

I shove it on my ring finger. It barely makes it all the way down, and I probably won't be able to get it off. What is her issue?

"Have you been crying?" Mariana asks.

"What? Why is that your business?" I ask.

Mariana snaps a picture as I wipe a bead of sweat from my cheek. Oh God, what is she up to?

After a couple of seconds my phone buzzes. I really need to turn off my Instagram notifications.

I open the app and nearly launch myself at Mariana. NWTruther has posted a photo of me, the one Mariana just took, where you can see the promise ring clear as day on my finger and it looks like I'm crying, with the caption #MadMeghan or #MeghanMourning? Mariana even took the photo in black and white so you can't tell what kind of stone it is. Jesus, whoever is running this account must have their fingers at the ready and their eyes glued to their phone 100 percent of the time.

"I'm going to k—" I stop myself. I definitely can't be throwing around the word *kill* when anyone could have a camera pointed at me and social media already thinks I'm an attempted murderer.

Mariana shrugs. "Now you look like the mournful potential fiancée."

"We're not engaged!"

"Yeah, but it really looks like it," Molly says from the sidewalk.

My phone buzzes with incoming texts. The same cadre of people who wanted to congratulate or castigate me for confronting Nate in the parking lot seem to have a lot of thoughts on the picture Mariana took.

I can't deal with this. I'm about to shove the phone into my backpack when a text comes in from the one person I want to hear from the most and the least.

We must have the same birth month.

How does Robin know that it's peridot? The photo is in black and white. It could be any stone.

She follows up: He gave me that promise ring sophomore year. Peridot. Size 5 1/2. Are we the same size?

I'm a six. And so fucking stupid. Of course he didn't get me something special. Everything was hers first. From the ring to the jersey to the guy.

A third text pings. I won't tell anyone. Keep wearing it. It's getting you a little sympathy. Can get it resized at my family's jeweler overnight for free. V discreet.

Well, if I'm going to convince people that Nate wanted to be with me as opposed to umpteen other lovers, this is one way to do it. But can I trust Robin? Even though I want to?

I take a deep breath. Okay. Meet in an hour?

Sure. I'll pick you up. We have business.

I don't ask how she has my address. I'm not sure I want to know, even though it makes my stomach squeeze in a pleasant way. I do wish the business we had was more enjoyable. But hey, once we're both cleared, *if* we're both cleared, maybe we can actually hang out, do something fun, finally get those pancakes.

**IT TAKES EVERYTHING TO SUPPRESS THE SNORT THAT** threatens to explode from my nose. Nate always told me it was cute, but now it feels wet and snotty, like I might hock a loogie in exchange for a laugh.

Robin and I are parked behind the jewelry store, our heads pressed together over her phone.

Bria has turned our travails into a compelling self-promotion. In it she stands proudly, wearing a blue-and-white blazer paired with a bold red lip. She stands in front of the school crest, her arms folded across her chest.

"They tried to silence your vote," she says, never clarifying who *they* are, though we can guess. "They tried to remove your democratically elected leader, reversing decades of precedent without even a student-led hearing. But I said no. I, Bria Kelly, will always stand up for *you*." Then she holds out her hands, proudly displaying a legal pad with her statement from earlier: I'm keeping my position. —President Bria Kelly.

She really is incredible. No reference to the reason Principal Turner tried to remove her, no protestations of innocence, simply a call to arms that a nebulous "they" wants her gone. She really is a politician. It's impressive and more than a little chilling. But hey, I guess we all cope differently.

"She terrifies me, but I sort of love her," Robin says. "Whenever she has something going on personally, she amps up the politician stuff tenfold."

"Aren't you friends?" I ask.

"Frenemies? We were friends as kids, the only two Black kids in the grade. But once I went the jock route and she started doing the politics thing, we grew apart. At least we were still cordial until..."

She doesn't have to finish for me to figure out the end of the sentence. *Until Nate.* Our lives are divided into before Nate and after Nate. The after Nate seems to be the worse option, based on our current circumstances.

We've been sitting in Robin's car for the last half hour while the jeweler's assistant resizes the ring. Robin hasn't brought up that the ring used to be hers again, and she didn't even chuckle when I had to force it back up my finger to get it off, leaving a clear indentation in my skin.

"Thank you for this," I say. "I appreciate that you're helping me."

"Of course. Like I said, I don't believe you'd hurt a fly."

Maybe not a fly. They're just annoying. But a wasp like Nate, who keeps stinging long past the need to? Maybe I would. I've certainly thought about it.

My phone buzzes with a text. My heart stops when I catch his name.

Nice bling. Ring makes you part of the fam? Noah texted.

I angle the phone toward my chest so Robin can't see. Don't tell your mom. *winky face*

You've got it, sis, he replies.

Robin clears her throat.

"So you don't think I'm a black widow like his friends do?" I ask, turning my attention back to her.

Robin rolls her eyes. "They're bitter Betties who want Nate all to themselves. Anyone who distracts him from coming to their countless parties and getting them invited them to NBA games is on their shit list. They hated me too. They just had to keep it quiet because we were in the same social circle. And they were afraid to say anything about Bria."

Fair. Maybe I should abandon niceties and just cultivate fear. It seems a lot more effective than the path I've chosen.

"Do you miss him too?" I ask.

"Of course I do. We were partners."

"Where were you Friday night? Between when you came to the party and when we woke up together?" I blush at the thought.

Robin leans back in her seat. "I went back to the school to confront Nate."

My heart thuds into my toes. *Shit. Is she about to confess? Am I supposed to keep her secret at my own expense?*

"I see." I swallow even though my throat has never felt more arid.

"I walked because I had snuck a flask into the pep rally, and I finished it while waiting for you in the bushes. By the time I got there, you were already laying into him."

*Oh my God, so she may have seen where I went next. And if she's telling the truth, that means she couldn't have been the driver of the car I got into.*

"Did you recognize the car I got into? How did I get to your house?" I ask.

Robin knits her brow. "You didn't get into a car," she says. "I live half a mile from the school; we walked together. Nate pushed you away from him, and I grabbed you and took you away."

I get a flash of that night. It's hazy, but it fits with what I've seen in the videos. Oh my God, am I finally going to remember what happened? The videos all cut off before what Robin just described.

*I stick my finger in Nate's face. He backs away from me with his hands up.* Just like in the videos I've seen.

"You're just like your parents. You *think* you're like your dad, cheater extraordinaire, but you're more like your mom. Trying her best to screw over Black women in every area of her life, starting by getting her hairdresser fired from the salon for going to a Black Lives Matter protest," I say.

"Stop fucking taping," he yells at the kids watching us. And they do. They listen to him.

I laugh sullenly. "The great Nate Walker. King of our world." I start a slow clap, moving my hands closer and closer to his face.

He pushes me back, harder than he needs to, and I stumble onto the pavement. Well, that explains the scratches running down my back and the pieces of gravel I found embedded in my bra strap.

Cameras flash. People are taking pictures, but no one is helping me up. Not even Nate.

I lie on the ground while he stares at me with contempt.

"I hope you die and I get to watch," I say. I'm sure I could physically get up, but something is chaining me to the concrete. It starts in my stomach and slowly works its way up into my head, a slithering, vibrating worm, oozing panic into every crevice of my upper body. Impeccable timing for my PTSD to kick in. The sense memory of being shoved never seems to go away.

A sister loc swings into my line of vision, and a hand pulls me up as though I'm weightless. It's Robin.

"Are you okay?" she asks. Before I can answer, she turns to Nate. "You're such a slimeball. You shove her and just let her lie there on the ground? How would you feel if someone put you in the ground? You'd better hope I'm never given the opportunity."

"You threatened him," I reply.

She cocks her head. "*Threatened* is a strong word. I simply asked how he'd feel if someone put him in the ground. But yes, witness accounts of that are really biting me in the ass right now."

"Ah. So that's why we got restraining orders and Bria didn't. We both basically implied we wanted him dead in front of witnesses," I say.

Robin nods and stares down at her lap. Unless she went back

to the school after bringing me to her house, which is technically possible, she couldn't have been the one to attack Nate. But given the way she looked at him in the parking lot, I bet she was angry enough to. Honestly, we both were.

I pull out my phone and try to ignore the influx of texts still coming in. I scroll until I find the picture that's supposed to be of me getting into a car.

Robin takes my phone and zooms in. She moves the picture back and forth and zooms back out.

"That isn't you," she says.

"You can confidently identify my ass?" It slips out before I know what I'm saying.

Robin fiddles with the bottom of one of her locs. "Actually, yeah. I've spent enough time checking it out."

Heat spreads across my lower extremities. "Very funny."

"I'm not joking. And anyway, the person in this photo is wearing what looks like a jersey. You weren't wearing one when I got to the school, or at the party," she replies.

I peer at the photo. The person's hair is the same length as mine, and it falls in front of their face, obscuring their features. But I can see that the maroon jersey, which hangs a little too loose, is the same one I was wearing earlier that day at the pep rally. At least it's the same design. I can't be sure it's actually Nate's.

"I threw away the jersey I was wearing when I left for the party," I say.

"Threw it away where?" she asks.

"The trash can behind the bleachers."

There's a knock on the driver's side window. The jeweler's assistant stands outside, holding up a small bag.

Robin rolls down her window and grabs the bag. "Thank you so much!" She slips the assistant a roll of bills. It definitely doesn't cost *that* much to get a ring resized. She rolls the window back up and turns the key in the ignition.

"So do you think I should wear it just at school or all the time? Who are we trying to convince?" I ask.

"Definitely at school and anytime you're out in public. If you make any social media content, wear it to be convincing."

"Thanks for the ride. I can grab an Uber if it's too out of the way to go back to my place," I say.

Robin pulls out of the parking lot and turns the opposite direction of my apartment complex. *Um . . . where is she taking me? This isn't even the way to her house.*

"We're making a pit stop," she says.

"To?"

"That trash can is only emptied once a week, and I have a key to the athletic complex. We're going to see if your jersey is still there. Check the console."

I open the console in between us. It's full of hand sanitizer, disposable gloves, and Clorox wipes. Not suspicious at all . . .

"What am I looking for?" I ask.

"Gloves. We can't just touch trash. Our classmates are disgusting." She pauses. "I'm a bit of a hypochondriac."

Touché. It still seems a little weird, but I resolve to give her the benefit of the doubt. She's the only person who has any faith in me. She believes in me more than my own mother.

She turns off her headlights as we pull into the parking lot closest to the athletic complex. She reaches into the back seat, where her field hockey bag sits, and pulls out two jerseys. She stuffs the one that has her last name emblazoned across the back into her shirt, making it look like she's wearing a particularly lumpy padded bra. She hands me the other one. It has *Walker* across the back.

When I raise my eyebrows, she says, "It's from last year. I kept it. Stuff it in your shirt."

"Why?"

"In case someone saw you throw Nate's jersey in the can and they tell the police. It's a solid replacement," she replies, as though it's obvious.

She hands me a plain black sweatshirt and a lacrosse stick. Apparently I'm pretending to be a fellow field hockey player in case we get caught.

"You've really thought this through," I say.

"What am I supposed to do, *homework*? We're being accused of attempted murder; yeah, I've thought of some things we should look into."

I do as she says and try not to let the heels of my boots click too loudly on the asphalt as we walk to the closest door that leads to the gym. If someone pretended to be me, that's a whole new level of conspiracy. I know someone is trying to set me, maybe even all of us, up. But why? And did they really intend for Nate to die?

Robin takes my hand as we walk, and I wonder how many other girls she's done this with. Sneaking around, holding hands, letting them wear her clothes. Does Nate know? Probably not. He isn't expressly homophobic, but he definitely has some weird views on bisexuality. That's why I've never told him that his gender never mattered to me, that I love him for who he is on the inside and that the outside doesn't determine who I'm attracted to.

Robin looks above us at the hinges of the bleachers. *Cameras*, she mouths, pointing at two that are trained on the court. They appear to be motion activated, but we're safely behind them.

Unfortunately, the trash can is located smack-dab between the two cameras, a couple of inches behind what I assume is their purview. Robin, who has been tiptoeing about as subtly as Tom in a *Tom and Jerry* cartoon, freezes a few steps behind the can as one of the cameras starts to move. It stops, and I watch her calculate what to do next.

She motions for me to come forward and points to the trash can. She mimes rifling through it.

I point to the cameras, and she shakes her head, even as they come to life. Is she setting me up to get caught?

She takes a deep breath and surges forward, her leg muscles rippling with every movement. As she passes the trash can, she kicks it over, scattering garbage across the ground close to me. The cameras immediately buzz and begin following her.

I almost laugh. She's running suicides across the court, and the cameras can't get enough. They continue to follow her even as I move toward the trash.

The gloves were a fantastic idea. I've never seen so many empty yet unbelievably sticky Gatorade bottles, airplane bottles of booze, and a distinct smell of parking lot–grilled hotdogs. I dig and dig, past stale popcorn and weirdly a pair of girls' underwear. Nate's jersey isn't here.

I shake my head at Robin and back away from the can.

She nods and runs toward the locker room. Once she disappears from view, the cameras stop moving.

A couple of minutes later, Robin peeks her head out of a side door close to me. She folds her jersey over her arm as we walk back to the parking lot.

Ah. So the jersey is a cover in case anyone asks why she was here, besides to run suicides at seven thirty p.m. on a weekday. Smart. Weird as hell, again, but smart.

"I'll take you home," she says. "But keep your phone on in case we need to communicate. And try not to ignore my texts this time?"

There is definitely someone conspiring against us. And we're officially on their tail.

## 10

**THE NEXT MORNING, EVERYONE STARES AT ME AGAIN,** but for a different reason. I keep my left hand prominently affixed to my cheek or my chest, and I rest it on my locker while I use my right hand to pretend-rifle through it before first period. Officer Nichols hovers down the hallway, always within sight.

Robin truly avoids me for the first time since this all started. Does it hurt, I wonder, to see me wearing her ring? To hear people whispering about how Nate and I were more serious than they previously thought? I saw her leaving what was, presumably, an interview with Officer Nichols in the main office earlier. He hasn't called me back yet, and I'm waiting for it.

Bria, meanwhile, has been seething. She stomped past me, hanging *Bria IS Pres* posters in the ten-foot radius surrounding my locker, at least seven times. Her glare is legendary, and while I'm somewhat used to it, it's still discomforting.

Someone taps me on the shoulder, and I turn to see Jess fake-smiling at me. She leans in to give me a hug.

"I'm *so* sorry," she says. "I didn't realize you and Nate were expecting."

"Expecting what?" I ask.

"I was playing around with you before, but now I realize that I could have caused stress to your baby," she replies.

"Excuse me?"

She rubs my belly conspicuously, grinning at each passerby. It takes everything in me not to shove her off of me. I don't know that I've ever felt more desire to hit someone than I do right now.

She lowers her voice to a whisper. "If Nate gave you that ring, he'd only do it because you were pregnant. That's just the type of guy he is. You trapped him, you whore."

"I'm not pregnant," I say loudly. "Nate and I were more serious than you are willing to accept. But it's good to know that you would use a brutal attack on a Black man to further negative stereotypes about Black women. When people can record any interaction for social media? Truly a mistake to be *racist*."

Jess drops her hand from my stomach like it's on fire.

Bria freezes as she presses her stapler against the wall closest to us. That bulletin board already has four of her posters, but she's nosy. She smashes the stapler down as boisterously as possible, causing Jess to jump.

"There's no chance Nate would risk getting anyone pregnant, which you'd know if he wanted to fuck you, which you tried to get him to do, despite dating his teammate," Bria says so that the entire hallway can hear.

A couple of people snicker.

"Andy and I are very happy and in love. Nate was—is—a mutual friend," Jess replies awkwardly.

"Well, you should have mentioned that to Nate, who thought you were an annoying brownnoser who he only tolerated because Andy is the AP's son and his teammate ... even if said teammate is the least talented player on the team," Bria adds. She smiles and mimes shooting a basket. "Swish. Just kidding. He's missed one hundred percent of the shots he's tried to take."

This time I'm the one fighting back laughter. When Bria's ire isn't directed at me, I love it.

"You're a bitch. Both of you," Jess says, shooting me a look of disgust.

"Every time a bigot calls me a bitch, I double my power, so thank you," Bria replies, blowing Jess a kiss.

Bria and I exchange a look, one where she raises her eyebrows and makes pointed eye contact with me before shifting back to Jess.

I think I understand what she's putting down. Whoever is doing this to us has a personal vendetta and the ability to sneak into the school after hours. Jess has enough spite, and Andy, while not the greatest basketball player, is an accomplished tennis player. He could have the physical strength to have taken Nate down, *and* he's the assistant principal's son. School keys must abound in that household. But why would he want to hurt Nate? Even if he hates me, Nate is the reason the team does well. He's the star.

As if I've conjured him, Andy appears beside Jess, grabbing her elbow to lead her away. He whispers something in her ear, then glances at Bria and me.

*You're off the bench?* Jess mouths.

Bria and I exchange another look. Apparently, I'm not the only one who can read lips. Bria mouths, *Point guard,* then *Backup*.

I knew it! There's our motive. Now that Nate's out of the picture, Andy gets to play his position. But it can't be just the two of them. Andy may be the muscle, but Jess isn't exactly the brains. Someone, or someones, must be helping them. Someone who has reason to dislike both Robin and Bria as much as me so that we take the fall.

I could see Jess being the face behind NWTruther. She seems basic enough to be obsessed with the idea of true crime without actually thinking of the real-life people behind the stories, and according to Bria, she is obsessed with Nate. I'd bet his teammates are allowed to visit him in the hospital, which explains how someone could have gotten that photo of him attached to a ventilator.

I tear up even thinking about it. I haven't called him since that first time, and I'm scared that someone will find out if I do. What if the police are listening to the calls, hoping the perpetrator will dial in? Am I setting myself up to take the fall for what happened if I keep hoping he'll hear my voice and wake up?

Bria sidles up beside me once Jess and Andy are out of earshot.

"Suspects number one and two," she says. "But they're too dumb to pull this off alone."

"Exactly what I was thinking, except meaner," I reply.

"Yeah, that's my brand. But seriously, what are we going to do about them? They've targeted you since the beginning of the year. They targeted me last year. The only person they don't hate is Robin," she says. "Nate hated them, by the way. In case he didn't tell you."

No one hates Robin, as far as I can tell. People are intimidated by her, in awe of her, but no one seems upset that Nate had been with her, despite what she's implied. Once again, the thought floats through my mind: she could be setting us up. She and Nate were willing to use me until the charity benefit; maybe this was all part of a plan. But Nate ending up in a coma couldn't have been in the cards. Whoever attacked Nate had to want him dead, right?

"Is throwing digs at me the most effective coping mechanism?" I ask.

"I don't need to cope. I need to fix this," she replies. "Besides, Janet was getting too much of my good shade, and I thought I should start saying it to your face. Come with me."

"Why would I—"

Bria guides me into the nearest corner and lifts up her shirt. There, across her left side, is a black-and-blue bruise that shows no signs of healing.

I flinch, instinctively reaching for my side. Somehow, whenever I've been bruised, it's been on the right. I dig my nails into my hand to bring myself back to this moment. I'm not bruised. I'm safe now.

"This is what happened in the tunnel. It was before any of

Robin's other teammates came out; she told them I tripped and that's why I was on the ground," Bria says.

The bruise goes from the bottom of her rib cage to her hip, but she doesn't wince as she moves her shirt back down. Most people would wince. I'd wince.

"How do I know that's real?" I ask.

"Why would I lie to you? You're not important enough to lie to," she replies.

*Ouch.* "Why didn't you tell anyone?"

"I tried. But Robin is queen bee, and no one cares. I get why she did it, but don't underestimate what she's capable of. I'm not the only one she's gone after."

Before I can ask Bria to clarify, Robin walks up behind us, her eyes wide.

*Oh, perfect timing. How are we supposed to explain this to her?*

"Guys," she hisses. "It looks like you're conspiring; what is going on?"

Officer Nichols seems to be hovering closer.

"Maybe we have to *conspire* to keep ourselves safe from you and your desire to assault everyone with your field hockey stick," Bria replies.

Robin looks at me. "Meghan, do you believe her?"

Why do I have to be involved? And why is that the first question Robin wants to know the answer to? I'm just trying to figure out who would frame us so I can get off academic probation and get out of this hellhole they call a private school.

"I think . . . I think we need to stick together, and eventually whoever did this will reveal themselves. But we can't turn on each other; that's what they want," I say.

"Ever the peacemaker," Bria says. "I think you're a suspect, Robin. Not the only one, and maybe not the main one, but I have my eye on you, and if anything happens to me, I do have a trigger plan."

"Well, in that case, I guess there's no reason to hide it," Robin says. "I think *you're* a suspect."

Bria snorts. "Yeah, okay."

I hold my hands out between them as if I'm going to arbitrate this fight. I don't want to be here or in this at all. I'm still gravitating toward Andy, Jess, and a third person as my main suspects, but there's a part of me that thinks it could be Robin.

"The drama club was here rehearsing *Macbeth* Friday night. They were here well past nine, well past Meghan's fight with Nate. They're doing *Macbeth*, and they like to prank each other by hiding their props around the school, like in the athletic office or trophy cases. It'd be very easy for someone—say, the actress playing Lady Macbeth—to sneak her sister into the school unnoticed so she could attack Nate from behind with a prop." Robin looks at us both triumphantly.

Earlier Robin wanted to partner with Bria, but Bria could be why we're in this mess now? What the hell is going on? He's in a coma; whoever swung at him must have hit him with a fair amount of strength at the right angle.

"Are you kidding me? Bringing my sweet baby sister into this?" Bria asks.

From the little I've seen of her, Janet is not that sweet. Robin's theory is a little far-fetched, though not out of the realm of possibility. Still, I firmly believe that if Bria were involved, Nate would either be dead or sufficiently warned against further screwing around. Though I suppose a coma could be a hell of a warning.

Robin fumes. "Sweet? She barely has to act to play Lady Macbeth. Maybe the two of you were enacting 'Out, damned spot' with our boyfriend."

"Oh, fuck off," Bria snaps. "You are so full of it. What about you and your army of minions? The girls' field hockey team has been known to play dirty."

Rumor has it that the team was almost disqualified from competing in regionals last year because of a mysterious string of career-halting injuries to members of other teams. It escalated to the point that the majority of Burke High assumed that Robin was basically leading a ring of field hockey stick–wielding Tonya Hardings around the county.

We never got the full story. No one fessed up to anything, perpetrator or victim, so it was squashed, and our team won state with Robin at the helm. But now that I've seen what she did to Bria, I wouldn't be surprised if some of it was true.

"You don't believe that, do you?" Robin asks me.

*Why does it matter to her what I believe?* If I'm honest, I assume it's the same reason that what she thinks matters to me. Because there's some puddle of feelings that neither of us is quite able to articulate yet. But physical violence is a deal-breaker for me. I've been through that, and I can't risk getting involved with another person who uses violence—verbal or physical—to keep their power and status.

"I've seen the bruises, Robin," I say. "I can't be with someone who does that."

"Be with?" Bria repeats. "What the hell is going on between you two?"

"Be aligned with," I clarify, but the damage is done.

Robin's face falls. Her gaze drops to the floor, and she takes a step away from us. When she looks up, she is staring only at me, as if Bria doesn't exist.

"Yeah, I hit her. I lost it, for the first time in my life. I have quite literally never put my hands on anyone else except in defense of *you*, Meghan," Robin says. "I apologized to Bria. We were supposed to be good."

Bria rolls her eyes. "Can confirm. All of it."

"So you were just trying to stir up conflict by mentioning the rumors from last year," I say.

Bria snaps at me. "Conflict between two people who are about to make it look like we all conspired together to get rid of Nate so the two of you could have your lesbian affair?"

Well, theoretically, if that were the case, why would we have involved Bria? She isn't a fan of either of us, especially not me. She'd sell us out in a second to protect herself. Plus, she seems strictly hetero.

All of our phones ping.

*Jesus, what kind of* Pretty Little Liars *situation is this?*

NWTruther has posted again. This time, it's a carousel that

begins with a blurry photo of the three of us—taken while we've been standing here. We're being watched. Is it by someone who is nosy and loves drama, or is it the attacker? Or both?

I look around to see who could be watching. It could be anyone. Everyone has a phone, and the account is already well followed. Maybe in part because Nate's was made private by his family. I've been blocked.

The next photos are individual ones of me, then Bria, then Robin leaving the auditorium yesterday from different doors. Anyone could have taken these pictures. The halls were full; it was right before the first bell.

We don't have a lot of time to take back our story. Even if it is revealed that someone else committed the crime, no one will believe that when there's a juicier story on the line.

Bria huffs loudly. Her grand plan to sneak us in and out of the lighting booth didn't work, and now we all look bad.

"Fantastic," I say. "Thanks, girl."

"We need to take control of the narrative. Like the child bride," Bria replies, gesturing to my ring.

"Don't be jealous," I say.

Bria snorts. "Why would I be? He offered to buy me one, but I told him I only accept lab-grown diamonds that are a minimum of three carats."

Robin covers her mouth to smother a laugh, then shoots me an apologetic look. At least Bria knows her worth. I can't even sell it. We're bonded until Nate hopefully wakes up.

"What did you have in mind?" Robin asks.

"We sell this team-up. We're the Birds of Prey, joining together to clear our names and figure out who hurt Nate, despite our clear differences. I'm Huntress, obviously, out for revenge against those who've wronged us. You, Robin, are the Black Canary, hand-to-hand combatant with a scream that can tear your enemies apart. And Meghan's Harley Quinn. She's the crazy one," Bria replies.

Of course I am. She keeps dropping hints like she knows about my past. As long as she keeps that information to herself, I'm fine. Plus, this wouldn't be the strategic time for her to reveal whatever she's uncovered. Maybe if I play it cool, she'll never use it as blackmail.

"You're still into comic books?" Robin asks.

"Literally always," Bria replies. "But only the female-oriented ones. Especially now."

It doesn't escape my notice that she happened to pick sort-of-reformed villains as our superhero alter egos. Who does Nate get to be? Batman or the Joker?

"And Meghan's not crazy; she's just been through a lot with Nate, right?" Robin says.

"Megsy, you want to take that one?" Bria asks. "I'm sure your new crush would love to hear why you got expelled from your last school."

I clench my jaw. That expulsion was supposed to be kept quiet. It's not even on my academic record. So how does Bria know? And how long has she known? Who else has she told?

How long until this ends up on NWTruther's account?

"For being a badass, I bet," Robin says.

I take a deep breath. If we're going to team up, I'm going to need to be a little honest. Drop a nugget of truth. Not the whole truth, since that will surely get me kicked out of this messed-up friend group, but something.

"I was dating someone, and he... he sucked. He said awful things to me, then love-bombed me into submission. There was some physical stuff that went down, and I got blamed even though I was defending myself," I reply.

Robin gasps. "Oh my God, Meghan, I'm so sorry." She takes a couple steps toward me and pauses, searching my face.

I nod, and she wraps her arms around me in a hug. It feels good to have her support.

Bria shoots me a glare. She knows that I'm only telling half the truth, but she's willing to overlook it.

For now.

My phone buzzes with a text from Noah.

Didn't I tell you to stay away from them?

I shake my head at my phone. I can't. It's not like he's helping me clear my name, so I need Robin and Bria.

Sorry, Noah.

# 11

**SITTING IN AP PSYCHOLOGY FEELS PARTICULARLY** ridiculous after everything that has happened today. How am I supposed to care about the biological link between the brain and behavior when the entire class is staring at me? What's the biological explanation for someone creating an Instagram account to accuse three potentially innocent girls of attempted murder? Hell, what's the biological basis for someone wanting to kill Nate?

Fine, I guess there could be several.

I find myself zoning out, pondering which lobe of the brain would make someone snap after a game. And who exactly could snap.

I feel a kick at my ankles, and my spine readjusts so that it's pin straight. Mrs. Houston, our teacher, stares at me expectantly.

Great. Another thing I can't do right.

A light breath touches my ear. "Parkinson's," a voice whispers.

I turn a bit. It's the student government yearbook liaison, the one who told me about the envelope of photos someone left for Lily, the photos she ambushed me with at the yearbook party. I think his name's Allen?

"Parkinson's," I say loudly.

"Correct," Mrs. Houston replies. "Keep paying attention, Ms. Landry."

*Thank you*, I mouth to maybe-Allen.

He winks at me, and I feel a stone settle in the pit of my stomach. This better not be some kind of trick or way to get me into the nearest storage closet.

In all my life, which admittedly hasn't been as long as it's felt, I've never had a boy treat me kindly without an ulterior motive. Even Noah, when he gave me the phone number to Nate's hospital room, must have some other reason. I know he dislikes Robin and Bria, but is that all it is? It could be a trick. Just like maybe-Allen here.

The members of the yearbook staff are compelling suspects for who's behind the NWTruther account, if it isn't Jess or Andy. Lily is brazen enough, from what I've seen, but she's not the type to get her hands dirty. I'd bet she's delegating, and the account, if run out of the yearbook, is a group project. We definitely need to figure out who's allowed to visit him. I don't know that a yearbook editor would make that list.

When the bell rings, I take my time packing up my bag, waiting for maybe-Allen to approach me. He spends a few seconds chatting with the other people around him. Is he ... popular? Who is he connected with? Yearbook isn't particularly prestigious in the world of high school politics. However, he is aligned with the student government, which means...

Another check in the column supporting Robin's theory that Bria is somehow more involved than we know. But it's not proof.

"Hey," I say finally. "Thanks for the assist."

"Of course. You're going through a lot," he replies, smiling at me.

"Have we formally met on yearbook yet? Meghan Landry. I swear I did the reading, and I don't intend to mooch off you again."

"Alain Hayes," he replies. "I'd *definitely* let you mooch off me."

Okay, so I was close. You'd think that, given the French connection, I'd have remembered his name. I refrain from gagging at his enunciation of *definitely*. I do not like the way he's looking at me right now. A chill crawls up my spine, lodging itself at the base of my neck.

"Thanks." I try to ignore what feels like blatant flirting on his part.

"But only if I can mooch off you in AP French. My mom was born in Montmartre, and I'm fluent in conversation but hopeless at writing."

"Maybe we can form an alliance," I reply, trying to choke down my growing dread. "Plus I bet you could get me on the right side of the yearbook editors."

Anything would help my image. I swear the yearbook staff was cold to me before my relationship with Nate went public, let alone after he landed in the hospital. Robin and Bria are both chock-full of connections in every clique. I need some acquaintances of my own.

Alain snorts. "I wouldn't count on that. Lily and I are in an on-and-off situationship, and at the moment, we're very off."

I restrain the urge to groan. Mrs. Houston clears her throat at us. The second bell is about to ring, and I've got to get to calculus before all the good seats are taken. If you're in the front row, you're sure to get hit with the hardest questions, and also maybe a little bit of spit.

"Ah, well, it was worth a shot," I reply.

Alain reaches out to touch my arm. "You really don't remember?"

At his touch, my brain lurches back to the night of the party. The night Nate was attacked.

*I've pounded an untold number of shots, and I'm leaning against a tree outside. I can barely keep myself up, and there's a real chance that these spins could turn into a puke session.*

*A figure comes toward me in a tragic green-and-yellow flannel that has no place at this party. They're not even the school colors, and they are not flattering.*

*"Hey, you don't look so good," the figure says.*

*"I'm fine," I reply, but my voice sounds far away, like it's echoing back to me.*

*"We have some classes together. I've always wondered . . ." The rest is garbled.*

*A face comes into view, but I still don't know who this is. We have classes together? I literally cannot remember having seen him before. And I'd certainly remember this level of fashion tragedy.*

*He puts his hand on my arm. "I've always—"*

God, why can't I hear him?

*I shove him away.*

There's a piece of the memory missing. I didn't push him for no reason.

"I was pretty drunk," I say. "Enlighten me."

"Nah, you were pretty aware," he says. "Maybe you're just embarrassed?"

My face flushes with anger. Everything around me has melted away, and I find myself counting the yellow stripes across the pocket on his chest. This is exactly what happened last time. And last time, someone ended up dead.

The second bell rings, and it somehow sounds both twice as loud as usual and muted. It shocks my body into awareness, and I push past Alain, hoping Mrs. Houston didn't hear any of our quiet conversation. Whatever happened with Alain, I want no part of it.

As I make my way into the hallway, I run smack into Janet, whose head is buried in her script. Alain barrels after me and knocks the script out of Janet's hand when he tries to reach for me.

"Don't *touch* me!" I whip my arm back.

"Excuse you two," Janet replies, snatching her script off the floor.

He grabs my arm. "Meghan, wait. I realize how it sounds, and I—"

Janet sticks out her foot, and Alain clatters to the linoleum, the buttons of his flannel making a particularly impressive smack.

"When a woman says not to touch her, don't touch her," Janet says.

"I tried to help you up at the party," he says. "You were falling back against the tree, and you vomited a little. When I tried to grab you, you stumbled. Then you started crying and talking about Nate, and you asked me to take you to the school, to him."

*So that's how I got to the school.* I now know the broad strokes of my own movements that night, and it's looking more and more promising for me. And since Janet is standing here, Bria will soon know where I was too, and probably half the school.

Janet is already tapping on her phone, half shielded by her script. A few seconds pass before I get an Instagram notification.

Someone has posted a photo of me, taken straight from my Instagram, with the caption: Which way does Meg sway? She arrived in Alain Hayes's beat-up Beemer and left in Robin Ellison's Mercedes. Should we call it a ménage et quart?

The Francophile in me wants to die. *Quart?* Like the unit of measurement? It's *quatre*. And I'd never be in a ménage of anything, let alone with Alain Hayes. He is certainly not my type. Plus I wasn't in Robin's car. At least not that night, so someone needs to get their story straight.

"I'm literally right here," I say.

"Yes, and?" Janet replies. "You should be happy that the rumors are switching to sexual innuendo as opposed to murder theories."

I glare at her. They're both bad for a myriad of reasons. I'm not ashamed of my sexuality, but I know how this could look. If people know I'm bisexual and that Robin is also interested in girls, they're going to put two and two together and assume that we teamed up to get rid of our troublesome boyfriend so we could go public.

I'm sure Janet, and certainly Bria, would love that turn of events. Bria not only gets proclaimed innocent, but she'd be seen as a victim of our sordid scheme too. If—when—he wakes up, maybe they'll even get back together and be the power couple reigning over my own personal ring of hell.

I walk down the hall towards the math wing. Another Instagram notification pops up on my phone. Great, I'm going to be even later to calc.

This time, the post features Bria's campaign poster with devil horns drawn on top of her head.

> President Privacy Violation? Our esteemed president is the one who submitted the hospital photo of our dear Nate.

I nearly drop my phone. I can't believe that Bria would do something so dark or that she'd betray Nate and us like that. Before my shock can fully give rise to anger, my blood runs cold. If there's anything more terrifying than being spied on by one of our classmates, it's Bria's impending wrath. Janet runs up behind me.

The door to my calculus classroom swings open, and Bria stalks into the hallway, her eyes full of fire.

Janet's jaw drops theatrically, and she starts toward Bria. Doesn't she know her sister? Bria is aware of everything that happens in this school, pretty much the moment it happens. Of course she's immediately ready to throw hands for this.

Bria screeches, her scream ricocheting off the nearby lockers. She holds up her phone and waves it in the air. I think she was wrong about who the Black Canary is in our little trio.

"Whoever runs this account, you're fucking next," she says.

And just like that, our phones blow up with Instagram notifications. Teachers have begun coming into the hall to send us all back to class. But who cares about derivatives now? Bria Kelly is officially at the center of the school's true crime obsession: the girl who somehow still has access to Nate.

**I HAVE TO HAND IT TO HER: BRIA REALLY IS THE BEST AT** everything she does. In response to NWTruther's post accusing her of submitting the hospital photo, she has spiraled hard enough that there have been ramifications for the entire school.

Cell phones, which were loosely tolerated in the hallways and study hall, are officially banned on campus, including during lunch. The student body is livid at President Bria. She stormed the main office and unleashed a tirade so legendary that the principal abruptly adjusted the phone policy, and the entire senior class is under increased scrutiny while the school investigates the NWTruther account. *And* the police are here, nosing around to see what they can find out about our very own true crime lover.

If anyone is caught with their phone out, barring an emergency, it gets confiscated until the end of the school day. If it happens a second time, a warning is sent home. A third time could result in disciplinary action.

I can respect that Bria goes scorched earth. If you're going to screw her over, she'll make sure the entire class is collateral damage.

We never did get to that lesson on derivatives.

The student government secretary/social media liaison had to make an emergency school-wide broadcast, which somehow took the entire forty-eight-minute class period and had the tone of a hostage tape. Bria is usually the one to make broadcasts, but she wasn't about to be the face of an unpopular policy. Plus, I think the administration refused to let her explain her position.

Samara Sligo, usually the definition of cool, calm, and collected from her bleached-blond bob to her pastel baby-doll dresses, was sweating for what was possibly the first time in her life. She kept looking behind her, like her kidnapper was telling her what to say. When she went off script, trying to praise Bria's leadership, she was cut off by someone in the background clearing their throat. Bria, who was back at her calculus desk not long after, looked like she was going to implode.

The second the screen goes dark, everyone starts to chatter. Our teacher doesn't even stop us. The bell rings, and we all pretend we're so interested in going to our next classes that we don't miss sticking our heads in our lockers and checking our phones.

No sooner do I step out into the hall than an arm yanks me back into the classroom.

"Could you clear the room?" Bria asks our teacher. "We'll only be a couple of minutes."

Inexplicably, he leaves, closing the door behind him and standing just outside, keeping the next class from entering. Is this how I die? Bria is looking at me like she's about to take a chunk out of my flesh.

Bria truly runs this school, and I'm even more convinced that she wasn't the one who attacked Nate. She has enough minions and barely contained hostility that she'd have succeeded in any mission unless she was somehow incapacitated, which seems impossible.

"I thought we weren't supposed to be seen together unless we were putting up a united front?" I say.

She's still gripping my arm, her nails pressing into my skin. There's no sign that she plans to let up. How much tension can a single person hold? I thought I was supposed to be the unhinged one.

"What did you say? Who did you tell?" she asks.

"About what, Bria? Contrary to whatever you believe, I don't really talk about you."

"You must have said something. No one would think I was involved unless they knew that I was there. *You're* the only person who saw me," she hisses.

*What? I saw her at the school when I came back for Nate? Before Robin showed up? When the hell could I have seen her?*

I really need to remember that night. It might be the difference between safety and all of my secrets being revealed to the school.

"I have no memory of that," I reply.

"You're such a liar, Meghan," she says. "Like how you told us something physical happened with your last boyfriend. The only physical thing that happened was you pushing him down the stairs."

My mouth goes dry. How did she . . . ? And I didn't . . . How much does she really know? Not a word of this can get beyond the two of us. But what am I going to do to keep her from spreading this around? I may not think she hurt Nate, but she has a worse alibi than I do. Best believe I'll use that if it means protecting myself.

"That's not what happened," I reply. "And you can stop trying to deflect from what we know *you've* done. You were the last one of us to see Nate. You were the one with the most access to the school and each of our items. You were in the office with Robin and her field hockey stick, and you have the key to the trophy case. I bet my locker combination wasn't hard to find in the secretary's records."

As I list all the strikes against her, I realize that, once again, they could all fit Andy and Jess. Both of them would have been there after the game, and Andy has unparalleled access to the school. They could have tag-teamed this.

"*I'm* deflecting? You're the one trying to turn the heat on me," Bria says.

She glances at the door, where our teacher is peeking through the window. She shakes her head like a freaking Mafia boss, and he turns around. The next bell is going to ring any minute, and I doubt Bria's going to write me a late pass for study hall.

"You took that invasive photo of Nate and submitted it to NWTruther. Like a soulless ghoul. How could you? I thought you cared about him," I say.

Bria snorts, and I want to wring her neck. She really is so smug, as if there's not a clear link between her and what happened to Nate. Even if I have reasonable cause to be upset with Nate, maybe even hate him a little, I would never do something like that. I wouldn't hurt him. He's in a coma. Who could do that?

And if she didn't take the photo herself, then who did?

"I'm playing the long game here, but let's stick to the right topic. You already know I was with him that night. *After* you freaked out at him. We went back to my house." Bria says. "And now you're trying to act like I'd hurt the one person I actually care about." Her glare sharpens.

"So why are you pissed about me allegedly seeing you at the school?"

She doesn't respond. Did I get this wrong? I could have seen her somewhere else, I suppose, but that would mean there's another gap in my whereabouts that night. I know how I got to the school and how I left. But did I come back? And where does Robin fit in?

Oh God, if there's time I don't remember, could I have been here when Nate was attacked?

The bell rings and Bria dashes out, careful to preserve her perfect attendance record. Of course she's going to hold whatever she knows close to the vest. Especially now that she feels like everyone is against her. What have I done besides be a little snarky and try to help?

I reluctantly head to study hall, as if I'm going to be able to focus on my English lit paper. My head is swimming with questions about how Bria knows what happened to my last boyfriend and how much she cares about what happened to our current one.

Why don't I remember seeing Bria that night? Did it really happen, or is she making it up? Can I trust my own memory, or am I filling in what I want to be true?

I can't answer that, and that's the scariest thing. The only people who know what really happened that night are the attacker and Nate. And only one of those people is conscious, as far as we know.

I sit in the back of study hall, counting down the minutes until the bell rings and I can go home. Normally I'd try and make the yearbook meeting, but I can't be around those people right now. The last time I popped into an after-school meeting, they barely looked at me. Only Alain, whose motivations I seriously question, paid any attention to me at all.

Before the text ban went into effect, Robin wanted to meet after school, in between last bell and the start of field hockey practice. I don't mean to stand her up, but I do. She'll survive. She probably doesn't remember that we were going to meet, given all the bustle of the day. I push this internal narrative all the way to my car and as I drive away from school.

I pull over in a gas station and park in the farthest corner of the lot. I take a deep breath before dialing.

There's a pause before I hear the nurse's voice. "Hello, you're on with Nate Walker. Name?"

I clear my throat. "Um, Liv Forrest."

"Hi, Liv. Go ahead," she says, and I hear her line click off.

There's that heart monitor beeping steadily. I fiddle with the ring, which finally moves on my finger now that it's been resized. But I guess even that isn't really mine. It was Robin's first. Nate was Robin's first, and maybe last too. Who am I to him anyway?

"Hey, baby," I say. "I miss you. I've been wearing the promise ring you got me. I know, *I know*. But it reminds me of you, and it's gotten people off my back a bit. In the interest of being honest, I know that you originally got the ring for Robin. It's beautiful. She's beautiful. I get it; I do. I get why you'd love her. It just makes me wonder if you ever really loved me too. I'm really sad. Everything is so messed up and horrible, and I wish you were here, really here to talk. Even if you chose Robin or, God forbid, Bria, I'd want to talk to my friend. I love you, Nate. I'm so sorry if I did anything to hurt you and your heart that night, and I will do everything I can to figure out what happened to you. I love you, even if you don't love me back."

I pause for a moment. It might be the hopeful part of my brain creating an illusion, but I really think I hear the heart monitor skip a beat before I hit the end button.

**THE NEXT DAY I TRY TO SLIP INTO SCHOOL EARLY AGAIN** to avoid the crowds. As far as I know, there aren't any team or theater meetings scheduled, so I should be safe. Fingers crossed student government only meets after school. I don't want to see anyone, but I really don't want to see Bria or Alain.

I make it to the library before I feel a hand on my shoulder. I jump and swat it away before I see who it is. I'm on edge. When I turn, my stomach flips.

"You blew me off yesterday." Robin folds her arms across her chest, which drags her already cropped shirt up, revealing her taut stomach muscles.

I have to remind myself that we're having a conversation and I'm supposed to respond and not stare at the waist of her jeans.

"Um. Phone ban. I forgot, sorry," I say.

Robin raises her eyebrows. "You forgot about me?"

I nearly choke on my own spit, which is rapidly filling up my mouth as I try not to drool over her. Of course I didn't forget about her; how could I? At this point, I don't know if this stupid promise ring makes me feel closer to Nate or to her.

"I couldn't deal yesterday. Bria confronted me, and I-I don't want to go through it," I say.

"And I do?" She shakes her head at me. "This is freaking hard for me too. He and I were partners for years, and this is the longest we've ever spent apart. And you and I—I thought we were friends."

Weirdly, I'm having trouble figuring out who she missed more, me or Nate. There's pain in her eyes.

"Are we?" I ask. "Friends?"

She takes a step closer. "Is that what you want?" The sadness is replaced by a craving.

"Don't ask me what I want right now."

We stand in silence for several moments, neither of us daring to make the next move. I want to pretend I don't know what that next move is, but it's so obvious. There's something between us. Something that could blind me to who she really is...or be more wonderful than anything I've ever known.

The library door swings open, and the librarian jumps, startled to find us standing there, staring at each other intensely.

"You really think that reading *The Hunchback of Notre Dame* in the original French is going to help me with my verb conjugations?" Robin asks. She widens her eyes in an effort to get me to go along with her.

"Whatever you can do to immerse yourself in the language, so the conjugations come up more naturally in your memory," I reply.

"Ms. Verona, you can help us with that, right?" Robin asks the librarian.

Ms. Verona is still rattled, as if the two of us together are a threat. I wonder if it's because we're quite literally suspects in an attempted murder or because we're Black. She's looking around as if she's worried for her safety. Officer Nichols is still stationed in the hall, and every time I pass by, he scribbles something in a notebook.

"Um, I'll have to check. Can you come back later?" she asks.

"Of course," Robin says, shooting her the megawatt smile that lowers all of my defenses. "Thank you, Ms. Verona." She cocks her head toward the lockers across the hall.

I follow her, trying to remember to keep it cool. This situation is fraught enough without my hormones and general longing for her getting in the way.

"You take Spanish," I say when we're out of earshot.

She smiles. "Knew you cared. Why else would you know that?"

"Nate mentioned it, and I was intimidated by how he talked about you."

Her smile fades, and we both seem to remember why we're even speaking to each other. A week ago, this wouldn't have been a possibility. It wouldn't have crossed either of our minds. We're only connected through Nate, and who knows if that link will outlast his time in a hospital bed?

Nate took both Spanish and French. He wanted to prepare in case he ended up playing in Europe for a year or two. I suspect that he had more than a little help in Spanish, given our tutoring in French, but I haven't figured out who would have helped him.

Could his Spanish tutor be his attacker? *Or his French tutor, amour?* I try to shake the intrusive thought from my head. It couldn't be me.

"Have you noticed that the account has stopped posting since the cell phone ban went into effect?" Robin asks.

"Yeah, I guess the account owner has to pay attention in class now," I reply.

Robin smirks. "Yes, but have you thought about what else it means?"

"Enlighten me."

She leans in, and I think maybe I'll die right here. Just leave my body and watch from above, hoping for a kiss I know is never coming. At this point, I know that I would let it happen. Robin's the question mark, though I know she feels this too.

"The cell phone ban is only in school. So it stands to reason that whoever runs the account is someone who stays at school late, perhaps in an after-school activity? Then, by the time they get home, they're busy or tired enough that they're slacking on posts."

Damn. I hate that she's smart too. In any other world, I'd have met her before Nate. We'd be the true power couple, and I bet she'd cause me less heartache.

I nod. "That sounds plausible. But how are we going to

narrow it down? There are at least six or seven clubs that routinely stay after dark."

"Well, between the three of us, we're in at least half, if not more, of the clubs. And we have friends in the others."

"I don't have friends," I say. "So count me out."

"You have a sort-of friend," she says. "Don't count *me* out."

I smile despite myself. She's so charming, and it almost makes me forget that she said the three of us. *Almost.*

"I can't work with Bria," I say.

"You have to. Suck it up. She has more influence than the two of us multiplied *and* magnified."

"You have no idea what she accused me of. *And* she's the one who submitted that photo of Nate. Robin, that's freaking diabolical." She couldn't even give me a real excuse for why she had that picture. Whether she can get into the hospital or not, how could she invade Nate's privacy like that? Show everyone how vulnerable he is?

"No offense, but I'm certain she's accused you of way worse than whatever she's said to your face. We can't do this without her," Robin says. "And we can't believe everything that some Instagram account posts."

What else could Bria have accused me of behind my back? According to her I have at least one murder under my belt and am working on my second. If I were rich like Robin, I'd consider suing her for defamation. Why not make things more chaotic?

It irks me that Robin is defending Bria's behavior. Bria has screwed her over more than anyone, *and* they used to be friendly.

She should be willing to cut Bria out. It's what I'd do. Hell, it's what I did to the friends who betrayed me at my last school. Bria submitted that photo of Nate and accused me of reporting her movements on the night of Nate's attack without remembering it. I don't trust her at all.

"Well, have fun then," I reply. "I work better alone anyway."

"Come on, that's a bit much," she says.

"I've had friends like Bria before. It never works out, and when shit hits the fan, guess who's never there? She's out for herself only."

"And we're not?" Robin asks.

Of course we're out for ourselves. But not only. I'd never let someone go down for a crime they didn't commit if I could find evidence to the contrary. Even if Bria didn't do the crime, she was definitely more involved than we know. Barely anything happens at Burke without her tacit approval. Robin may be the queen bee popularity-wise, but Bria runs the show behind the scenes.

"Not like her," I reply.

"Why do you hate her so much? If anything, we're all just as bad as each other. Well, except you because you never knowingly cheated," she says. "How bad did it get at your old school?"

I shake my head. I can't get into that with her or anyone else. I can't stand the idea of her looking at me differently. I'm at Burke because I have to be, not because I want to be. I was fine where I was and could have happily been valedictorian there without a lick of true competition.

I was happy with *him*. I was so incredible at the psychological warfare in my own head that I convinced myself everything was fine. That I didn't need to stiffen up every time his hand moved toward me. That using bright makeup to distract from bruises was a quirk of the relationship. I thought that someday he would break up with me.

But he wouldn't allow that. He wouldn't leave. He wouldn't allow me to either. And that was nothing compared to her, my so-called best friend. She made sure I had to leave school. She made it sound as sordid as possible.

"If you trust her, good luck. That's all I can say," I reply.

Robin genuinely looks hurt. Like she wants me to stay with her, with them. Be a team. But it's better this way. I'm better off without them. After all, look what happened when I started to let them in. And look what Bria did. She was the first person to submit something to the NWTruther account. I bet she has some idea who's behind it. So it stands to reason that any clues she puts forth to Robin are probably distractions from the real culprit.

"I thought we were maybe—I thought . . ." Robin says.

"I have more to lose than anyone. And I'm done losing, Robin. I'm done losing to girls like you and Bria."

"You don't have to lose!"

"I already have." My eyes fill with tears, and I'm not entirely sure why. Am I overwhelmed by the past few days, or am I overwhelmed because talking with Robin feels fraught?

People have started to trickle into the hall, and there are at least three camera phones turned on us.

A flash nearly blinds me, and Robin reaches out to steady me. I hold on to a locker instead.

Robin walks over to one of the offenders. "Don't forget about the new policy." She snatches the phone from their hand. She lets it fall to the ground over their protests. "Leave her alone."

I hang my head. Robin isn't like my former friends. She's trying to protect me. But we have to figure out from who.

# 14

**MY SISTERS CORNER ME NO SOONER THAN I SET MY** backpack on the floor. Mom has an overnight shift, so they're acting as though I'm the only person who can feed them, as if she didn't leave a note recommending Indian takeout. Well, Mariana and Molly are. Mila has offered to make a cauliflower and tempeh stir-fry to save Mom's money, and they are firmly against that idea. There's a reason Mila is Mom's favorite and Molly's least favorite.

"I'll order us a pizza," I say.

"Hold off; we have questions," Mariana says.

I sigh. For people who don't attend the same school as I do, they're dedicated to following the drama there.

"You and that Robin girl are gay for each other, right?" Molly asks, as though it's the most casual thing to drop into conversation.

Mila exhales as loudly as humanly possible. "*Molly*. We've

been over this. You aren't 'gay for someone,' and attraction exists on a spectrum. Pull it together, please."

"Bisexuality is real," Mariana adds. "Obviously. The real question is: How long have you and Robin been in lurve?"

*Oh God. Which account has started posting fan fiction about me and Robin?*

"We're not in anything," I say.

Mariana shows me her phone, which is tuned into a TikTok hashtag that says #Robghan. A handful of accounts have posted stitched videos of Robin and me from around the school. Some of them feature commentary from blurry heads that I think I recognize as classmates.

Several of them have emojis that refer to the items found with Nate. The book emoji appears most often, which apparently is an indication that the majority of posters think I'm the one who did it.

"To give you the rundown, people think that you and Robin are into each other and that you're either trying to cover up what one or both of you did to Nate or that the tragedy of his loss-esque situation is bringing you closer, which is romantic," she says.

I close my eyes. "Do I want to know how many people are leaning in either direction?"

"It's a growing number, but I'll keep you updated. We've got to get in on the narrative. You're already late," Mariana says. "Molly has some TikToks ready to go about your excellent academic record and professional accomplishments, and we're searching for any content of you and Nate, which . . . if you are willing to part with pictures . . ."

I don't want to get involved in this social media war. But unfortunately, I can't stay out of the online fray, not anymore.

I hand Mariana my phone. "Take what you need, get my social media passwords, and leave me out of it as much as possible. I don't want to know what you're doing."

She practically jumps with joy. I've never seen her so happy as when she's scrolling through my photos, as if there is anything interesting there.

Molly shows me her screen, where there's a TikTok playing. Oh great, NWTruther has migrated. The text says, Bria Kelly and her phone ban are done, with a knife emoji afterward.

Robghan's coming out the gate, with a blurred-out cartoon of two Black girls kissing. The police are investigating.

"Good call," Mila says, scrunching her nose up at the video. "You've lost control."

"I'll start dropping TikToks tonight," Molly says.

"And I'll get started on dinner," Mila adds.

"*No!*" Molly and Mariana say at the same time.

Mila rolls her eyes and concedes. Now for the inevitable sisterly argument over where we should order dinner from and how bad the delivery fees are going to be.

Molly is doing some hand motion that must have something to do with a TikTok trend I'm not up on. Mariana is *ooh*ing and *aah*ing over what I assume are the selfies I've taken of Nate and me. The only photos I could get him to be in with me.

Mila taps my leg and nods toward our bedroom. The littles are occupied enough with my social media that we should have at least ten to fifteen minutes of uninterrupted time. This is almost always how we nail down dinner choices.

As I sit on my bed, Mila closes the door behind us. She does so as quietly as possible so the others can't hear. Then she softly clicks the lock. Never a good sign.

"You're in a lot of trouble," she says.

"I know," I reply.

"If word gets out about what happened at your last school..." She purses her lips for a moment. "It'd be bad."

"I know."

"So we need to figure out who did this. Where are you in the investigation? What are the facts so far?"

She takes notes in the back of her planner as I talk. I see her drawing lines to connect events and scrawling notes in the margins. Being an overachiever runs in the family, clearly. When I finish, she takes a deep breath. I've even told her about what's really happened with Robin, including this morning.

"So? Do you have any ideas?" I ask.

"I agree that Andy and Jess are compelling, but I think you're overlooking other potential suspects," she says.

"Like who?"

She circles something in her notes before holding the planner up to my face.

*After-school club members. Friends?*

"Your school has that Big Brothers Big Sisters program

designed to pair kids from underrepresented or underprivileged backgrounds with current students," she says. "When all of this started going down, I filled out an application with fake information. I got approved a couple of days ago, and I have to fill out a survey of some of the experiences I want to have. Which clubs stay late?"

I almost laugh. Mila must be losing her mind. She can't come to Burke and snoop around without raising suspicion. On the other hand, there are so few Black kids that as long as no one sees two of us at the same time, they may mistake her for "one of the other ones." It happened to me often enough before Nate and I got serious. But still, it's not safe.

"You will never get away with it; it's not a good idea," I say.

"Try me."

"How will it look if someone figures out you're my sister?" I ask.

"We haven't taken a photo together in the last decade, and there's no overlap between our neighborhood and theirs. I'll keep a low profile, and I'll only be there after school. Trust me."

What other choice do I have? I don't have any other allies. Mila is about as level-headed and chameleonic as I am. If anyone can do this, it's her.

"Okay. You'll have to hit theater, newspaper, field hockey, student government, debate, and quiz bowl."

"Perfect. I should be able to start next week. Mari and Molls have the social media thing covered, and they can get home on the bus after school. Anything you find out, let me know, and we'll handle it internally," she says.

"Thank you."

"Sisters do anything for each other, haven't you learned that?" she says.

I really have. Doubting my sisters has always been the wrong move. Even last year, they didn't know everything, but they knew enough, and they handled a lot. Mila was the only one actually in the same school with me, and she was a lifesaver. She saw right through the narratives others were trying to spin. She saw my bruises, physical and psychological, and made sure that it would never happen again, at least not at that school.

Mila protects me the way a mother is supposed to. Ours was working, of course, but part of her always believed that I could have done it. She definitely thinks less of me now. She thinks I'm a wild card because of my trauma and that even if I had a good reason for doing what they think I did, it's somehow my fault for not handling it earlier.

If I had gotten out of the relationship sooner or told someone, maybe none of it would have happened. I tried to do both of those things though, more than once. Being a sports star really helps you get away with quite a lot. My ex and Nate had that in common.

"Have you been in contact with Robin since this morning?" Mila asks.

"No. She's texted once or twice this afternoon, but I'm avoiding her."

"Look, I know you like her. It's obvious. And as much as you should keep your distance, you can't afford to have her as an enemy, especially if it turns out that someone on the field hockey team is involved. So keep it cordial, give her bread crumbs, but *do not* kiss."

She's not wrong. Why is my younger sister never wrong? Ugh. Time to get my phone and actually respond to Robin's texts. But what do I say? I look to Mila, and I can tell she knows.

I reach out and give her a side hug. Thank goodness for sisters.

## 15

**THE ONLY THING PARTICULARLY THIRSTY ABOUT THIS** Thursday is that I am starting to get attention for the reason I always wanted. My sisters' social media escapades have actually granted me a bit of favor with some of the student body.

The quiz bowl team has started circling me near my locker. At first, I thought Bria had sent them as a warning. But it turns out that they sort of hate her. Sure, she's their captain and a large part of why they won the district competition last year. But she's also apparently more abrasive than I knew.

I've learned more about Bria from being cornered by these four trivia nerds than I have from my own nerdy penchant for research. For example, she apparently has a brother she doesn't talk about. Janet's perfect in her eyes, and Bria has been campaigning to make her the first Black Juliet in school history. Lady Macbeth may be the better role, but Bria wants Janet to be seen as a romantic lead. It would be great for people to see a Black girl who gets the guy. Minus the whole ending-up-dead thing.

Is Bria supplying the drama teacher with perks in exchange for her sister's success? I wouldn't think so, but apparently that's the rumor on the quiz bowl team. What are these perks, exactly? No one will say, but they like to leave it open-ended for the worst interpretations. They also think she could be blackmailing him. (Blackmailing *plus* perks sounds like a lot of unnecessary work, but who knows?) What would she have to blackmail him with? Again, nothing is confirmed, but they really want me to know about it.

From what I gather as they swarm me after three different class periods, they want to force Bria out of quiz bowl, and my sisters' TikToks make me seem smart. I didn't realize they had snuck so many pictures of me studying. Under Mariana's direction, Molly has apparently stitched several of them together along with videos from my phone that I recorded while practicing for my French oral exams, my freshman-year speech contest, and my brief tenure on the debate team. The girl they've created is too busy being an intellectual to attack anyone.

Mariana has been updating my Instagram with photos of my book collection, my desk, and me studying on my bed with my hand on my cheek, prominently displaying the ring.

I thought the quiz bowl team would be the most annoying clique, but no. I've also caught the attention of the vague religious group on campus. They won't outwardly identify with any denomination, but I have a sense of where they're evangelizing from. At lunch, when I try to sit alone on an outdoor bench, three of them sit next to me, practically shoving my hip into the armrest.

One of them takes my left hand in hers and holds it to her heart. I have literally never met this girl before. I don't know that I've ever seen her. But she's bubbly, bottle blond, and blathering on about the beauty of promise rings. I would chuck this thing into the garbage can in a second if it meant she'd let go of my hand.

They also seem glad that I'm not Bria. They don't like Robin either, but they at least respect her and the long-term relationship she had with Nate. Bria has a certain reputation because she's always been seen as the other woman. There are whispers of all the places she and Nate supposedly hooked up behind Robin's back. Was their first make-out under the bleachers? Or was it in the janitor's closet? And have I heard about how, during her first campaign, she tried to appeal to the religious kids by playing the purity angle against her opponent?

When it didn't work, Bria did what she always does. She pivoted. She wore that scarlet letter on her chest and eviscerated anyone in her path. For that, I envy her. Bria is herself, warts and all. If anyone has anything negative to say, it rolls off her back. She's the one of the three of us who could actually handle the public glare of being Nate's girlfriend, maybe even thrive in it.

Speak of the devil, she's storming toward us, her eyes wild. Has the seemingly unflappable Bria Kelly finally lost control?

"Holding court, princess?" Bria asks as she reaches the bench.

"I wasn't trying to," I reply.

Bria sits down on my lap and glowers at the girls until they scurry away to another bench. She is scary like this. This is the Bria I would believe attacked Nate. My pulse quickens.

"What are you doing? Besides drawing more attention to yourself with this ridiculous stunt," Bria says.

"They approached me." I shift so that she slides onto the bench. "Apparently your constituents are divided, Madame President." I clap theatrically.

"Sure. I know you hate me. You think I'm the one behind all of this," she says.

Robin didn't think withholding that opinion might be helpful for our proposed partnership? There was really no need to sell me out like this.

"And you return the favor. You hate me and think I'm the unhinged one in the equation," I reply.

"*Of course* you are! This is your second boyfriend to turn up worse for wear on school property in the last six months. What else am I supposed to think?" she asks.

"How do you know about that?"

She purses her lips. "When you started dating Nate, I messaged some of your former classmates on social media."

"Who?"

I ask even though I already know. I don't even need to ask why. Who wouldn't do a bit of light stalking?

She scans the area, making sure there are no administrators around. Then she slips her phone out of her pocket and shows me a couple of names. Someone who was in my French class, a guy on the football team, a former debate captain. Then she pulls up a familiar profile. One I've since blocked.

My former best friend. The one who was there when my then-boyfriend fell down the stairs. She knows what really happened. But she had her own back, never mine, and she bent the truth to make sure the chips fell in her favor.

The only reason I'm not in juvenile detention is because everyone thinks I'm so traumatized that if I pushed him, maybe I had a good reason. It was self-defense—that was the argument. But this girl, my ex-best friend, is holding the company line: I pushed him in cold blood because he was cheating on me. With her.

"She has a ton of photos of the two of you together, so I assumed she was a reliable source," Bria says.

I should feel hurt. I should feel that prick of sadness like I did after it all happened. But I don't. I just feel rage. Rage at the friend I thought I had. Rage at Bria for dredging up the past. Rage at whoever is putting the three of us through this now. Rage at the boys who have tried so hard to make me a victim. Rage at myself for continuing to fall for them.

"She wouldn't give you the whole story. And I'd think that as a fellow Black girl, one of very few in this school, you'd give me the benefit of the doubt, given how people have talked about you," I say.

For maybe the first time in her entire life, Bria seems at a loss for words. It's ironic, I realize. She and I have been called the same names. We've been perceived similarly, except everyone thinks I'm fake nice, and she's unafraid to be mean. We're two sides of a coin, more alike than I imagined.

"I'm sorry," she says. "I know it isn't easy being in Nate's shadow. Or Robin's, for that matter. And I should have told you that ammonia is a good way to get black paint off of your locker. The custodians will usually lend you some if you're nice to them, which I'm sure you are."

It's the closest I think we can come to a truce, and it's entirely unexpected. And today I'm tired of weird sycophants who want to pit me against Robin and Bria. I need someone in my corner when my sisters can't stand beside me.

"I'm sure you didn't come over to be nice to me," I say.

"Actually, I came to invite you on a mission," she replies. "Mother Robin says we have to play together."

"What are we doing?" I ask.

"Tomorrow night we party. It's at Samara's house. All three of us are going, and we're going to investigate."

She glides a Post-it across the bench like we're in a *Charlie's Angels* escapade. On it are two letters: *NW*.

There are a lot of people with the initials NW, including our boyfriend. What is she getting at?

"We're each watching a suspect," she says. "You're on Noah duty."

"*Noah's* a suspect?"

"Noah is in several clubs, and people are trying to glom on to him. He's already met with the good officer three times. Since you're the only one of us he actually likes, you're in charge of keeping tabs on everyone he talks to. We'll narrow the pool from there."

She's not wrong. Noah, who I've never seen speak to more than three different students, has become almost popular. He seems grotesquely uncomfortable with this new reality, but everyone wants to get close to him. It's really proximity to Nate they're looking for, and they think Noah is their ticket.

He sort of is. He was for me, over the phone at least. I wonder if he'd FaceTime me from the hospital. I miss Nate's face. I'm mad about all the trouble it's gotten me into, but damn if I don't miss it.

I refocus. "Who are you and Robin watching?"

"I have Lily, the yearbook editor, since she's famously acerbic, and Robin is supposed to be cozying up to Samara. Her idea, but it makes sense since Samara is nosy and loose-lipped."

I flush. Samara is the government secretary that Robin has been hooking up with. The one who told her about the meeting on Monday. Jealousy bubbles in my stomach and rises up to my chest. I don't want her near Samara, and I certainly don't want to see it.

Bria rolls her eyes. "It was a one-time thing, and Robin is only flirting in exchange for information. Chill."

"I don't know what you're talking about," I reply.

"Yeah. Play it cool. You are hopelessly obsessed with her. You even dress like she did when she and Nate first got together. And the ring? It's uncanny."

When has Robin ever worn Peter Pan collars? I don't think I've even seen her in a dress. Have I somehow been morphing into her? Why does that thought make me feel warm?

"Nothing can happen," I say.

"When Nate wakes up, dump him. Wait a month or two, and then soft launch your relationship with Robin. I have a whole timeline. I can be your campaign manager. Clearly you already have someone running your social media."

"Sisters."

"Aren't they the best? Like, who needs any other siblings?"

I try to stifle a laugh. "What about your brother?"

She draws back. "Why would you ask?"

Okay... mark that in the column of things I need to follow up on. Is he a creep? Strange? Did he once get a B on an exam and tank the family reputation? For now, I let it go. I've got to figure out how to get Mom to let me of the house on a Friday night after what happened on my last night out.

# 16

**IT TURNS OUT THAT MOM DIDN'T TAKE MUCH CONVINC-**ing. She's working overnight again and only asks that I try to keep out of trouble. Even via text she sounded exhausted, so that's how I end up heading to the party in a car with Bria and Janet. Conversation on the way is minimal, and I'm relegated to the back seat. I've taken off my sweater and am sweating it out in a strapless bodysuit and jeans.

We park a block away from the party so as not to rouse suspicion, as though thirty kids walking toward one house is inconspicuous. The moment Bria steps out of the car, she's greeted by almost every person in the vicinity. I can't tell if they really like her or are terrified of her. Knowing her, it's probably the latter and she likes it that way.

I follow Bria and Janet into the house and scan to see if I can find anyone remotely familiar. One of the quiz bowl members tries to catch my eye before noticing I'm standing next to Bria. He backs into the crowd.

"Hey. I definitely didn't expect to see you here."

I turn to find Noah, my mark. "You didn't think this would be my scene?" I ask.

"Not at all."

"It's not. Pretty sure it isn't yours either," I say.

He holds my gaze for a few seconds, like we're the only two people in the room. Unfortunately, we're not, which means we're being watched.

He makes a big show of lifting my left hand to look at my ring. Only I can see the smirk on his face. For a second he looks like Nate. My breath catches.

"Good to see you, sis," he says loudly. He lowers his voice. "It's not my scene, but I'd rather be here than at home."

"How bad is it?" I ask gently.

"Well, Dad is still going out on the road, mostly to avoid dealing with Mom, who alternates between keeping vigil in the hospital and locking herself in her bedroom. They sort of hate each other but can't bring themselves to admit it given the situation."

He exhales, like he's been holding on to that for a long time. The Walker home situation was already a tenuous one; I can't imagine how much more this stress has torn them apart.

I put my hand on his shoulder. "I'm so sorry, Noah. And I'm sorry I haven't been checking in on you like I should have. As your *sister*."

He snorts, then covers his nose like he's embarrassed. "Sorry, the sister thing is funny. But smart." He gestures to the ring. "Good call."

"He gave it to me," I say, as if I have something to prove.

"Of course he did. He can be generous sometimes," he replies.

Nate's shadow is a hard one to shake for both of us. It's elevated Noah but dragged me down. I wonder if I'd have made friends, real ones, if I had never accepted that tutoring assignment.

It breaks my heart to think about. Maybe I'd have friends. Who, I'm not entirely sure, given that no one besides Robin has made a particularly positive impression on me thus far. But when it was just the two of us, Nate made me happy. He made—makes—me happy. Is he worth all of this, though? Would I trade my moments with him for organic friendships, unlike whatever is going on between my sister wives and me?

"Thank you for giving me that number. And for being so kind. I can never express how much it means to me," I tell him.

He smiles, and his eyes start to well up. "I knew it would. You're the one who really loves him. I can tell," he replies. "And that means the world to me."

Out of the corner of my eye, I watch Robin, still in her field hockey uniform, make her entrance. Her school-mandated skirt looks itchy, and the matching polo she's had since (I assume) freshman year barely stretches over her midsection. She's a dress code violation waiting to happen on campus but perfectly dressed for this event.

She waves hello to people, playing the cheerful team captain off the field. The other field hockey girls don't look particularly thrilled. But they just clinched an important win, according to the school's Instagram account.

Robin nods at Samara from across the room, and Samara blushes. She snaps a photo of Robin with a bulky camera. What is their deal? Are they really casual, or should we be taking a closer look at what Samara might have been willing to do for Robin? How long has this been going on? I've got to figure it out. For Nate, of course.

Noah rolls his eyes. "Bit much, don't you think?"

I nod. Internally, I seethe. Jealousy is a powerful emotion. The kind of emotion that could be a motive. Samara is giving pseudo cool girl, dressed like a Candyland-themed Barbie doll with a carefully scavenged vintage camera.

*You're on Noah duty*, I remind myself. *No making up conspiracy theories right now*. I turn back to Noah, but I've lost him.

He can't be *that* hard to find. There's only a handful of Black people at this party, and I came in with two of them.

I spot Bria leaning against a sparsely filled bookshelf, forcing herself to smile at something Lily is saying. Lily is showing her something on her phone while pointing and laughing. Bria is not laughing. Bria could not be further from laughing. She looks like she could leave her body in this moment.

Janet seems to have vanished too. Maybe I should find her and get the scoop on their secret sibling. I don't actually have to *talk* to Noah the whole party. I just need to know where he is and who's going out of their way to be around him.

I grab the nearest beverage to fit in. My stomach curdles at the mere thought of drinking after what happened at the last party. I hike up the chest of my bodysuit, which is hanging on for dear life. Mariana made me do a photo shoot in front of the only bare wall in the apartment before I left home. She and Molly directed the poses. I'm nowhere near tall enough to be a model, and with them trying to contort me into squats and leans that I'd never imagine for myself, I should have known I'd be adjusting the top all night. When I got into her car, recounting my exploits, Bria told me to always use tape, and that was that. She didn't offer me any, even though, knowing her, I'm sure she's ready for anything.

I make my way toward the back patio, where people are gathered around what I assume is a keg. Robin sits on the short brick wall surrounding the patio, smiling at Samara, who is chattering her ear off. Robin clocks me almost immediately but doesn't react. Samara turns too, and when she spots me, her face turns sour.

Alain slides into my line of vision, and I try not to roll my eyes. I hate his vibe. There's something about him that doesn't sit right with me, but not in a murdery way, an annoying one.

"Whoa, there. Be careful with that," he says, gesturing to the drink. "You can get dangerous on those." He mimes taking a picture with his fingers.

"Hmm?" I try my absolute hardest to keep my veneer of composure.

"You know...last time?" His smile starts to fade as he realizes his attempt at humor isn't landing.

"Alain? Word of advice. Don't call Black girls dangerous as a joke. Especially when they're being tried in the court of public opinion for violence," I reply.

He turns bright red and backs away from me. Dropping the hint that a white person may be acting a little racist is a surefire way to get them to leave you alone. He literally bumps into someone's back, then lurches forward into me, knocking the beer in my hand all over my top.

Perfect.

Now I'm going to be soaked in stale beer for the rest of the night, *and* Mom is going to kill me if she beats me home and smells it.

Robin hops off of the wall and rushes over to me. She nods toward the street, and I feel a rush of satisfaction that she was ready to rescue me even when she was supposed to be with someone else.

Samara glares at both of us. Then her face brightens as she notices someone else across the patio. She waves, and I follow her gaze.

Noah grins back at her with a smile bigger than I've ever seen from him. That smile tells me they are, at the very least, good friends. But how? When?

When she notices me watching her, her smile fades.

*Well, that's interesting.*

Robin leads me around to the front. "You really can't stand to see me talking to her, can you?"

"Not as much as she couldn't stand you looking at me," I reply.

She snorts. "Touché. I don't love seeing you with Noah either. He may not be his brother, but you two seem rather cozy."

I laugh. "Unfortunately, I've always gravitated toward jocks."

My body heats as I realize what I've said. What I've implied. As if every implication between the two of us doesn't feel painfully clear.

"So you're saying I still have a chance," she says.

I lightly swat her arm. "Don't even."

She shrugs. "Don't be scared. I'll only bite when you want me to."

She is torturing me. Truly tormenting me for the fun of it. It just makes me more determined to do the same back. Flirting is harmless, right? Especially when no one can see us.

"When? Ever the confident one, aren't you?" I say.

She runs her tongue over her teeth. "You like confidence, don't you?"

"On some people."

She laughs. "And here I am, trying to help you find an alternative to these wet clothes. Except this time, I don't have a tracksuit. Where are you parked? I know you must keep a change of clothes with you."

"My sweater is in Bria's car. We came here together. Teamwork makes the dream work, right?" I reply.

"Oh, perfect. I passed it after I parked."

She leads the way. Always the team captain, always the leader. For someone who wanted to keep all of us on the hook, Nate couldn't have picked three more strong-willed girls. It's like he wanted to tame us. Oh boy, did that not work out.

"So you're into Samara?" I ask.

"She's fun, cute. It's nothing serious."

We stop in front of Bria's car, neither of us daring to say anything else. I try the driver's door, which is surprisingly open. But Bria has dash cams, one pointing through the windshield and one pointing at the back seat.

Robin waves to the camera that is now recording the two of us, then points it down at the floor. She slides into the back seat and pats the space next to her, knocking my sweater onto the floor.

I reach past her legs to grab it, but it's caught on something.

Robin leans down and starts digging. My sweater is caught on the zipper of a bag. She maneuvers it out and hands it to me. A glint of maroon catches my eye. I pull the bag onto the seat.

Robin sees it too, and she looks at me, her mouth gaping.

Someone's been digging through the trash, and they have Nate's jersey.

## 17

**MY HAND SHAKES SO BADLY THAT I DROP THE JERSEY** onto the floor. My eyes fill with hot, angry tears. I was starting to trust Bria, at least a little. I thought we'd come to a truce, and all this time, she's the one who had the jersey. The stolen jersey. *My* jersey.

"Whose bag is it?" I ask. "Is it Bria's? Or her secret brother's?"

Robin swallows. "No. It's Janet's. There's a theater pin attached. And they don't have a secret brother."

"But Bria has a brother?" I confirm.

"She did. He died when we were in middle school."

Oh God. I can't imagine. My sisters drive me up a wall, but I wouldn't trade them for anything in the world. No wonder Bria rides so hard for Janet. She knows what it's like to lose someone. But if she knows that pain, why would she keep this? It's a symbol of everything that happened that night.

"Why would Janet have Nate's jersey?" I ask.

Robin sighs. "There are at least five different reasons I can think of that don't involve murder. But I'll admit, it does look bad."

Neither of us makes a move to touch the jersey. What are we even supposed to do with it? It's not fully incriminating, but it would certainly raise some eyebrows. The jersey was in the trash can after the pep rally. Bria or Janet could have taken it. They could have found it afterward too. But did they hold on to it because they were guilty or because they thought it made them look guilty?

Now that we know they have it, what would they do if they found out what we've discovered?

My mind runs through several scenarios, and I snap a picture of the jersey and the bag with my phone.

"I need a minute," I say and step out of the car and out of Robin's sight line.

"Well, make it fast. She could come out here looking for us, and then we're both screwed," she calls after me. She sounds genuinely scared, like she knows something about Bria that I don't. Like how dangerous she truly is.

Robin has already proven that she can take on Bria. Now it's my turn. If she was hoping to mess with me, two can play that game.

I text Mila the photo: Found jersey in B's car. What should I do?

She texts back immediately. Leave it how you found it and get away. I've got you.

"Just put it back the way it was. Then we can figure out how to approach Bria and Janet," I tell Robin.

"We?" Robin asks.

If I have learned one thing from horror movies, it's *never split up*. Secondly, never confront a potential murderer alone. I'm not an idiot. If Bria or Janet attacked Nate and kept a literal souvenir, then we are in serious trouble.

"Are you not with me on this?" I ask.

"Come on," she says, wedging the bag under the seat. She holds out my sweater, and I snatch it from her. "I'm sure there's some other explanation."

I slam the car door and start walking back toward the house. There is no room for the benefit of the doubt. This is fucking serious. I thought we were all being set up, which was scary enough, but if Bria is the one who attacked Nate, it's only a matter of time until she comes for us.

Robin grabs my arm and spins me around.

"What?" I snap. "What could you possibly say to defend her?"

I hear a siren in the distance. *A siren in the distance, me stumbling down a sidewalk. Seeing . . . seeing . . .*

The siren approaches, along with another, and I realize this isn't a memory. Those sirens are coming toward us. Every time sirens have been this close, someone close to me has either been dead or injured, and I'm usually on the suspect list.

Someone yells from the patio, and a steady stream of partygoers heads in our direction. All the oxygen leaves my lungs as people push past me. It feels like a stampede, like I'm going to drown in a sea of my fellow students.

Anyone could sell me out. Bria could have spread rumors about what happened at my old school.

The police could start looking at me. They could reopen the old case. Make connections. Then I'd truly never see Nate again. My entire family would be ashamed. Robin wouldn't...

Whatever is happening here would be over, good and bad.

Robin grabs my arm and pulls me in an unfamiliar direction. Of course she'd know the best way out of here. This isn't her first rodeo at Samara's house.

We end up crouched behind a bush several feet from Bria's car while the police start to comb the property and, presumably, interrogate whoever is still inside. Are they asking about the party, or are they asking about us?

"You okay? You look like a deer in headlights," Robin says. "Have you never been at a party that's been busted up?"

I roll my eyes. Of course I have. I only *look* like a stick in the mud. I usually don't worry that I'm the cause of it though. Is it a coincidence that the party is being broken up a few minutes after Mila said she'd take care of it? Probably not. I suppose there are mostly rich white students inside, so nothing too crazy is bound to happen. But Noah is inside. So are Janet and Bria. Robin and I aren't that far away, and I reek of the beer that was dumped on me. This could get unnecessarily way, way worse.

I yank my hand out of Robin's, ignoring the tingles shooting up my wrist from the skin-to-skin contact.

"I'm fine. *I* haven't done anything wrong," I say.

"Are you sure? You seem pretty shaken. We're okay. It's okay," she says, rubbing my back.

I move a couple of inches away from her. "I'm ready to go home, but I need a new ride."

"I'll take you. The cops are roaming, so we have to be careful with our timing," she whispers.

As if she's conjured them, a pair of officers starts peeking into the row of cars in front of us. She squeezes closer to me and motions for me to keep quiet.

Some people have begun to gather, and Robin takes the opportunity to drag me off to the side, around the commotion. We stay low, trying to be as subtle as possible.

"Do you think we'll be dragged into this?" I ask.

"We're already in it, babe."

Soon we are three blocks away from the house and safely out of view. Her car is parked on a dead-end street. Almost like she knew something was going to happen at this party.

Have I been suspecting the wrong girl?

**BY THE TIME ROBIN DROPS ME OFF AT MY APARTMENT,** I'm so exhausted and emotionally sick that I go straight to bed sans shower. I don't say a word to Mom, who's actually home, as I pass her in the living room. In my defense, she doesn't say anything either, even though we both know I smell like I bathed in a container of beer, then sat in the sun for several hours.

I wake up the next morning smelling worse and feeling like I have a colossal hangover even though I didn't drink. Fantastic.

Mila is standing over me, her nose scrunched up. "Please shower. And do laundry. I'll give you quarters myself, but I will *die* if you continue to smell like this."

"Sorry," I groan. "It got hectic."

"Yes, Burke social media is abuzz with the revelation that Nate Walker's jersey was seen in Bria Kelly's car. However, I may have miscalculated submitting that tip," Mila says.

Of course it was her—and of course NWTruther's post with my photo has made the rounds on half the senior class's Instagrams.

"Miscalculated how?" I ask.

"You were seen wearing his jersey during the pep rally. Robin wore it multiple times in the past, but Bria was seen in it that night, with him."

"That night?" That's new.

"Yeah, someone saw it in her Insta stories from the night of Nate's attack," she says.

So Bria took it out of the trash. She wore it with him, for some probably disgusting reason. But that doesn't implicate her any more than before.

Except...

Why would she keep it hidden? And why was it in Janet's bag? Could there be evidence on it connected to what happened to Nate?

There are just so many questions I have no clue how to answer. But answering them is the key to clearing my name. Maybe I should be taking a closer look at social media. If someone found the jersey in Bria's old stories, what clues could I dig up?

Mariana bursts in, then catches a whiff of my smell. "Ew, what died?"

"Megs's second-favorite top," Mila replies.

Mariana snorts, then shoves her phone in my face. "Bria is on a warpath, and Robin is caught in the crosshairs."

I look at Bria's Instagram. Apparently, at one a.m., Bria went live and revealed several things.

Number one, when she was the "other woman," Nate told her that he and Robin were broken up and only playing at coupledom for appearances until the fall-winter sports season was over. She provided copious text messages from Nate saying so, as well as a video she had sneakily taken of him right before the holidays last year.

Number two, she was with Nate earlier on the night he was assaulted because he came to her house begging for her help. He knew he had messed up with all of us and wanted her spin doctor skills. In exchange, he offered to publicly admit to misleading her to restore her reputation.

And number three, the big one: Janet was the one who saw me throw away the jersey. She rescued it from the trash can and returned it to Nate, who in turn gave it to Bria as part of his apology. Bria felt it was important to emphasize that it still smelled like Coca-Cola from the trash and my BO specifically. Apparently, I smell fruity but in a negative way.

But none of that explains why she kept the jersey a secret. There were so many times she could have turned it over or left it with other sports gear at school. Why would she keep it unless she was planning to use it to her advantage?

I don't realize I've said that final part out loud until Mila grits her teeth.

"So she could plant it on you or Robin at a later date, *obviously*," Mila says. "New number-one suspect engaged."

"That's diabolical." Even though, as of last night, I was looking sideways at Robin.

"Not as diabolical as her revealing that she wasn't Nate's first mistress. He hooked up with Robin's cocaptain first," she says.

*Liv? The same Liv who quite literally kicked me when I was down? Oh my God.* Another notch for the Robin-could-be-the-suspect theory that's been building in my brain for the past twelve hours.

"Liv? That cocaptain?" I confirm.

"That's the one. Then *she* went live to try and deny it, but then Bria introduced receipts. There are *pictures*, a lot of pictures of the two of them," Mariana replies. "Robin has yet to respond."

I whip out my phone and text Robin. I've seen her and Liv hanging out. I can't imagine Robin keeping up the friendship if she knew.

She texts back: I'm hanging in there, but it hurts. I thought one of them would have told me.

What are you going to do?

If she wants war, I'll bring war.

Robin's reply causes a shiver to shoot down my spine.

Mariana's jaw drops. "Ohmigodohmigodohmigod. Bria apparently told the police this morning that she refused the apology jersey and that you were in the car with her last night."

Um... are you allowed to release your police statements on social media in the middle of an active investigation? Can't they get her for interference or something? Well, likely not, with her family money and connections. Great.

Molly comes running in, nearly colliding with my bed frame. I don't know how the students of Burke are making TikToks so fast. Don't we have college applications due?

Mom follows her. She turns her nose up. "It smells awful in here." She looks me up and down. "Are those your clothes from last night?"

"What's up, Mom?" I ask.

"The police are here with some questions," she says. "Again."

"I'll be right out, just let me change," I reply.

She closes her eyes and presses her fingers to her temple. There are bags under her eyes that I swear have become deeper.

"You can't keep getting into these situations, Megs," Mom says.

"I didn't *do* anything," I reply.

"Just . . . why him? He screamed trouble and—"

"It's a bit rich to blame me for my taste in men, given our mutual history."

Her lips purse into a tight line. Only Mila and I are old enough to remember what happened with our father. What happened with Mom's attempts at dating. If anything, I'm just repeating the mistakes she made, only on steroids.

"Her picker may be damaged as all heck, but she's not a killer, Mom," Mila says. "We all know that."

Mom's mouth tightens again, but she concedes with a nod. "I'll put on a pot of coffee. Be quick."

As the door closes behind her, my sisters get to work. Mila picks out my most conservative pink dress, with a square neck and long sleeves, while Mariana grabs the promise ring and unearths a cross necklace from the depths of my bedside table. I did one summer of Vacation Bible School, and oof. The sandwiches were bad, and let me tell you, the jewelry was even worse. I swear this necklace will turn my skin green.

Molly takes a look at my hair and sighs loudly before putting her phone down for the first time in probably three years. She makes quick work of throwing my hair into two braids and pinning them to the top of my head like some sort of Pollyanna-Heidi hybrid.

Mila cleans the remnants of last night's eyeliner from my face with a makeup wipe, then fogs me with some body spray.

I couldn't look less like a murderer if I tried.

Sisters. Can't live without them.

They gather by the door to snoop as I make my way to the living room. Officer Nichols and another officer are waiting, each holding a steaming mug of coffee. Great, they've fully deputized the SRO. School arrests must be imminent.

Mom sits across from them and pats a space next to her. She looks mildly amused by my appearance but seems to approve. What else can I do besides look as innocent as possible? The police either think I'm vindictive or crazy. I might as well try to appear angelic.

I slide in beside her, cross my ankles, and fold my hands in my lap. "Hello, Officers, how may I help you?"

"We have questions about a party that occurred last night," Officer Nichols says. He raises a tape recorder.

Mom puts her hand on top of mine, and her grip is a silent message to keep it together, even if it involves a little lie. She nods at the recorder, and I follow her lead.

"Of course. Ask away." I shoot them my brightest smile.

"How and when did you arrive at the party?"

"I arrived with Bria and Janet Kelly at around nine."

"And why did you elect to go with them?" he asks.

An image of these two men laughing at me over TikTok conspiracy videos flashes in my mind. They think they already know my story. Everyone thinks they know me, but no one really does. I don't throw people under the bus, even if this is my opportunity. And I can't shake this nagging feeling that Bria isn't the one who attacked Nate. It just doesn't feel right.

"We're both in a unique position by virtue of what happened with Nate, so we've tried to find some common ground. I thought going with them would be a sign of goodwill," I say.

"Despite your concurrent relationships with Nate Walker?" Officer Nichols asks.

I swallow hard. I hear the implication in his voice. He doesn't have to call us sluts for me to know that he's thinking it. The derision in his eyes is palpable.

"*In addition* to our mutual interest in Nate. As highly accomplished young women, we shouldn't be reduced to our connection to a man." I smile again.

Mom squeezes my hand, and I can't tell if she approves or is telling me to shut up.

"And what about Robin Ellison?"

I shrug. "She was in her uniform at the party, so I assume she came directly from practice."

"Have you three interacted much?" He watches me like he thinks he's caught me in something.

Tension radiates off of Mom. She was here last year when I was interrogated by the police, in this very spot. Neither of us wants to be doing this again.

"We've been commiserating about how difficult it has been without Nate, without him being able to tell his story, and all of the attention and false accusations that have come from this," I reply.

"Accusations?"

"Yes, rumors are being spread on social media, distracting us from our education. We've been discussing whether or not it would be prudent to file a Title IX complaint against the school," I say.

We haven't actually discussed it, but now I'm wondering if it might be a good idea. We could keep it in our back pocket to scare the administration. Though we'd need a lawyer to take our case.

Plus, anytime I've tried to report the misdeeds of an athlete, I've been summarily shut down.

Maybe this time will be different. But knowing the people in charge, it won't be.

"Tell me about the jersey," Officer Nichols says.

Mom clears her throat and takes a sip of coffee.

"I threw the jersey in the trash can after the pep rally. Bria was spotted wearing it later that night, with Nate. I saw that on

Instagram. I'd be happy to consult with you all on the social media posts and the information they have provided," I reply.

"Did you tell anyone about getting rid of the jersey?"

"Just my sisters," I reply.

"And your ring? The ring from Nate?"

Mom's head snaps toward me, and her eyes bore holes into my skull. I've never told her about the jewelry, and she's barely on social media. This is definitely not the way I wanted her to find out.

"We are not engaged." I flash my left hand. "He gave me this promise ring a couple of weeks ago as a sign of his commitment."

"Ironic, considering," the second officer says, speaking for the first time.

"I'm aware," I reply.

Officer Nichols elbows him. Apparently snarky comments aren't part of police procedure.

"And what about Liv Forrest? What do you know about her connection to all of this?"

My throat goes dry. What if those calls I've been making to Nate weren't private? And even if the content was, it's only a matter of time before they figure out it wasn't the real Liv Forrest calling.

There's a pang in my chest. If I call again, I'll need to switch names. Or stop calling. That feels even worse. *But why? You're already starting to move on.*

"I can only speak to rumors, since I wasn't at Burke during the initial situation with Nate, Robin, and Bria. But there is a rumor that sometime last year, Nate was unfaithful with Liv in addition to Bria. And Liv is Robin's cocaptain of the field hockey team."

"And what is your connection with her?"

"She has been particularly unkind to me, which I guess makes more sense now." I blink a few times, trying to conjure the appearance of tears.

"Unkind how?"

I lower my gaze. "I don't want to get anyone in trouble."

The officers whisper to each other a bit, giving me the opportunity to bite the inside of my cheek until tears prick in my eyes. Good. Crying will sell my story even more. Granted, my story is true, but who will believe me? No one ever believes me.

Mom seems to sense a way out. She nudges me gently. "Meghan, sweetheart, you have to tell the officers what Liv has done."

It takes a lot of willpower not to flinch at her *sweetheart*. I wish I thought she meant it.

"Um... I don't want to press charges," I begin.

"We'll decide if that's warranted. Go ahead."

"Liv assaulted me on our first day back after Nate's accident. She shoved me and kicked me. Robin had to intervene, or it would have been worse." I pull the nearest blanket over my lap to cover my bare legs and pull up my dress to reveal the sickly yellow bruise on my stomach.

Mom gasps.

"Would Robin Ellison confirm your story?"

"I'm sure she would. As would anyone who was in the hallway

when it happened. I'm also willing to bet someone caught it on camera," I reply.

"So you're saying that Bria Kelly had Nate's jersey and wore it after you, with Nate, the night of his attack. And subsequently, Liv Forrest, who also had a relationship with Nate, physically assaulted you, and Robin Ellison defended you."

"Yes. And Liv may be behind the Instagram account NWTruther, which has posted inflammatory and offensive content about all of us." I take a deep breath before adding, "Including a photo of Nate in the hospital sent by Bria."

If Bria wanted to screw me over with that jersey, I can return the favor. The police can figure out the rest.

"According to Bria Kelly's dash cam footage, you came back to the car with Robin before the police were called to the party."

"Yes. We felt uncomfortable being there, and I wanted to get my sweater. Someone spilled . . . Red Bull . . . all over my top," I reply.

"Uncomfortable?"

"I was frustrated with the guy who spilled his drink on me," I say. "And I needed space to vent about some girls being catty without our gossip session being overheard."

We're teenage girls. Adults always think we're gossiping about one thing or another. Plus, it's the only excuse I can think of while my heart is pounding out of my chest. I can see the handcuffs dangling out of one officer's belt.

Officer Nichols clicks his pen. "Thank you."

The second officer looks at me thoughtfully. "You seem like

a nice girl. I'd advise you to find new friends and stay away from girls like those."

That sick feeling in my stomach comes back. *Girls like those.* Ten minutes ago, I was one of those girls. Now I've used whatever power I have to put the attention on other girls who may or may not deserve it. Some feminist I am. But I have to save myself, right?

**BRIA AND ROBIN ARE WAITING FOR ME AT MY LOCKER ON** Monday morning. Bria looks ready to breathe fire, and Robin... Robin just looks disappointed. With whom, I have yet to decipher. As I approach, Bria steps over so that she is physically blocking my locker. Nate's been in a coma for over a week, as the NW Truther account keeps reminding us.

"You really don't support other women," Bria says. "For all your talk of solidarity, you're a violent, backstabbing b—"

"B, don't go there," Robin says.

*I'm* violent? As if these two haven't played WWE for the school to see. What are they going to do now? Excommunicate me from their group again? My defenses prickle as I see all the ways this could go. Almost every single path involves them turning their backs on me so I take the fall. Just like at my old school.

Bria rolls her eyes. "I thought we had a truce."

"So did I, before I found out you had Nate's jersey hidden in your car and you sent the police to my house."

Bria lets out a loud puff of air, and Robin closes her eyes.

My guard is up for good reason, but it's ruining the closest thing to friendship that I have. Even if that friendship is with a girl who is willing to let me take the fall and another who maybe committed the crime.

"Do you really believe everything you see on social media? Now the police think I teamed up with freaking Liv Forrest, who I literally cannot stand," Bria says. "She tried to *call* me yesterday. What a psycho."

"Look, the police were questioning me again, and I freaked out," I say.

"They questioned all of us again. Nate's vitals spiked for a few seconds. They think he could wake up," Robin shares.

*I thought Noah was on my side, but he didn't even give me a heads-up. Why wouldn't he? Did his parents find out he's been talking to me and...*

I take a deep breath. "How do you know?"

"Our Instagram friend DMed me," Robin replies. "I would have told you, but you were too busy throwing us under the bus."

"I didn't throw *you* under the bus. I have been through this before, and I have a lot to lose if anyone is too suspicious of me. I'm scared, and I reacted." I add, "Maybe too quickly."

"And that's why you don't have any friends," Bria replies. "And the one you had, surprise, turned on you."

Of course she'd use that against me. I actually told her

something real, something in sort-of confidence, and she's throwing it in my face. What about our ceasefire, huh? What really hurts is Robin not standing up for me this time.

I snap, "Because she sided with my abusive boyfriend instead of me. Is that really how you want to play it?"

"You're both hitting below the belt," Robin says. "Let's meet up after school and talk this out. When there aren't people watching."

Bria steps toward me, and even though I have a couple of inches on her, it feels like she's towering above us all. Her hands are balled against her sides. Here's the Bria I always expected. Not the snarky one or the one who I actually connected with. The one who looks like she could nail me in the face.

Robin tries to pull Bria's arm. She doesn't account for the fact that Bria has secret Hulk strength and is able to push her away.

Then the vice principal arrives with Officer Nichols at his side, and we all freeze.

Bria's eyes flick up and down, from Robin's eyes to her chipping nail polish. Her upper lip curls until it almost touches her nose.

"For appearances only," Robin whispers so only the three of us can hear. The two shake hands.

Gosh, they're good at this. Everyone knows they've been fighting, but they turn it around to act as though it's all a façade.

Bria puts her arm around Robin, and they flash twin whitened smiles at the rapidly growing crowd. Bria even takes a bow, drama queen that she is.

"And that's why my platform for this year will be female empowerment. We're going to make sure you're watching us for our accomplishments, not who we're dating or who you *think* we're fighting over," Bria says.

In another life, I would want Bria as a true friend. We could rule this school. But in this life, I need to get out of here. Only the most oblivious of the student body and staff will believe Bria's bald-faced lie. I don't want to be the center of attention when I'm still getting tagged the most in the NWTruther comments. Even with my sisters' incredible PR blitz and my seeming alliance with Robin and Bria, most of the school still thinks I'm the one who hurt Nate.

"Come on, Meghan. Don't be shy." Robin shoots me a pointed look.

I bow too, trying to ignore the embarrassment I feel for being a part of this charade. But what can anyone do?

"That's what real friends do," Bria whispers. "Take notes, girly."

As the crowd starts to hesitantly disperse, Robin turns back to me with a wounded look on her face.

"I wish you'd trusted me," she says. "You could have told me what was happening, and I would have reassured you that Bria didn't screw you over. I tried to tell you that at the party."

*But did she?*

Bria steamrolls ahead. "Our alliance is over. Figure out who attacked Nate on your own, or 'fess up to being the attempted murderer, since that's your track record. You've made an enemy, darling. Don't forget what I know."

What more could she know? She has the gist of what happened at my old school, courtesy of my fake former friend. There isn't much more to the story. If and when she decides to go nuclear, I'm screwed, regardless of what the truth is.

"She doesn't mean it," Robin says.

"Oh yes, I do. I submitted my last app yesterday, and the student government is basically running itself. I have plenty of fucking time to dedicate to figuring out how Meghan was involved in all of this. And if it involves digging up past dirt, then buckle up." Bria flips her braids over her shoulder and starts down the hall.

Then she turns around and looks back at us. Robin takes a single glance at me and follows her.

I really am on my own here.

**IT TAKES ANOTHER TWO DAYS, BUT MILA IS FINALLY** approved and scheduled to visit my school. In her infinite wisdom, she wrote the biggest sob story about her family history and educational experiences, using only one or two pieces of actual truth. Sure, she grew up without a father, but not because he dropped dead of a heart attack in the hospital right before her birth. And yes, her public school could be stronger academically, but she wasn't denied the opportunity to take AP classes because no one believed she could handle the tests.

Her story is so moving, so convincing, that she is approved to spend an entire school day at Burke, shadowing one of the juniors and then bouncing between after-school activities.

Thursday morning rolls around, and Mila has me drop her off a couple of blocks from the school. I know she can handle herself, but if anyone figures out that she's not Milan Baker, her alter ego, we're both going to be in deep shit.

Though the Burke administrators didn't do a lick of research or check any of the details she provided. They simply trusted that a school in "that area" must have failing ratings and unqualified teachers. It works in our favor, but I feel a little guilty about it without fully understanding why.

According to the NWTruther account, Robin and Bria have been spotted together on several occasions over the last few days: in the hallway, in the student government office, outside sipping coffees from their lunchtime Starbucks run. Every time someone posts a photo or a TikTok of them, I feel a debilitating pang of jealousy. Robin won't speak to me, which I thought would be the worst part. But the worst part is knowing that the only club I was ever really a part of here has kicked me out. Or that I, in my paranoia, kicked myself out.

Every time a photo of them is posted without me, Noah texts me a thumbs-up or some encouragement. I appreciate the sentiment, but it still stings. He's a silent ally, but I need someone to vocally defend me.

The NWTruther account posts pictures of me sitting alone in various corners of the school. Creative filters make my focused expression look like a murderous one and pencils look like knives. Any sympathy I was gaining from the online community has rapidly disappeared. The quiz bowl team has stopped trying to recruit me, and the religious kids now avoid me in the hallway. I'm back to being suspect number one in the court of public opinion.

Liv Forrest has been pretty quiet ever since the news came out about her and Nate. She and Robin still have to play together, and I've seen more than one TikTok of them at practice, trying not to look at each other. The girls' field hockey team has never been this popular, and that's *really* saying something given how their popularity has only ever been surpassed by the boys' basketball team.

Robin's social media presence has remained pretty consistent. She posts on her Instagram grid every other day and reposts stories frequently. She mostly sticks to field hockey news but occasionally throws in a cryptic quote like, who are your enemies but former friends? or only trust yourself. It's most likely a subtweet towards Liv, but I can't help but feel as if she's talking to me as well. Not that I'm checking obsessively. Thank goodness she hasn't blocked me yet.

Bria's social media has stabilized, but she goes live every evening, even if only for a few minutes, to talk about her political goals for the year, often with Janet beside her. Her TikToks are even more pointed. She's taken to stitching herself into other peoples' conspiracy videos and debunking them. However, she only debunks the ones that accuse her and occasionally Robin. The ones where I'm implicated, she seems to ignore, even though I know she really doesn't. Her likes are strategic across platforms, never enough for me to confront her but pointed nonetheless, and pointed in my direction.

I pretend to fiddle with my locker combination while waiting to see Mila enter from the corner of my eye. Andy and Jess are canoodling across the hall, blocking access to several peoples' lockers. Ugh, they're so performative. No happy couple actually acts like that.

In everyday life, Mila dresses more preppy than I do. She has an enviable blazer collection, foraged from Goodwills and thrift shops across the area. Milan, however, isn't as put-together as Mila. Milan is wearing an oversized flannel sourced from Molly, who almost exclusively wears men's shirts, and a pair of ripped jeans that I recognize from Mariana's closet. Her usual understated hoop earrings have been replaced with faux black pearl studs. Her combat boots are from my closet, but I've only worn them to Burke once or twice, so I don't think anyone would recognize them. To polish off the look, she has thrown on a pair of her own blue-light glasses, which are chunky, red, and huge on her tiny heart-shaped face. Honestly, her whole look is a vibe, and she's selling it—though she's going to have to sleep in a houndstooth skirt suit tonight to regain her sense of self.

She pretends to look around as if she's unsure of how to get to the principal's office, despite my very specific directions.

A blond on the yearbook committee jumps out of the nearest classroom, startling Mila. Her mouth starts moving before Mila fully registers her presence. This must be her buddy for the day, which means she's already secured an invite to the yearbook meeting.

Mila forces a smile, which is somehow so unlike her actual one or the strained one she reserves for family pictures. She hates attention, but she may need to get into theater. She is transforming herself into a character before my very eyes. *Take that, Janet Kelly.*

Mila and her student buddy begin walking toward me, and I hold my breath. Have we already been found out? A security camera blinks at us, and my heart starts speeding up, even though technically I haven't done anything wrong.

We've lied, but that's not a crime. At least, it wasn't last year.

Andy snorts as they pass him and Jess. Jess pinches her nose, as if Mila has ever had body odor a day in her life.

"Hey, Megs, are you related to this chick?" Jess calls. "Both *underprivileged*?"

She makes *underprivileged* sound like a slur. There's so much venom behind it that Mila, even with all her preparedness, freezes for a moment. I've told her some of how bad it's gotten, but I neglected to tell her how bad it was before Nate's attack.

Mila swallows. "There's actually a word for girls like you where I'm from," she says to Jess.

Jess raises her eyebrows. "Oh, really? What is it?" She taps Andy on the shoulder as if they're about to hear a really great joke.

The ghost of a smirk flashes across Mila's face. It's an expression I've never seen from her before, and I have no idea what's about to happen. Mila is the most controlled, self-possessed person I know. She drives me up a wall sometimes, but it's why I trust her so implicitly.

"*Racist,*" Mila replies.

Jess lets out a strangled noise, and Andy covers his mouth to keep from laughing. She tries to swat his arm, but he moves away.

"That is *so* offensive. I am a well-known ally," Jess proclaims.

*Well-known to whom?* is the real question, but I keep that to myself. Mila's got this without me. I'm proud. She may be my younger sister, but I admire how quick-witted she is. When did that happen?

"I'm sure that discussing how tragic it is for you to be called racist for thinking all Black people look alike will be a wonderful addition to the diversity addendum on your college essay," Mila replies. "Real special."

Mila's student buddy, who has turned four different shades of purple, motions toward the foreign language wing, and Mila follows her.

Jess starts trying to push Andy toward the two of them as if he's going to intervene. "You're supposed to stand up for me," she hisses loudly enough for the entire hall to hear.

"I'm not getting involved," Andy says. "Good luck."

"You sure didn't have a problem getting involved when it came to decorating lockers," Jess says.

My fingers tighten on my locker door. *Decorating lockers* is definitely code for spray-painting *Black Widow* on mine. Here they are, mentioning it casually because they never faced actual consequences. It makes my blood boil. People like them never face consequences. I learned that at my last school.

"Prove it," he replies.

Jess takes a step back from him. I guess it never occurred to her that he could turn against her or whatever couple's agreement they have. That her beloved boyfriend may not always take her side. This piques my interest even more. Could Mila have been too quick to dismiss them as suspects? This visible tension is out of character for the two of them.

I take a deep breath and close my locker firmly. Mila has inspired me. I turn around so that I'm facing them and the rest of the hallway.

"Maybe he's just afraid of the black widow's wrath." I bare my teeth at her until she looks physically ill.

"You're a psycho," Jess says. "We all know that."

"And you're a racist," I reply. "We all know that. Maybe Wellesley should too? Shall we make a TikTok? Or is X/Twitter still the way to secure cancellation? A Jess Hanson Is Over party?"

"You wouldn't dare," she says.

"Oh, you have no idea what I'd dare to do. None of you do. Leave all of us Black girls alone, and maybe I'll let it go. But don't underestimate how much I want to screw you over," I reply.

Jess gasps as if I've mortally wounded her. My classmates are sneaky, but their phones are out. We're being recorded, probably for a series of after-school posts. I hope the recordings have captured the full conversation, all the way back to their admission of guilt. Maybe if the two of them get exposed, especially as racists, the police will start looking at other leads.

There are plenty of people with personal reasons to want Nate out of the picture, and they're not all romantically oriented.

In the corner of the hall, as if summoned by someone else being the bitch, I hear clapping. Bria steps out of the shadows, smiling. Oh, here we go. She's starting. What, I don't know, but I'm already intrigued.

"Incredible show. Hate the messenger, love the message. Watch what you post on social media, folks. I've got quite the collection of questionable past posts ready to go the next time your racist tendencies slip out," Bria says. "Want to test me?"

Jess drags Andy by the arm down the hallway. The rest of the crowd thins until it's only Bria and me standing a few feet apart while the clock above us ticks toward the first bell.

"Thanks for the assist," I say.

"I don't assist. You're the one channeling me, not the other way around," she replies.

"Look, I'm sorry for—"

"Oh, I don't care. I expected you to backstab us at some point. I did think it'd take you a *little* longer, since you're a user and you've barely gotten anything out of us. Robin is the one who wanted you out. You really hurt her feelings," Bria says.

And that's the nail in my coffin. Part of me knows she's saying it to dig in the knife, but it's effective. I hate that I hurt Robin.

"Can you tell her—"

"Tell her yourself. How are you ever going to have a relationship with her if you can't own your shit? God, the two of you annoy me. Kiss already, and stop circling around each other."

"Wouldn't that be convenient? Then when Nate wakes up, he'll be all yours."

"Yeah, someone else can have him. I'm over all of this, and he was never worth the trouble. You all could lose my number and I'd live a better life."

I don't have her number to lose. She wouldn't give it to me after she gave me a ride to the party. Not being friends with Bria won't make or break my existence, but I don't want her as an enemy.

"You're right. I was protecting myself, and I did it at your expense. I'm sorry," I tell her.

"Ah. My two favorite words. A step in the right direction. Maybe I'll pause your position on my shit list."

I've technically already apologized, but maybe Bria wasn't ready to hear it. Honestly, I can't blame her, given how I acted.

"That's all I can ask," I reply.

She takes a step closer and leans in. "Nice job sneaking your sister in here, by the way."

*Damn it.* She really does know everything. If anyone could figure out who attacked Nate, I'd expect it to be her. So why hasn't she? Why haven't any of us? Are we looking in the wrong places?

"I have no idea what you're talking about," I say.

"Sure you don't. Let's see who figures it out first."

I don't know if she's referring to Mila or to our continued search for who attacked Nate. I guess I won't figure it out now, since she's already halfway down the hall. But in this moment, I'd give up my search for Nate's attacker if it meant I got another chance with Robin.

**AFTER SCHOOL, I HOVER AROUND THE GIRLS' LOCKER** room. It's about as creepy as it sounds, though I'm trying to be casual about it. Mila is watching *Macbeth* rehearsal and sneaking in as many questions as she can before heading over to the school newspaper headquarters. The newspaper, which is weekly, is woefully behind on current events given the state of the students' social media. It's impossible for them to catch up at this point, and there's no way the faculty advisor will let them really get into the weeds.

Even the local news seems to be slipping. Most of its focus is on the hospital and Nate's potential recovery. It's for the best. I'm sure that my former friends have seen the headlines, but hopefully they're not aware of my connection. They'd love nothing more than to sell me down the river.

I keep waiting for the other shoe to drop. Eventually, someone is going to make a social media post about my past. I know it. Just because it hasn't happened yet doesn't mean it won't. And whoever reveals it or submits it to the NWTruther account will probably wait until we're closer to figuring out the real attacker for maximum damage, which is almost comforting. The day my life blows up could be the day I learn what actually happened to Nate.

I pretend to be filling out a French worksheet, half-heartedly translating sentences in my composition notebook. As the seconds tick on, I recognize several mistakes, even though these sentences are well below my actual French literacy level.

The door to the locker room swings open, and I jump, dropping my notebook on the floor. One of the field hockey players looks at me like I'm a horror show come to life.

I bend down to grab the notebook.

"Stalking me now?"

I look up, and there she is, slightly sweaty from practice. I think she might be perfect. "Hi."

"What?" she asks, folding her arms across her chest. She leans against the wall and fidgets with the glove on her left hand. "I heard you were here and thought I could wait you out. Apparently not."

She won't even look at me, and it hurts. It hurts more than finding out about Nate. I think part of me expected that he'd cheat on me, or at least betray me in some way. But in the time I've known her, I never thought Robin would turn on me, even if she thought I'd turned on her.

"I'm sorry for not trusting you. I was looking out for myself, and I should have known that you wouldn't screw me over, even with Bria in your ear," I say.

"Bria can be in my ear all she wants, but I can pick my own friends," she replies.

"Friends, huh?"

"Not anymore."

A few more players stream out of the locker room and seem to be staring at us for longer and longer periods.

Robin's focused on a spot across the hall. Apparently, the tiles there have been discolored for as long as anyone can remember. The rumors that have proliferated over the years range from the incredibly likely to the impossibly salacious. The most rational among us believe that it's water damage. The schemers are convinced it's some kind of bodily fluid spilled during a fight between two former cheerleaders. Rumor has it that one girl came out with a concussion and the other had to have stitches put in her head.

Obviously, they were fighting over some no-good athlete they found cheating on both of them. No one has confirmed if this story is true. But it's a perfect parallel for where we are now.

Robin groans. "Come on." She takes my arm and leads me down the hall to another door.

The back entrance of the locker room. The hall around us is empty, and I feel an eerie sense of déjà vu. We've been here before. I know it. I flash back to that night.

*Robin leads me down the hallway, her hand in mine. Oh God, am I going to puke in front of Robin Ellison? That would be too* embarrassing. It's Robin freaking Ellison. She's so popular. She's so pretty. She's cooler than I'll ever be. I have to seem normal.

She pulls me through an open door, and we're in the girls' locker room. It's not the main entrance, though. I didn't even know this door existed. Is there a similar one for the boys? Do they sneak girls in there? Does Nate?

He probably does. I bet he's cheating with every girl he can. How could it be only the three of us? God, even my thoughts are bitter. I bet he sensed them and that's why he did this to me.

It's somehow all my fault.

Robin sits me on a bench and opens one of the lockers. Her locker. Of course.

She leans forward and I flinch. She dabs an antiseptic wipe over a cut on my shoulder. It's such a tender move on her part that I find myself tearing up.

When she turns her back to get a Band-Aid, I reach for the field hockey stick that's leaning next to me. I pretend to swing it.

"Can we get a Nate piñata?" I ask.

"We were here together," I say. "The night of Nate's attack."

"I don't know how you got that cut, but yeah," she says.

"You always take care of me. You have no reason to, but you do."

"That's what you do when you think someone could be your friend."

I reach for her perfectly pointed chin. For a moment, it seems like she's going to resist as I turn her to face me. My heart skips a beat. *Am I really doing this?*

"What do you do when you think someone could be more than a friend?" I ask.

She closes her eyes. "Meghan—"

"What would you do?" I ask.

With my hand still on her chin, she closes the gap between us. Her lips are softer than I'd imagined, and her hands are already searching for something I'm eager to provide.

There are fireworks I've never had with Nate. This feels like no kiss I've ever had before. It's better. It's unbelievable because it's with her.

Robin pulls away first, ending the fantasy I swear was coming to life. I've wanted her to do that since I first saw her.

"We can't..."

There's a small sound on the other side of the locker room. I shiver. It's probably nothing. Not that I'd have noticed if someone had come in while we were kissing.

"You're unfair," I say.

"*I'm* the unfair one?"

"How was I ever supposed to keep from falling for you?"

"The same way I was supposed to resist you," she replies. "We have—had—the same boyfriend."

So she's had the same feelings, noticed the same things, even before Nate complicated the picture.

My phone, which has been buried in my bag for most of the day, starts going off. I could have sworn I put it on silent. The only people who can get through are emergency contacts.

*Shit.* My only emergency contacts are Mom and Mila. I had to take Mariana off after she sent me too many TikTok fashion hauls during school hours.

I dig until I find it. Thankfully, it's not Mom. Mom only calls me if she needs me to pick up one of my sisters or if she wants to remind me that she can't afford this school without my scholarship, so I'd better behave.

"Hey, Mila. Where are you? What's—"

Her voice is muffled, but I can sort of make her out. "In the girls' bathroom on the second floor, hiding. That girl Liv just gave a statement to the student paper about her involvement in Nate's case, and she's about to post it online. Where are you?"

"In the girls' locker room with Robin. Come meet us."

Robin whips her phone out of her pocket, having overheard, and opens Instagram. Her eyes widen.

Liv has posted a black-and-white photo of her field hockey stick lying in the grass. In the caption she simply wrote: Today I made the difficult decision to step away from the field hockey cocaptain position. I can no longer play alongside someone who dedicates their time to spreading falsehoods. Robin claiming to have no knowledge of my relationship with Nate is untrue. Due to her family's close relationship with *certain* members of the administration, the note she left in my locker—a smiley face with X's for the eyes and Nate's name crossed out on top—went unaddressed, despite our coach finding it threatening. Since then, she has enlisted someone to terrorize an unconscious Nate with phone calls to his hospital room pretending to be me. She is a dangerous human being, and I will be reviewing my options.

"What the actual fuck is she talking about?" Robin asks. "Terrorizing Nate's hospital room?"

Oh no. She thinks *Robin* has been calling Nate's room? And that the calls were somehow malicious? How did I make this situation worse?

"Robin... I have to tell you—"

"Have *you* been harassing Nate? Seriously? Bria was right about you being cra—"

"I've been calling, but just to talk to him. I think it's been helping. I heard the heart monitor, and it... His heart skipped a beat for me, Robin."

She rolls her eyes. "Seriously, Meghan? Don't be ridiculous."

There's that pang in my chest again. Even if she has feelings for me, she doesn't believe me. No one ever does, and that's why we're here. That's why I'm at Burke. No one ever believes that I have good intentions. That I'm not the bad guy.

"I'm not kidding. You'll see. What about you? Did you know what was going on with Liv? Then you lied to me too, pretending last week was when you found out."

"I didn't *know*. I saw him flirting with her once, and yes, I wrote the note. It wasn't a big deal."

"You *lied*, Robin!"

"*So did you.*"

We're at a stalemate, and I'm not sure that either of us will bend. It's part of what I like about her so much, but it could be our downfall before we've even started.

"When you broke up with Nate... was it because of Bria, or was it because of Liv?" I ask.

Robin sighs. "I didn't break up with Nate. We had a fight

after I caught him flirting with Liv, and two days later, he dumped me, claiming he had feelings for someone else. Bria started soft launching him the next week."

"So you never knew that anything had actually happened with Liv?"

"No, otherwise I would have gone after *her* in the tunnel. Or at practice. Or at any of the three million other places I could have gotten revenge on her in the last year."

I never know if I should look at her sideways for those comments. Her go-to seems to be violence, but there's only been the one incident. At least, one that I know of.

Robin couldn't have—*wouldn't* have—hurt Nate. I think. I hope.

There's a creak on the other side of the locker room, like a door slowly being eased open. We both freeze, and I'm very aware of how close we are. How my hand hovers over Robin's thigh.

It could be a janitor coming to empty the trash. All of the janitors seem to like me, since I'm one of the few students who actually acknowledges them. Or it could be one of the field hockey girls grabbing something she forgot. This will look weird, but maybe they're scared of Robin enough to keep it to themselves.

Who am I kidding? A photo of us would be all over Instagram before I made it to my car.

Or what if it's Nate's attacker? What if they're ready to repeat the crime? We're basically sitting ducks.

Mila tiptoes over to us, checking around every corner like a field hockey boogeyman is about to appear. I have never been happier to see her. She immediately clocks the energy between us and raises her eyebrows at me.

"Mila, Robin. Robin, this is my sister Mila," I say.

"Underprivileged, huh?" Robin says.

"Compared to you, absolutely," Mila says. "Though I guess privilege isn't totally working in your favor right now. The paper is still figuring out how to spin it, but basically, they're investigating your, quote, history of violent behavior."

Robin's face falls, but she forces her veneer back into place. The fall, though. It means something, I know it does.

Robin has done more than I know. There must have been other incidents, probably smaller, given that they haven't come out, but they're enough to cast doubt on her character. Cast doubt on whether or not she would have attacked Nate for yet another transgression. It also provides an opening. She'll need an ally, and so do I.

"Anything happen in the theater?" I ask Mila.

"Janet is an absolute diva nightmare, but very talented. The others seem to hate her. She stays later than anyone else rehearsing. *And* she makes at least one member of the crew stay with her because she insists on using props," Mila replies.

Robin and I exchange a look. It's so extra, but such a good anecdote for Janet's future *Playbill* profile.

"What props?" Robin asks.

"Sometimes just a rosary or something small, but for one she was swinging a hammer. I swear she's pulling random items from the props closet, which is a *disaster*. A hazard waiting to happen."

Mila pauses. "Also, I'm pretty sure some of the set paint has gotten on several of the props. One of the fake boats has red stains all over it. It's truly disgusting."

My stomach drops. *Oh my God, we're such idiots! Where better to hide a murder weapon than backstage at a high school production of Macbeth? No one would think twice about red paint, and it'd be so easy to hide.*

"Um . . . are you sure it was paint?" I ask.

Mila's eyes widen. "Oh no."

"Oh yes!" Robin exclaims. "If Janet was here late, the props closet was probably unlocked. Meaning it'd be very easy to stash a weapon in there, especially given that Nate was attacked only a few doors down. How could we miss this?"

All we need is to find a prop that could have done similar damage as one of our three items. But to do that, we need to know what kind of head injury he sustained.

"Well, there was a gap between when Nate was attacked and when he was found. The weapon was probably cleaned, so we need to know what kind of item could have caused the injury he has—and if any cleaning supplies have mysteriously been moved," I suggest. "His hospital room is in the trauma wing, meaning that his injury was substantial and likely to cause serious acute damage."

Robin gives me a curious look. "Why do you know where his hospital room is?"

I avoid her gaze. "Noah gave me the number."

"Of course he did. You're his favorite," she says.

It's not like I was Nate's favorite. He clearly had more respect for every other girl he was involved with. Bria and Robin both had more information than I ever did. They may not have known the extent of his cheating, but they knew something was up. And they knew that I was being led on, even if they didn't realize he was leading them on too.

"At least I'm somebody's favorite," I reply.

"You're mine," Robin says, quietly enough that I almost miss it.

"What happened with you and Noah? I would have assumed he liked you," I say. *I would assume that everyone liked you.*

"He did at first. But Nate and I are both alphas, at least in this school. When we started dating, Nate was a basketball star, sure, but he wasn't as popular. He stuck to himself and his training. After a few months, we became a commodity together. When that happened, Nate changed. He was so sweet in the beginning, so dedicated to us. That's when he gave me the ring. When he got a taste of popularity, he became more like the rest of them, and it drove a divide between him and Noah, and Noah and me," she says.

*Like the people who would vandalize my locker because they thought I wasn't worthy. Or the people who would make fun behind our backs, knowing Nate was betraying all of us. But hey, at least it wasn't them.*

"The narrative is bad," Mila says. "The tides are turning against you, Robin, but plenty of people still think that it was Meghan or Bria, or the three of you together. The evil lesbians theory is really gaining traction, because God forbid that girls like girls without there being some secret devilish deal to take down a man."

I'm pretty sure Robin and I are both blushing at this point.

"Do you think you can get backstage and look for a potential weapon?" Robin asks.

"My visitor pass is up, but I have ideas. We need to figure out what kind of head injury Nate has." Mila glances over at me. "And I know someone who can get us that information."

Robin's eyes light up. "Look at you with the connections. Who?"

I close my eyes. "Our mother."

## 22

**I SIT ON THE COUCH, BOUNCING MY KNEE AND PRETEND-**ing to reread *Les Misérables*. It's late, late enough that Mom will probably be more angry that I'm awake than interested in why I want to have a conversation. But this is her earliest-ending shift, and I made sure to have a box of cookies and her favorite grocery-store sushi waiting on the coffee table.

She comes in at 12:23 on the dot. Her shift ends at midnight, and she always gets home at exactly this time. Her routine is impeccably consistent. She clocks out, grabs a cup of tea to go from the staff lounge, and is in the car with her Broadway playlist by 12:07. I strive to be as consistent as she is, and I almost meet her standard. I even listen to the same Broadway playlist.

We really are a lot alike, deep down. Maybe that's why she resents me so much. I could be just like her, but in her eyes, I keep causing trouble.

When Mom sees me on the couch, she pauses, and for a second, I think she's going to turn and go right back out the door.

"What's wrong? Are the girls okay?" she asks.

As if I'm not one of the girls. There's me, and then there are my sweet, innocent sisters. The ones who matter. I never get to be the one who matters—not in a good way, at least. At home, at school, with my friends, or with the people I love.

"Everyone is fine, and nothing is wrong. Well, beyond all the things that were already wrong," I reply.

She sits beside me and notices the sushi. I even laid out a pair of chopsticks and poured the soy sauce into the compartment. She hesitates before picking them up.

"What do you want?" she asks.

"Hey, Mom. How was your day? Oh, good. My day? Yeah, that was fine, just trying to deal with being accused of murder."

"Meghan, I'm tired. Come out with it," she says.

"I know you can't look at his records..."

Mom groans and rubs her thumbs into her temples. She eats a piece of the sushi, but chews slowly, like she's reconsidering every bite.

"No, I can't. So don't ask me to," she finally says.

"I was only wondering if you knew anything about his injury. Have people talked? I know the other nurses like to consult with you, especially since you're one of the few nurses who consistently works overnights in trauma."

Depending on when Nate was found, she might have been on

duty when he was brought in. It's something I should know, but I don't because we barely talk.

"I was one of the responders when he was initially brought in. As soon as I recognized who he was, I had someone else step in. But she still had to report to me as the supervising nurse," Mom says.

She says it so casually that I almost miss a key point. She never told me she was promoted to supervisor. Did she tell my sisters?

"Congrats, Mom. You never said anything about the new title."

"It doesn't come with more money, so..."

"I still care," I say.

She picks up a cookie, squinting at it for a few seconds before taking a bite. They are obviously store-bought, and I hate that she looked at them like I might have poisoned them. I feel like she thinks so lowly of me.

"What is it you want to know?" she asks. "Without breaking HIPAA, of course."

"About his head injury. Do you have any idea what kind of object could have caused the damage? I know he was found with—I just... I have some ideas, and I wanted to see what's actually feasible, given the medical situation."

"He has a severe head injury, a depressed skull fracture that went untreated for several hours. He had to undergo emergency surgery immediately. Given the extent of the fracture, your book could not have caused it—unless he hit his head on something else afterward. The base of the trophy could have, but it probably would have broken. The field hockey stick is the most likely culprit."

I didn't realize she'd seen the picture. Then again, it was all over social media, and I'm sure someone at the hospital would have shown her. So this whole time she's known that it couldn't have been me. At least not in the way people think.

"So it had to be something hard with a somewhat blunt edge?"

"Most likely. And it was swung hard, probably bottom-up," she replies. "Do I want to know why you're asking?"

"Probably not."

She swallows. "Please be careful. Your sisters need you."

*And you don't,* rings unsaid in my head. My own mother doesn't need me. Why would Nate? Why would Robin? Who would?

"Yeah, I will. Thanks, Mom."

I scoot away from her and pick up my copy of *Les Misérables*.

She reaches out and touches my shoulder. "I never thought that you hurt him or anyone. I just see how this looks. I'm worried. And I'm frustrated that you're in this position but not frustrated because of you. None of this is your fault."

My eyes fill with tears. God, it feels weak to want my mom to tell me that I don't completely suck. But it's what I needed. We may push each other away, but I still want my mom.

"I got so drunk that night that I don't remember what happened. I have flashes but—Mom, I could have done it. Anyone could have," I say.

Mom holds up a finger and walks over to the storage closet. I don't think I've looked in there since I thought I could play soccer in middle school. I couldn't. Athletics were never my strong suit. Honestly, they weren't even my mediocre suit. Maybe I gravitate toward athletes in my personal life because they're able to do the one thing I truly can't.

She opens the door, and I swear I can see a dust monster hiding out behind the forgotten soccer net. She pulls out a collection of sports equipment: a baseball bat, a golf putter, and a bowling ball. What a depressing version of a Dick's Sporting Goods.

She hands me the bat and motions for me to stand in front of the couch. When I pause, she leans down and drags the coffee table back a bit.

She leans three of the pillows against each other. "Okay, you're going to swing. Hit the pillows as hard as you can."

"Are you serious?" I ask.

"Yes. You're going to do it with each of these pieces of equipment, and we'll see how strong you actually are. Then I'll spin you a couple of times to simulate you being drunk and we'll see how well you do."

She's so chill about it. Like this experiment is a regular part of being a nurse or a mom.

I try to take myself back to that night and visualize Nate. Nate in the closet with Robin. Nate in the hallway with Bria. Nate telling me that he never really loved me. I get a flash of him up against a locker, but I don't know if it's from that night or if I've conjured the image. I channel my inner Robin. When she takes a swing, she doesn't miss.

Neither will I.

I let my shoulders guide me as I drive the bat into the pillows, which seem to moan on impact.

Mom nods. "You're stronger than I expected."

Her phone buzzes.

"Hold on." She answers it. "Hello? Yes? Yeah? You sure? Um... did you check with—okay, I'll be right there." She hangs up.

"Is everything okay?" I ask.

"I'm being called in. A patient is having a change in status, and the family requested a supervisor. Even though that supervisor is me." She gives me a pointed look.

*Oh shit. Something has happened with Nate.*

"Is the change in status good? Or..."

"I don't know. But the family has specifically requested me, even though they know that I'm your mother." She bites her lip. "Try the bowling ball."

"What?"

"Go ahead," she says.

I pick it up and am almost certain I'm going to have an allergic reaction to both the dust and the corroded metal embedded in this ball. Why do we even have this? I can't remember the last time we went bowling.

I swing, trying to not throw the ball into the wall behind us. The pillows jump up, and a feather comes out.

Mom squints at the pillows. "I think it was something smaller and heavier," she replies.

*Like something you could find in a props closet?*

"Would there have been blood?" I ask. "On impact?"

"Not necessarily. But there would have been blood afterward." She glances at her watch. "I've really got to go."

"Thank you, Mom. I really appreciate this. You've helped. More than you know."

She nods and is out the door before either of us can say another word.

Why am I only able to bond with the women I want most in my life when it's about possible murder?

**THE NEXT MORNING, I TEXT ROBIN AND ASK HER TO** meet me in the back of the library before school. After a few seconds, I send a second text telling her to invite Bria as well. She doesn't respond, and I don't really expect her to. I just hope she'll show up. I hope they both will.

I find a small table tucked behind a pair of bookcases. The books back here look like they haven't been moved in at least forty years, though the school has been open for only twenty.

Bria arrives first, surprisingly. She slides in across from me, her nose turned up.

"You summoned me?" she asks.

"We can wait for Robin."

"Who says she's coming?"

"I'm hopeful."

Bria smirks and pretends to pick something out of her nails.

What is *her* endgame here? She agreed that we all needed to work together, but I feel like she does whatever she can to let me know that she doesn't think I belong on the same playing field as the two of them.

There's a rustle behind the bookshelf, and Robin ducks into the corner. She leans against the nearest shelf instead of joining us at the table.

"You called?" Her mouth twists into a tight line.

"I did. First of all, I'm sorry. I truly am. I was looking out for myself because I didn't trust that either of you would. And to be honest, I don't think Bria would, but Robin, I know you would," I say.

"Oh, I'll go so you two can make out in peace," Bria snaps. "And for the record, I wouldn't accuse you of murder without just cause. At this point, I'm convinced you're unhinged enough to have been successful in any attempt, so it's unlikely that you made this messy situation."

At least she concedes that I'm competent, I guess? It's not the best thing she's said about me, but it's far nicer than most of the things she's said.

"I feel more of a bond with Robin, yes, not only roman—not only because of *that*. But I understand you more now, Bria. And I'm sorry for making you feel less than. Even though you do that to me too," I say.

"Getting in the dig is very me-coded, so I'll accept that," Bria replies. "Why are we here?"

"My mom works at the hospital, and she was called in last night because something changed with Nate."

Robin takes a step forward. "Is he . . . ?"

"Dead?" Bria finishes. "He's dead, isn't he?" Her voice cracks a bit, betraying the emotion she tries so diligently to hide.

Robin shoots her an offended look, as though it isn't a logical question. Of course, it is possible that Nate woke up. Though after all of this time in a coma, is that the most likely outcome?

"I don't know exactly. My mom hasn't said anything yet. It sounded serious, but that's only part of why I asked you here," I say.

"What's the other part?" Bria asks.

"She said that Nate's skull fracture was deep enough that it's unlikely any of our items were the murder weapon. If any were, it'd be the field hockey stick, but she believes the item was heavier. She had me swing a baseball bat and a bowling ball—"

"Your mom is whackadoo too! Explains everything," Bria says.

Robin reaches over to swat her with the nearest book. I hold my hand up and take the book from her, laying it back on the shelf.

"Basically, she thinks that it was something smaller and heavier than Robin's stick. And it may not have blood on it, depending on impact. But there could have been blood after the impact," I say.

"And you think you know what the weapon is?" Robin asks.

"No, but I assume that it's still in the school. That'd be the fastest, probably least risky way to get rid of it. What do we know for sure about that night and Nate's whereabouts?" I ask.

Bria takes a deep breath and reaches into her backpack. She pulls out a spiral notebook and opens it about three-quarters of the way through. In it she's detailed the timeline that we know so far, along with question marks where she wants more information.

> 8:57 p.m.: ML starts
> 9:01 p.m.: RE arrives
> 9:04 p.m.: RE and ML leave
> 9:07 p.m.: NW goes to rehearsal, finds JK
> 9:10 p.m.: NW finds BK in office
> 9:30 p.m.: NW and BK go to BK's house
> 10:01 p.m.: NW gets text from?? that he left something @ school
> 10:05 p.m.: NW leaves, says he's coming back
> 11:10 p.m.: BK calls, no answer
> 11:13 p.m.: BK calls, answer, but just breathing and hangs up
> 11:15 p.m.: BK calls, phone turned off

I look over at Bria. She established a whole timeline and never mentioned anything about it to either of us?

"So we think that he was attacked sometime between ten and eleven?" Robin asks.

Bria shrugs. "I don't know."

"The breathing, though. You think it was whoever attacked him?" I ask.

"*I don't know.* That happened a couple of times, lining up with when he was with"—she swallows—"one of you."

My stomach heaves itself into my rib cage. Disgusting. Now I can't stop hearing Bria's ringtone in my head.

"So it was either his attacker or you think that he was with—with someone else?" Robin asks.

"I think he was with someone else." Bria's clenches her teeth for a few seconds. She's actually tearing up. "Right after he was with me."

"I'm sorry, Bria. That's a terrible feeling," I say.

"So Liv's a suspect, obviously. Or someone else who had business in the school that late. Janet is scoping out the theater kids. Don't you *dare* suggest that it was Janet. She would never betray me like that." Bria adds, "And she finds Nate physically repulsive."

"Can your police contact figure out what happened with his phone? Maybe someone figured out who texted him?" I ask.

"It was a spam-likely number. I saw it when he went to the bathroom," Bria says. "When I tried calling it, the call could not be completed as dialed."

*And that wasn't a wake-up call? Nate was sneaky, but I highly doubt he was getting his sidepieces burner phones.*

Robin's eyes light up, and she finally sits beside me. Our arms brush against each other, and there's a jolt through me. She scrolls through her phone, stopping at several images before choosing one.

It's the photo of the alleged weapons in the storage closet where Nate was attacked. I hadn't thought about it being one of the "secret" hookup places in school.

*Shit.* So Nate really was hooking up with someone. And that person, or someone affiliated with them, must have attacked him. We need to know who she was.

Robin zooms in even further, and Bria's hand flies up to her mouth. She snatches Robin's phone and holds it close to her face. She taps the screen.

The closet is full of equipment: deflated basketballs, extra field hockey sticks, even an old soccer goal that more than one of us has gotten tangled up in during a make-out session ... at least, I assume.

Bria's pointing to the floor, where it looks like something has shattered. There are small shards of glass on the linoleum. Though ... if my memory isn't faulty ... there's no glass kept in the storage room.

"Talk me through it," Robin says, motioning to Bria.

I almost smile. It was hard to believe they used to be friends until now. But Robin intuited something from Bria so quickly, so casually. There's something deeper there than I've seen before. Something way beyond Nate Walker.

"I'm thinking ... if someone swung at Nate and he hit the floor, what would he have with glass on it?" Bria continues, "He never wore glasses, and his backpack barely had two notebooks and three broken pencils. What could have broken?"

It hits me. If he accidentally answered the phone during his ... entanglement with the yet-undiscovered *other* other woman, then ... he probably didn't put it back in his pocket. So maybe when he was attacked, it was out. Or he was holding it in his hand when ...

"You think those are the remains of his phone screen," I say.

"Meaning that the phone was probably completely wrecked.

Because he was holding it, trying to call someone when he was attacked," Bria says.

"But who was he calling?" I ask.

Robin closes her eyes. "Me."

Bria and I swivel our heads toward her. *What?* How could she leave that out? And where was I? Passed out in her bed while she took a call from our boyfriend?

"I'm expecting an explanation," Bria says. "Post-fucking-haste."

"The call dropped before I could answer it. I didn't think anything of it, and when I called him back, he didn't answer."

"Was I with you?" I ask.

Robin closes her eyes again. This is going to be really bad for both of us.

"No. You took off after a little while at my house, and you came back around an hour later. You passed out after that, and I never asked. I . . . honestly, I didn't want to know."

Bria sucks in her cheeks as my eyes brim with tears. I knew it was possible, of course. But deep in my heart, I never thought that I would have hurt him. I'm sick. I'm so sick. After everything I went through in my last relationship, after all the walls I put up to keep myself safe, after all I did to make sure this would never happen to me again . . .

There is a very real possibility that I hurt the person I thought I loved most.

Panic rises up in my chest until it's clawing at my neck, threatening to choke me into oblivion. I almost want it to. The idea of having hurt Nate is too horrible to face. I can't face myself, my family, *his* family. *Noah.* Oh my God, Noah, who has been so kind to me. Who gave me the number of the freaking hospital so I could call him.

And Nate. Nate's heart skipped a beat when I was talking with him, not because he was happy but because he was panicked. He was terrified, and now he might not be okay because I simply had to talk to him.

Stupid, selfish, *evil* Meghan. I'm terrible. Like they all said.

I'm shaking when Robin takes my arm and tries to hold me still. Or hold me back. She must be scared of me too. I'm a monster.

"There are cameras," Bria says suddenly. "There are cameras all around the school, including outside. That particular closet is out of view, but we could see if you came back to the school during that time period."

"Don't tell me you know how to hack the security system," Robin replies.

"I don't. But I have an in with the security guard," Bria says.

What's left unspoken about Bria's extensive connections? She's probably going to sic the security guard on me in the most public and embarrassing way possible. I'll go to jail. Am I old enough to be sent to an adult facility? Does this state have capital punishment?

"And does your connection with the security guard extend to the actual police officer who's been hovering around us at all times?" Robin asks.

"Well, it's not exactly *my* connection," Bria explains. "I maybe implied that I'm a steward of the underprivileged student program and that I helped bring in Meghan, who has always been so kind to security. And Officer Nichols isn't here today. There was an incident at the public school."

I'm so panicked that I don't have room to be offended, and it doesn't occur to me to ask what happened at the public school.

Robin takes up the mantle in my stead. "Do you realize how that sounds? Meghan is middle class, and she earned her spot here more than either of us. Besides, how do you know what's going on at the public school right now?"

"Technically, she *is* underprivileged, just like we're overprivileged," Bria says. "If we can see the footage, then we can see if she came back and could have been in the closet with Nate. As for your other question, the police are investigating a girl at the public school who claimed she saw Nate that night in an intimate capacity. She was super willing to get involved for a fee."

A fee? Bria's paying people to lie to the police? What the hell is going on? Is this to protect me, or is she protecting someone else?

"I can't believe I did it," I whisper.

I sit, still vibrating with horror, trapped in my own head. It's a hell of my own creation. And now some random girl has been dragged into our situation because Bria has money—and I have a temper.

"You didn't," Robin assures me. "There's not a single part of me that believes you could have done that."

"And logistically, we've seen the videos of you at the school earlier. Robin was with you. Physically, it's unlikely that you suddenly had the wherewithal to go toe-to-toe with Nate," Bria adds.

"Exactly," Robin says.

Bria shoots Robin a look that she doesn't seem to pick up on. Bria reaches out as if she's going to take my hand but reconsiders.

"Then why are you paying some girl to get the SRO out of school?" I ask, my voice rising.

"Because the SRO has been harassing me, trying to get information about you, and I'm not buying it," Bria replies.

"As if you'd really try and defend me."

Bria shakes her head like I'm missing the point. "If you were the girl in the make-out closet, you were blackout drunk. You couldn't consent, even if you were in a relationship with him. So if you attacked him, it was self-defense, after he…he sexually assaulted you."

I burst into sobs, the kind that cleave your chest in two. My body heaves. Not only is my entire sense of self being rocked, but my view of Nate as well.

Being terrible enough to cheat on all of us is one thing. Assault is another. I can't imagine that he'd ever do that. But then again, I didn't think my last boyfriend would try that either.

And still, I was the one who was blamed for his actions. I was the one whose life was torn apart when it happened and when he died. He was valorized, treated like a tragic hero, even though so many people knew what he'd done to me. What he'd done to her.

I've kept her secret for so long at my own expense. Because that's what friends do. But now maybe we're the same.

"Come on," Bria says. "We've got to see that footage to put your mind at ease. But whatever happened, it is not your fucking fault, Meghan. It is *not*. I promise you, if I thought it was you, I'd throw you under the bus."

She and Robin have to help me up, each of them throwing one of my arms over their shoulders. The height difference is apparent. Robin has at least two inches on me, while I have four on Bria, so we're all struggling. I can barely feel my own body, yet my feet feel like they're on pins and needles.

I may be blacking out. There's no sensation in my legs, even though I know we're moving. My ears feel as though they're stuffed with cotton balls.

I've never had a panic attack this bad before, and it seems to be lasting for ages. Maybe I'll be hospitalized. Maybe I'll die. That's one way to get away with murder.

All of a sudden, I feel something ice-cold on my neck. I almost jump out of my skin, but it shocks me back to reality.

Bria is holding an iced coffee cup against me while Robin tries to explain our situation to the security guard. Of course, she's lying. She can't very well say that I'm having a massive anxiety attack because I think I may have attacked our boyfriend. Apparently, I'm sick over my beloved grandmother's locket going missing, and can we see who was seen leaving or entering the school on the night in question, because I'm certain it fell off outside the front door when I was fighting with Nate.

I take a huge gulp of air. It's like I'm coming back to life but with a massive hangover. This feels worse than when I woke up at Robin's house.

Robin rubs my back while Bria hands me my water bottle.

I force a smile at the security guard, and he's sympathetic, like he believes the story we've concocted. I suppose it's obvious that I'm distressed. And why would we lie? Except for the violent assault accusation, I have a pretty sterling reputation. It's not like the police haven't already gotten a copy of this footage. Plus, the three of us together, getting along, is probably enough of a surprise that he's willing to go along with it.

He begins searching through the computer files, scrolling back until he finds the folder from the day of Nate's attack. He types for a few seconds, and the footage from that night appears on the screen, playing at double speed.

Nate walks outside and stands, scrolling through his phone. There are enough people around that this can't be from the time he was attacked. I glance at the time stamp, and then I see myself. Oh great, it's my confrontation with Nate.

Robin squeezes my hand. We both know what's coming.

Nate shoves me to the ground. It's rough. And then he stands there, looking off to the side as if I don't exist. Robin's superheroine entrance is incredible. She sprinted from somewhere off camera at a speed that would get her recruited to any college track team.

The security guard pauses the video. "Miss Landry, I have to ask—"

"It's already been reported to Officer Nichols, and I assume they have the footage," I lie. "We need to see the rest of the video, please."

The lies keep rolling off of my tongue. *Monster. Liar. Killer.* Who knows what else I could be lying about?

The video keeps going, and we watch as the crowds begin to thin. We're in the general time of Nate's attack. He reenters the school not long after Bria told us he left her house. He's looking around like he's waiting for someone. But then he goes inside. And he doesn't come back out.

The video keeps playing, and no one else appears to be coming in or out. All we can see is a shadow at the edge of the screen that seems to fade. The video keeps going until we see the flashing lights of the police sometime early in the morning.

"Are any of the other entrances to the school open that late?" Bria asks.

"No, the only way in or out after eight p.m. is through the front, even with a master key," the guard replies.

The three of us exchange a look.

Whoever attacked Nate was already in the school.

## 24

**I SOMEHOW MAKE IT THROUGH THE SCHOOL DAY WITH-**
out having a complete meltdown. Still, the universe tries me yet again. I'm packing up my backpack at my locker after calculus, thinking about how I'm going to watch one of my favorite Catherine Deneuve movies as part of my goal to immerse myself in something purely French for at least ten hours a week, when the crackle of the loudspeaker sends me right back into panic.

"Meghan Landry, Bria Kelly, and Robin Ellison, please come to the principal's office for an urgent matter."

My classmates snicker behind their hands. Samara Sligo looks particularly pleased before seemingly remembering that Robin was called too.

I glare at Robin's hookup as I swing my backpack over my shoulder.

"Clink, clink," someone says.

"Shut up!" Noah slams his locker shut.

Samara giggles.

I turn to her, anger coursing through me. If people want to make me out as a devil, then I'll do something actually mean.

I duck into a corner of the hallway and whip out my cell phone. After making sure that no one is around, I send a DM to NWTruther. They can decide what to do from there.

> Hey, fellow Nate lover. Word on the street is that Nate was hooking up with someone in school the night he was attacked. We both know he had a lot of groupies, but here's a name you might not know: Samara Sligo.

Yes, it's petty and vindictive to implicate the other girl my crush is hanging out with. But her snickers were rude, and there's a good chance she was at school late as a member of student government. Plus, she's suddenly friends with Noah, though I've never really seen them hanging out before. She's even been carrying his camera around, taking hallway pictures like the second shooter at a wedding.

But mostly I'm being mean. After the anxiety hangover I've suffered all day, lashing out is one of the few things I have energy for.

I slip my phone back into my pocket and jog to the principal's office.

Robin sits in the waiting area, biting at her cuticles, and Bria paces in front of the secretary's desk.

"What took you so long?" Bria snaps. "We had to wait until you showed up."

"I had something to take care of. You'll see," I reply.

"Ominous, babe," Robin says.

I smile. "Don't be mad. There's a method to my madness."

The madness is jealousy, and the method is rumormongering. We'll see how it turns out. It's not *impossible* that Samara's our girl.

Principal Turner peeks his head out of his office. "Girls, come in."

He doesn't open the door all the way, so we're walking into an unknown situation. Did the security guard tell him we looked at the footage? Have the police come back with additional questions? Are they going to make an arrest? My arrest?

Robin enters first and gasps. Bria follows and starts coughing like she's choking.

I walk in, trying to keep myself from spiraling into panic. At first, I think I'm hallucinating.

Mr. and Mrs. Walker sit across from the principal, staring at the three of us. None of us knows how to act. We all had entirely different relationships with them. Robin doesn't talk about them much, but I know she used to be close with his family. She attended dinners, parties, even a Thanksgiving or two with her parents in tow. Bria only met them once and didn't have a favorable impression. Nate Sr. seemed to take to her, though he warned Nate against getting too serious with a "girl like that." Mrs. Walker's feelings toward me remain eminently clear. She can barely look at me.

I wobble on my feet. Them being here can mean only one thing. He's dead. He's actually dead.

I start to pitch forward, and Robin catches me and guides me to the couch next to Bria.

Principal Turner sits at his desk and doesn't appear inclined to say anything. So here we all are with no one telling us what's going on. My ears start ringing as my heart races.

"Is he okay?" Robin asks. "Just tell us. Look how upset she is. We care about Nate, even if you want to make us the villains."

"Which is incredibly problematic from an intersectional feminist lens, but I should probably keep that to myself," Bria adds, making eye contact with Mrs. Walker.

My laugh helps me slow my breathing. Bria should really rebrand. Our classmates like to call her Bria the Bitch, which she has reclaimed on social media. In reality, she's Bria the Brazen or Bria the Brave. She'll say absolutely anything.

Mr. Walker shakes his head at her. "We're here to talk about our son."

"Is he okay?" I ask. "Please. He's okay, right? Please."

Mr. Walker looks sympathetic. "He isn't awake, but they think he may be soon. His body appears to be healing."

*Oh my God. Mom was called in because he's doing* better. *He's going to wake up. He'll be back and—*

Will the investigation stop? Will the three of us still talk?

Will Robin choose me over him? Will I choose her?

"That's amazing," Robin says. "You came here to tell *us* that?"

She's right to be incredulous. These people, under guise of loving their son, have made all of our lives hell at different points because they don't think we're the ideal partners for their son.

So many parents would be pleased if their son brought one of us home. Independent, ambitious, talented, intelligent Black girls who have goals—that's what makes other people see us as catches, including Nate. But it made us indigestible to the Walkers. Nate is the center of their world, but he was never fully the center of ours.

"When Nate arrived at the hospital, he wasn't wearing his family ring. We heard that he gave one, maybe two of you a ring, and we wanted to know if it was his," Mr. Walker says. "We want him to have it when he wakes up."

I hold up my left hand. "He gave me a promise ring. It's my birthstone. And Robin's."

Mrs. Walker purses her lips. She glances down at her own ring, and I have the darkly comedic thought that maybe her ring is a hand-me-down from one of Nate Sr.'s exes too.

"He didn't give me anything besides a bad reputation," Bria says. "And he was wearing his family ring when I saw him earlier that night."

Mr. Walker flinches. "This is delicate, but . . . do you ladies happen to know if he was seeing anyone else? Not only that night, but in general? We've tracked down Liv Forrest from her phone calls to his hospital room, but she has an alibi."

My face is on fire. I should have picked a random name instead of someone in Nate's extended social circle.

"We have the same question," Robin says. "Keeping track of the different ways we were each betrayed is complicated."

"And we apologize on his behalf," Mr. Walker says.

"Are you withdrawing the restraining orders too?" Robin asks.

"Yes, actually," Mr. Walker responds. "And we're inviting the three of you to see him at the hospital."

What is their endgame? Whichever one of us prostrates herself at his hospital bed first is the one who did it?

Mrs. Walker clears her throat. "Actually, Meghan, your mother and her incredible work at the hospital inspired us. The way she talks about you . . . we—you were underestimated."

Gotta love the passive voice. *She* couldn't have underestimated me. I was underestimated by some unseen force that influenced her perception.

"Thank you," I say tightly. "My mom is pretty amazing."

Mrs. Walker looks at Robin and Bria. "We realize you've been treated unfairly too."

All three of us turn to each other. Relief starts to creep in.

"The portrayal of your relationships with our son was demeaning to all of you, particularly as Black girls. You were unfairly adultified and criminalized because of what happened with Nate, despite the evidence to the contrary," Mr. Walker adds, as if he received coaching from a professor of African American studies before coming to this meeting. And this is coming from a man who barely acknowledged being Black during Nate's entire childhood.

Principal Turner chooses this moment to engage. "On that note, we're all hoping that you will drop your discrimination lawsuit against the school."

I glance at Bria, who holds up her hands. Robin looks surprised too. Who the hell filed a lawsuit on our behalf?

"None of us are involved in that," Bria says. "And if we were, we'd need a lawyer or a parent here to discuss it, given that we are minors."

"If you drop the lawsuit, you can have prominent summer jobs on my upcoming local congressional campaign," Mr. Walker says.

Mr. Walker is running for local election? What a terrible idea. Nate has never been specific, but it's pretty clear there are some skeletons in that man's closet.

Bria doesn't miss a beat. "Bribery is a bad look in politics. Take it from a successful politician."

"Can we see Nate?" I ask. "Like, right now?"

Mrs. Walker nods. "We want there to be peace, especially when he wakes up. It will be important for us to be calm to help him recover. The doctors say that hearing familiar voices is critical. They could make the difference." She looks at me, as if we share a secret.

Principal Turner leans over his desk and hands me a piece of paper. It's a legal notice accusing the school administration of defamation. It's pretty well written, and it's on what looks like official letterhead for Marcher, Andor, and Camina. But I never authorized a lawsuit to be filed on my behalf, and Mom wouldn't have had the time or the money.

Robin leans over my shoulder, reading. Bria takes the paper and squints. She mouths the firm's name to herself.

"I've never heard of this law firm," Robin says. "And I'm pretty familiar with the ones in the area."

"They don't have much of an online presence," Principal Turner says. "If this was a prank—"

"If it was, it wasn't by any of us. Though this accusation would give us ammunition for a real lawsuit, right, ladies?" Bria asks, holding out her hand.

Robin puts hers on top of Bria's and nods. They turn to me. Without really thinking, I put my hand on top of Robin's. She looks so proud of me.

"Noted," Principal Turner replies. "You are free to go."

Robin takes my hand as we make our way back to the hallway. I look over at her and smile. No one else is in the hall, but this still feels big. Publicly holding hands in school has to count as a new step in our relationship.

Bria leads us to the student government office, which she unlocks with her purple-painted key.

The office is basically a collection of four desks and an armchair older than we are. The campaign posters of all the former student presidents are affixed to the walls. Bria's is starting to yellow at the edges, due to the humidity in here.

Samara sits at one of the desks next to Vice President Chad. She seems to be showing him something, whispering in his ear. They both look up as we come in.

"Give us the room," Bria says. It's not a question.

"We're working," Samara replies. "Hey, Robin. Missed you last night."

"I need to talk to you," Chad says to Bria.

Bria may have run on a platform of female empowerment,

but she still needed to bring a rather generic white guy along for the ride to get elected. I don't think Chad has ever contributed a policy suggestion or made public appearances, but he can put VP on his college applications and is first in line to replace her when he's a senior next year. That and his internship at the police station last summer are sure to make him a shoo-in at universities that were all too happy to end affirmative action.

"Give us five minutes, and then you can tell me whatever you want. But first, *out*. Both of you." Bria's face is a bastion of steely resolve.

Samara practically has steam coming out of her ears. She looks to Robin as if Robin is going to defend her.

"We'll be quick. Promise," Robin says.

"And you'll call me later?" Samara asks.

"I'm really busy, hon, but I'll try," Robin replies.

"Bye." I wriggle my fingers at her. I take a step closer to Robin, just to be annoying.

This delights Bria, who claps her hands together while Robin tries not to laugh. Fantastic. I'm winning Robin over. Not that I've been struggling to do that, but it still makes me happy.

The second the door closes, Bria looks through the window set in it and shoos the two of them farther away. Of course, they were leaning by the door, trying to listen. She pulls down the curtain.

"That's not a real law firm," Robin says. "So why would someone serve the school with a fake legal document on our behalf?"

"As a prank. Did you catch the names, my little polyglot?"

Bria shows me the phone note she made in the hallway with each of the names.

Her phone desperately wants to autocorrect several of the words.

I snort. "They're all *Walker* misspelled in different languages."

"Ding ding ding," Bria replies. "So yes, a well-done fake. But is it from someone who was trying to help us, or is it a sick game by NWTruther?"

"We should look at the people with lawyers in their families," I suggest.

"Babe, that's the entire school," Robin replies. "We should see who had a summer internship at a law firm."

That's practically the entire school too. I swear half the senior class had internships in New York for the summer, courtesy of family connections.

Chad strides back in, his head held high and his eyes shining with entitlement. Bria shoots him a glare I know she wishes could actually kill.

As important as this all is, my thoughts keep going back to Nate. We can see him. Shouldn't we all be rushing over to the hospital? Why are we wasting our time with Chad or fake law firms? Soon Nate will be able to tell us himself.

"I'm calling a meeting," Chad says.

Bria huffs. "You could have said that when I invited you back in."

"It's been a few minutes," Chad replies. "And I want to discuss impeachment proceedings. You haven't been doing your job—"

Bria doesn't mask her disdain. It is rich, for sure, to decide now is the time to go up against Bria. With Nate on the verge of waking up and all of us on the verge of exoneration, our popularity stocks are set to rise. His timing couldn't be worse—for him.

"First of all, I always do my job. I do everyone's job. Second of all, this is *school* government. You can't impeach me. That's a legal proceeding. Do you know *anything* about politics?"

"We're going to go. I wanted to visit Nate anyway," I say. "I'm sure you can handle whatever this is without us."

As I close the door behind Robin and me, Bria is already laying into Chad. She is verbally eviscerating him. I almost want to intervene, but I have never heard such a creative collection of insults in my life.

Samara loiters in the hallway, waiting for Robin. When she spies us together, her nostrils flare.

"If you wanted me out of the picture, you could have talked to me like a *woman* instead of teaming up with your side ho to submit lies about me to NWTruther. Nothing ever happened between Nate and me. We're *friends*."

Robin's eyebrows go up. "I had nothing to do that with that. Is that what they're saying?"

Samara ignores the question and glares at me. "So you'll steal anyone's partner, huh? Textbook slut, swinging it around and ruining everything."

"I'm not the one sidling up to Nate's vulnerable brother for clout," I reply.

"Oh, fuck you. He's my best friend and has been since before you knew this school existed. I'm the one who has been supporting him through all of this. Where have you been, *sis*?"

Robin steps between the two of us, her hands up.

"It is not my job to manage *your* relationship," I reply. "I didn't ask to be dragged into this incestuous social situation. Call me a slut one more time, I dare you. See how it goes. I really will ruin everything."

Samara clutches her necklace as if I've threatened to stab her. She looks to Robin like, *Can you believe her? She's so scary.*

I've put Robin between a rock and a hard place, and for the first time I'm not sorry. I don't have any loyalty to Samara. As far as I know, they've hooked up once or twice. Why am I the one being blamed if Robin can't make her own decisions? The idea that I can bewitch the most popular kids in school and make them act contrary to their beliefs or personalities is absurd. I'm simply trying to survive here, and I keep getting dragged into drama that isn't mine.

Well, this one is partially mine. I sent the DM. But I didn't "steal" Robin, the same way I didn't "steal" Nate.

"But you were here that night, Samara. Pretty late, as I recall, based on your texts," Robin says. "So it's not impossible."

"I'm not interested in men, so yes, it is," Samara replies.

"I thought you were bi," Robin says.

"You assumed that because you can't conceive of someone who isn't attracted to Nate Walker," Samara snaps. "So keep my name out of your mouth and your fingers out of my DMs. Clearly, you've found someone else to screw . . . over."

She pushes open the door to the student government room. Inside, Chad is almost in tears.

That can't be good. Bria should watch her back. Her vice president and her secretary are both pissed, and I'm willing to bet they'll take it out on her. The only question is how.

Robin sighs. "That was messier than I intended."

"As messy as you accompanying me to see our comatose boyfriend together?" I ask.

"Somehow, no." She smiles. "Come on; I'll tell coach I'm sick. The team barely wants me at practice anyway. Let's go wake up our man."

## 25

**BY THE TIME WE ARRIVE AT THE HOSPITAL, THERE ARE** a couple of local news crews outside, and several members of the boys' basketball team are idling by the entrance. Did the Walkers give a freaking press release that Nate *may* be waking up soon? Jesus, why is everyone here?

Robin circles the lot and finds a spot between the entrance and the ambulance bay. We may have to find another way in. There's no way we can get through the front door without everyone noticing us. Plus, they're Nate's teammates, the same guys who spray-painted my locker and have been whispering behind my back for months. How many of them knew about his other flings?

"How are we going to handle this?" I ask. "We can't face all of them."

"Of course we can," Robin says. "We were invited."

"Robin... you don't know how it's been with them. I—"

"I do know how bad it's been. I could regale you with stories of what they did when Nate and I broke up or when Bria came on the scene. Or when Nate and I got back together. Or when you started dating Nate. I promise that you're not the only one they've targeted."

I know that I'm not the only one the guys have gone after, but this all feels so overwhelming. If Nate turns out to be okay, will things get better? Once he confirms that none of us attacked him, will we finally get a moment to breathe? Can I worry about my stupid college applications instead of a court date?

For the first time ever, I kind of wish Bria was here. If there's one thing that could scare Nate awake, it's the sound of all three of our voices in the same place at the same time. He worked so hard to keep us apart, to make sure that our paths barely crossed, but now we're bonded together, and he's going to have to deal with all of us before getting any one-on-one time.

When the Walkers said Nate was going to wake up, I was thrilled. I'm also completely petrified of seeing him. I started our fight. He shoved me. If he remembers any of it, I'm probably the last person he wants to see. Or second to last, after whoever attacked him.

How am I supposed to act with him? Should I be the dutiful doting girlfriend I was before, or do I have a right to demand answers? Do I wait until he's released from the hospital before airing my grievances? Am I still his girlfriend?

Robin tosses me a hoodie from the sweatshirt graveyard in the back seat of her car. There are at least seven thrown across the seat, from Burke field hockey swag and college sweatshirts to a random shirt from someone's Bat Mitzvah five years ago. I think I spot a Greenpeace logo on one, though I'm pretty sure Robin's family money originally comes from oil. The one she gives me is fitting. It's from the Shakespeare club's production of *Antony and Cleopatra*: doomed love, betrayal, and ultimate destruction. I feel called out, though I don't know why she even has it. There's no way Robin has ever been in the Shakespeare club.

"Um, did another one of your lovers leave this?" I hold up the sweatshirt.

"Nah, I did makeup for the Shakespeare club freshman year. Still do sometimes, when Janet asks me to help her out. You know they don't have *our* shades," Robin says.

"So you have access to the props closet," I say.

Robin's eyes dart sideways. "No. I'm not *that* involved."

I slip the sweatshirt over my head and try to settle the uneasy feeling building in my body. Here I thought Bria was the only one of us close to the theater because of Janet. But Robin has a secret connection. One she didn't mention. Bria didn't mention it either. Does she even know her perfect baby sister has been bonding over Fenty beauty products with the girl whose reputation she helped tank?

How much more entangled could we all get?

There's an urgent knock on the car window, and I nearly jump out of my skin. We've been found out, or we're double parked. *Oh God, was this all a trick to get us to the hospital so we could be arrested?*

Bria stands outside my window, her acrylics insistently tapping against the glass. Jesus, how did she get here so quickly?

I roll down the window.

"Are we going in or not?" Bria demands.

"Meghan is a little nervous because of the crowds," Robin says. "Basketball guys."

Bria snorts. "The guys are nothing. It's their freaking girlfriends I can't stand. Do you know how many times I had to pretend that Jess had an interesting thought? And I was only with Nate for a couple of months. Truly a hellscape."

"I don't want us to get swarmed if we're recognized," I say.

Bria grins. Of course she has a solution. Knowing her, she either has a security guard who can sneak us in or she's about to suggest we hide in body bags.

She holds up three plastic bags, and I open my car door to accept one.

I unzip it part of the way and stifle a cackle. She's brought what look like nun's habits. We're supposed to sneak into the hospital dressed like this?

"Janet's idea," Bria replies. "These are from when they did *Sister Act* two years ago. They were in the back of the costume closet. No one will miss them for a couple hours. Let's hurry up."

I've never felt more ridiculous in my life, and my body

is already on fire from the warmth of the sweatshirt. If the Walkers are here, they are going to love this. The irony is just too great. And if we're caught, NWTruther is going to have a field day.

Mila is going to flip. Actually, all my sisters will, but Mariana will find this funny, and Molly will send me TikTok jokes.

Robin adjusts my veil and then does the sign of the cross over my chest. I think Bria may pass out from a lack of oxygen to her brain, given the ferocity of her laughter. As if I look any more ridiculous than the two of them. We'd all be excommunicated from the Catholic Church with equal fervor.

"Maybe we should show our faces wearing these. It'd be transgressive. You know, reclaiming our innocence, our virtue." Bria adds dramatically, "For feminism."

"Oh hell no. This thing is polyester. Come on, sisters. Let's go," Robin replies.

We keep our heads bowed as we make our way through the parking lot. We have to nudge each other every few seconds when one of us gets the giggles. For the first time, I really believe that we're all friends. Maybe even the kind that could last beyond this.

When we pass through the double doors, I reconsider everything.

*Geez, is the entire basketball team here? Don't they have practice? And the cheerleaders... Wait, the field hockey team is here too, Liv included.*

Robin catches my gaze, and a chill passes through me. All

these people wouldn't be here on the chance that Nate could wake up.

"He must be awake," I whisper. "Nate is back."

"It's like this more often than you'd think," Bria replies. "Not that I've been hanging out at the hospital."

"Awww, Bria, should we tell Nate that you actually care?" Robin asks.

"Don't you fucking dare," Bria replies. "I have cultivated a certain image with him and everyone else that I'd like to keep going. Especially since *Chad* is trying to mount a challenge for my presidency."

Bria says *Chad* like his name is a slur. I don't know that I've ever seen her more disgusted, and she's been boring holes into the back of my head in AP Lit all quarter. Plus, she's eaten more than her fair share of questionable bake sale confections in pursuit of the presidency. Her stomach should be rock solid at this point, and her disgust tolerance should be off the charts.

"What does he have on you? Why does he think he can suddenly take over?" I ask.

"He's always thought he could take over. This is simply the moment I seem most vulnerable. But joke's on him. I have contingencies in place," Bria replies.

"Which are?" Robin asks.

"None of your business. You'll find out," Bria replies. "Keep on my good side, ladies."

I'm surprised she has a good side. I assumed there was only her bad side and a position of neutrality.

A couple of players are sitting, wearing pins with Nate's face on them. Who had pins made?

Bria glares at them, her eyes barely visible beneath the costume. "I had those made as a joke when we were dating," she whispers. "I don't know how they got them. They were in a box of stuff that I left at his door after our breakup."

So these buttons somehow made their way from the Walker house to the varsity basketball team. The Walkers may be a lot, but they're not tacky. And Nate definitely wasn't handing out buttons of his face to his teammates.

Robin clears her throat, approaching the guys. Bria reaches out to grab her by the veil, but the material slips through her fingers. Robin keeps her head angled toward the floor.

"Peace be with you," she says, throwing her voice up an octave and adding a regionally inaccurate Parisian accent.

"And with your spirit," several of the guys reply in unison.

*Since when does Robin speak Catholic?*

"May I ask you nice young men where you found those buttons? We would love to use them to . . . pray . . . for the young man," she says.

"They were for sale on Instagram from a fan account for our friend," one of the guys says.

Bria covers her mouth to rein in a gasp.

"Thank you," Robin says, and returns to us.

The receptionist watches us with a faint sense of bemusement. I recognize her. She graduated from my old high school three years ago. She hands us the sign-in sheet.

"IDs, ladies?" She looks us up and down and lowers her voice. "We were told three young women would be coming to see Mr. Walker, but I wasn't expecting the coordinated outfits."

"Have you been on social media lately?" Robin asks.

"I have." She looks at me, and her smile fades a bit.

Great, so she's heard *everything*. I don't remember her that well, but maybe she's someone's older sister? Or the news that one of our star athletes died last year has spread beyond the current student body.

She cocks her head toward the set of double doors behind her. "Room one forty-eight."

We hurry through the doors. The moment they close behind us, we each throw off the veils.

Bria makes quick work of folding them into perfectly symmetrical triangles and holds them against her chest. I wonder if she went to military camp or something. I've never seen creases that smooth outside of a movie.

Robin, standing between the two of us, holds out her hands. She nods, and we each take one. We're in this together.

She leads us the down the hallway. It's almost as if she doesn't notice the doctors and nurses who're watching our procession.

As we approach room 148, there are more medical staff milling around. Either there's an emergency or a medical miracle. Here's hoping for the latter.

"Ready?" Robin whispers.

"Ready," Bria says.

I nod. I don't know if I can force words out at this point. My heart is pounding. All of the blood in my body feels like it's rushed into my head.

We push open the door together, step into the room together. Wires are coming out of Nate's body. His face is a little ashen, and he looks thinner than when I saw him last. But it's been more than two weeks. It's not like he's keeping up with his macros right now.

I feel a swarm of emotions: care, love, anger, sadness, relief that his eyes aren't open. Fear that they won't ever open again.

I drop Robin's hand before she can drop mine. When I turn my head, I see that Bria has done the same.

The power he has over all of us is almost embarrassing. Actually, it's very embarrassing. But I love him. I still love him, and I don't know where this is going to go.

His eyelids flutter like he's in REM sleep. Like they could open at any moment.

I clear my throat. "Hey, Nate. It's me, Meghan. I've brought some friends. You won't believe this," I say.

"Hey, Pumpkin Head," Robin says. "I've missed you. I'm pissed at you. But as your day one, I'm here, ready for you to explain and to hear what you think about me and Meghan."

I shoot her a look of protest, but she shrugs. I wonder how much he knows about her sexuality. He knows nothing about mine beyond what he's been a part of. I always made it seem like I was Nate-sexual. As though I'd never been attracted to anyone besides him, even though I'm sure he knew that wasn't true.

I wanted him to feel like the only person in the room. Though I'm realizing he rarely made me feel the same way.

"Nathaniel," Bria says, dragging out the second half of his name. "It's your bae BK. I'll say it because of the situation we're in here, not because I endorse the nickname. But I'm here too. Shocking, right? The three of us are sort of getting along. Even with Meghan, which is surprising. She's more layered than I thought."

"Thanks," I say. "I think."

"I was talking to *Nate*." Bria playfully swats at me.

The heart monitor beeping seems to speed up, but maybe it's my imagination.

I walk over to the side of his bed, taking in all the freckles on his face. I've missed them—him. I pick up his hand and kiss it, forgetting that we're not alone.

Robin clears her throat, and I look over my shoulder.

Bria hangs back, looking uncomfortable. Not with Nate, but with the hospital in general. Every time there's a beep, she twitches a bit. And she keeps wrinkling her nose.

*You okay?* Robin mouths to her.

Bria shrugs again.

Oh . . . her brother must have been in the hospital when he died. This is bringing up something for her. Yet she still came. Even with whatever baggage she brings to the hospital, she showed up, not only for Nate but for us.

"I'm sorry." I'm not entirely sure who I'm saying it to. Partially it's to Bria for her discomfort. And to Robin, because she has to see me with Nate. It's to both of them for this open display of affection that neither of them seems inclined to get in on.

"It's okay to still love him," Robin says. "I do too. Something just doesn't feel right about it anymore. Not only because of you. Don't worry. Robin Ellison doesn't get whipped."

"I don't want him to get an even bigger head," Bria says. "Hey, Nathaniel—I'm over you. In fact, I'm doing a date auction with the basketball team. Who would you pick for me?"

"Nate, babe, I think I want to date your girlfriend," Robin adds. "Thoughts on that?"

My face burns with embarrassment and pride. I want to date her too.

"You're going to have to fight for me, Nate," I say. "You've got a hell of a competitor."

Robin smiles at me and something squeezes my hand.

I gasp and begin jumping up and down.

Bria looks horrified, like I've lost my mind.

I lift Nate's hand.

Robin's eyes widen. "Oh my God, did he—"

"He squeezed my hand," I say.

Bria shakes her head. "You probably imagined it. There's no way."

I look back at Nate. His face is still the same; at least, I think it is. Does he have the ghost of a smile on his lips? He always loves being the center of attention, especially with pretty girls.

"Nate, I bet you want to prove your bae BK wrong. She doubts you," I say.

"Call me that again, and I will use the power of my presidency to destroy you," Bria replies.

"Ooh, keep that language to yourself, or I'll tell Chad," Robin says.

"And how exactly can you destroy me? My reputation is already tanked. Unless Nate wakes up and proposes," I reply.

I probably shouldn't joke about that, given Nate's precarious health. He might flatline to avoid us.

Robin and Bria move closer, and Bria, after a moment, grabs hold of Robin's arm.

I squeeze his hand again while they watch. And we wait. And wait. And wait. It feels like an eternity. In reality, it's probably twenty or thirty seconds. Time is an illusion as we wait for some sign.

Then the sign comes. He squeezes my hand again, and we collectively gasp. This time he holds it for a few seconds.

One of the doctors bursts in. "We heard yelling."

"He squeezed my hand, twice! I'm Meghan, his girlfriend." I look at Robin and Bria, who both seem bemused. "One of them, I guess."

The doctor goes over to his heart monitor and begins checking his vitals. Everything is looking good, though his heart rate is starting to climb.

From what I can gather, this means he's probably going to wake up soon. But they don't want too much excitement around him, especially since we don't know how he'll wake up or what he'll remember.

He could have to relearn everything: walking, swallowing. Basketball. Who we are. Will he remember the night of his attack? Will he be able to tell us what happened? Will he remember our relationship? Who will Nate Walker be when he wakes up from this? And what will he want moving forward?

Will he want me?

Robin does. She has been nothing but kind to me, protecting me through all of this. Shouldn't that be enough? Why am I so confused about who I want to be with? Robin has shown me all the qualities I want in a partner. But Nate represents the life I've wanted for myself. The picture-perfect coupling and future.

Am I ready to be queer out loud after all of this? I'm not ashamed of being bisexual. My mom might be surprised, but she wouldn't be upset. My sisters have already accepted it. It's normal to them. But it's a shift from the life I envisioned. And after all of this, would people think I tricked Nate? Or would everyone think I'm confused and I don't know what I want?

The truth is, I don't know what I want or who I want. It's not because I'm bisexual. I'm in an unusual situation with two unbelievable and entangled options. It's also because of the choices I've made in how I present myself. I've played the stereotypical meek feminine role to perfection and almost never let on that it was a lie. Who am I in a relationship when you take impressing a guy out of it?

Decisions are hard. Knowing who I want to be when this dark cloud dissipates is harder. Whoever I turn out to be, I hope I like her. I've never truly liked the fake Meghan I've been projecting. Other people may have, but I've always felt a little sick, burying myself to play the perfect little girlfriend. And it hasn't saved me from abuse or bullying.

It's time for Meghan Landry to be the real Meghan Landry. Screw being liked for being someone I'm not.

Letting go of Nate's hand is hard, but I do it. I can do hard things. I'm not walking away, but it's time to start letting go.

**I GO BACK TO THE HOSPITAL THE NEXT DAY AND OVER** the weekend. Actually, I spend most of the weekend by Nate's side. I bring my laptop and talk him through the last of my supplemental essays. I read him the most ridiculous NW Truther captions and tell him our different theories. Part of me hopes he'll wake up if I read him the right one.

Robin and Bria stop by individually, but they don't stick around. Bria cracks a few jokes but retreats with a well-timed phoned call from Janet. Robin comes with her parents, who wait outside and decline to meet me.

I'm the one who stays.

I stay when his family visits and even force myself to make small talk with his mom. I pretend to care about basketball with his dad. I help Noah through his French lit project. It feels like they're finally starting to accept me, and I only hope that Nate can hear it.

Maybe it will be different when he wakes up. Noah and I have started texting since I started visiting the hospital, little things like memes. We're becoming actual friends.

We've been in limbo for days, since it seemed like Nate was coming out of his coma when he started responding to my touch. And, as if someone has spread it around, the NW Truther account has barely posted any stories. But Nate still hasn't opened his eyes, and that scares me more than any of the other stuff.

On Sunday afternoon, it's just Mrs. Walker and me sitting on either side of his bed, each holding one of his hands.

"I misjudged you, Meghan. Of all the young ladies, you've really dedicated yourself to Nate," Mrs. Walker says.

"We all care deeply for Nate, even if Bria and Robin aren't here to say so. It's a lot—and not the most conventional of situations."

"He should choose you," she says.

"And I have to choose him back. We'll see. But no matter what, I'll be here for his recovery, even if it's as a friend," I reply.

Mrs. Walker kisses the top of Nate's head. She nuzzles her cheek into his for a couple of seconds, then stands up to wipe the tears from her eyes.

"I'm going to get a cup of coffee. Do you want anything?" she asks.

I shake my head.

She gives me a small smile and takes a long look at Nate before leaving the room with her purse.

I lean into Nate's ear. "All right, she's gone. You can open your eyes," I joke.

"About to squander all that goodwill," a voice says from the doorway.

I startle. It's Noah, holding a container of cookies.

"Oh, you're baking now?" I ask.

Noah snorts. "In our home I'd never be allowed to do anything other than grilling and chilling on Sundays. That's why Mom likes *you*. You're the closest she can find to a Stepford wife for Nate. And you're not even that much of a pushover."

He makes cracks like this sometimes, and I pretend they don't sting. Even if I *dress* like a Stepford wife, I don't want to be one. And if that's what the Walkers think of me, I wonder why I stay.

"Oh, thanks, backhand-compliment me like you're my own sibling," I say. "Ow."

Nate squeezes my hand again, this time more tightly than before.

Noah notices. "With that hand strength, he'll be back on the court in no time. We should install a little hoop on the back of the door for when he wakes up. Make it homey while he recovers."

"And play '99 Chicago Bulls games on repeat on the TV," I reply.

Noah holds up the cookies. "Familiar smells are supposed to help. He has always loved macadamia nuts."

"If you didn't make them, they're safe from whatever atrocities I assume you'd commit in a kitchen," I tease.

He sticks out his tongue and moves the container underneath Nate's chin. He takes out a single cookie and holds it near Nate's nose.

I might be hallucinating, but I swear I see his nose twitch.

Noah drops the cookie back into the container. "I'm going to see if I can find some air freshener. Mom uses a special one on his gym bag because it smells like *ass*."

"It's not *that* bad. Just stale sweat. I wore his jersey, remember?"

"You got the cleaner one, trust me. I almost did an article about it as a joke at the beginning of the year before the season started," he says. "It was going to be 'Life as Nate Walker's Jersey.' He was superstitious about washing it, so it got used over and over but was never given that extra TLC, like his multiple girlfriends. But there was no space in the paper for it, and then once the season started, well... everything blew up."

"So am I a dirty piece of fabric or a good luck charm?"

As he chuckles, I go over his words in my head. He said "at the beginning of the year." At the beginning of the year, we didn't know that Nate was seeing all three of us. But Noah might have. So much for Noah being on my side.

He seems to recognize what he said, and his eyes widen. "Meghan, I'm so, so—"

"You *knew*. All those times we sat outside waiting for him to get out of practice, you never thought to mention that Nate was dating other people? I thought we were friends, Noah, I really did. Especially now."

"We are," he replies. "That's why I made sure you saw those photos at the yearbook party. I wanted you to know about the rumors."

"The rumors that you started? You pitched that idea, didn't you? That's how the entire school found out before we did. You slipped up at newspaper, and the other writers told their friends."

The guilt on his face tells me everything I need to know. The three of us looked like idiots while everyone else heard it from the horse's brother's mouth.

"I didn't mean to," he says. "I am sorry. I never would have if I knew how much I'd actually like you."

"Robin and Bria didn't deserve it either, no matter how you feel about them. We may have been pawns to Nate, but you should know better."

"So should he," Noah says. "Why does he get away with it?"

"He doesn't! Look at him!" I reply.

Noah folds his arms across his chest, glaring at me. His family ring catches the light, and he tucks it under his arm so it's out of view.

"You're always defending him. He cheated on you, humiliated you, but you're still here. Imagine if he had a fraction of that loyalty."

It's a slap in the face, even if it's true.

"Being here to support him is the right thing to do. Same reason you're here, right?"

"He's my brother. I'm here because I have to be. Family

is different. You can leave. You can be happy. Why won't you do it?"

"You know that's not fucking fair, Noah. I thought you liked having me around."

"I do. You just deserve better."

"*Stop it!*" Mrs. Walker stands in the doorway, shaking so hard that her coffee might spill. "Have some decorum, both of you. Meghan, I thought better of you."

I hang my head, ashamed. This isn't the place. And in front of Nate? He doesn't need this either.

"I'm sorry, Mrs. Walker. I got caught up, I—*ow*." I look down at my hand. Nate's squeezing it again.

I turn to look at his face. That's when it happens. The eyelid flutters that I thought were part of his sleeping start to slow. And then, over the course of seconds, his eyes start to open.

I scream, scaring the absolute bejesus out of Mrs. Walker and Noah. Noah's eyes widen as he figures out what's happening and runs out of the room, yelling for a doctor.

Mrs. Walker grabs the edge of the bed to keep from fainting. There is no doubting it now. Nate is waking up.

He stirs, his pupils dilating. He reaches for the tube in his throat.

*Oh no, I've heard that people feel like they're choking and have the impulse to pull out the breathing tube.*

I put my other hand around his to stabilize him.

His machines start beeping urgently. His blood pressure spikes like he has hypertension.

"It's okay," I say. "You're okay. Just keep breathing and the doctors will come in and help. I know the tube is uncomfortable, but it's to help you breathe. Your mom and I are here, together."

He seems to nod, though there is panic in his eyes.

I kiss him on the cheek. "Remember how we meditate together?" I tap my finger on the back of his hand to try and get our breathing in sync. "Just breathe. Noah's getting a doctor."

Three doctors burst into the room as Nate's hand goes limp and his blood pressure plummets.

"Oh my God, oh my God," Mrs. Walker starts sobbing. "My baby! My baby!"

"You both need to go," one of the doctors says. "Now!"

I drop Nate's hand and speed over to Mrs. Walker. She has a death grip on the hospital bed. I rub her back and gently pull her arm.

"We have to let the doctors work. He's awake. That's the big hurdle. Let's trust them, okay? It's going to be all right," I soothe her.

It's a lie, maybe. I don't know that everything will be all right, especially not with the image of Nate's horrified eyes lingering in my brain. But Mrs. Walker needs him to be okay. The alternative is too horrible to consider.

Noah appears on her other side, and he starts whispering. He pulls her hand with a little more force, and we're able to lead her into the hallway. His eyes fill with tears, which he keeps trying to blink back.

"We can't go to the waiting room," Noah murmurs. "There are too many people out there. Rumors will start."

"I'll check with one of the nurses," I say. "My mom has connections, remember?"

We end up being taken to a back waiting room that's shared with the neonatal unit. The wall is covered in storks and sunshine, the exact opposite of how we're all feeling.

Mrs. Walker won't sit. She insists on standing, her face pressed against the glass between us and the babies. She stays glued to the window, watching as those little humans try to figure out how to exist outside of their mothers. She's still crying, but silently. A few people are looking, but no one bothers her.

"You've been here for a long time," Noah says to me. "Why don't you go home and get some rest? I'll text you when there's an update. And I'm sorry for what I said. I don't think he'd be awake without you here. Thank you, Meghan."

"The moment there's an update." I tell him. "No matter what it is."

"I promise. I owe you that. You'll be the first to know, sis."

"Thank you. I'll tell Bria and Robin. Maybe come back with them," I reply. "I owe them that."

He doesn't respond.

Finally, I just nod at him. I'm going to do it regardless.

By the time I get back to my car, I'm ready to pass out. I haven't been sleeping amazingly. I haven't since last year. I'm emotionally drained.

I dial Robin's number first. She answers on the second ring, almost too eagerly. I know she's not answering because she wants news about Nate. She wants news from me.

"Hey, babe, you still at the hospital?" she asks.

"Yes, but can we loop in Bria?"

"A sentence I never thought I'd hear you say. Yeah, hold on; I've got you."

I'm almost certain that the call will go to voicemail. For someone who claims to always be available to her constituents, Bria takes an absurdly long time to answer her phone. By the time she picks up, I'm almost crawling out of my skin.

Before Robin or I can speak, Bria launches into what can only be described as a tirade.

"So you saw it, I assume?" She doesn't wait for a response. "I can't believe him. He's such a fucking Chad. Because he's Chad and he's, *ugh*, I hate him. I want his head on a spike, and I think you should support me on that. He's going to accuse *me* of corruption? Based on what? Racism, that's what. He is so entitled. He thinks he deserves to be president. This Nate stuff was just the excuse he needed. Can we get revenge on *him*? He can't spread lies like this."

Robin and I are both speechless. First of all, I have no idea what she's talking about, but I can put enough of the pieces together. I almost want to mute the call and look at Instagram, but that's not what's important right now.

Bria puts on a "bro" affect, mimicking a lazy approximation of a mid-Atlantic accent with a dash of stoner thrown in. "'Bria Kelly is a scammer who is using your hard-won votes to advance her own agenda.'" She returns her voice to its normal register, minus the hysteria that forces it up an octave. "He didn't give *any* indication as to what that agenda is, but I'm sure if you were to press him on it, he'd say the woke agenda or some shit. And hard-won votes? Like the students of Burke had to fight for the right to vote! He's a rich white dude. He's boring and unimpressive and jealous that I am so much more fabulous than him."

My head is spinning. But at the same time, how do I interrupt whatever stream of consciousness she's spewing? And how do I tell her that Nate is awake?

"You'll figure it out," Robin says. "Should we listen to what Meg—"

"Oh, here's the catch. Get this: he's saying that he has some information that would make my presidency completely untenable. Obviously he didn't use the word *untenable* because his vocabulary is limited, but that was the implication. It's something about the people I associate myself with, which obviously includes you two. So I think he's going to try and start another rumor about our coven of witches attacking Nate," Bria rants. "How are we going to get ahead of this?"

"We don't even know what *this* is. There's no evidence of anything. The three of us are clear, right?" Robin asks.

"Well, the only person who can vouch for us is unconscious, so we're not in a great position," Bria replies.

I clear my throat. This could not be more uncomfortable, not only because of what I know but because there's still a giant question mark in our timeline of that night. Two of the three of us are probably in the clear. I'm not. Also, I don't really give a shit about Chad. Like, sure, he sucks. He's annoying. He probably has nothing on us. He is truly irrelevant at this point.

"He's not," I manage to spit out.

"What? What are you talking about?" Bria asks.

"Nate woke up," I reply.

Robin gasps sharply, and Bria goes silent. We may have all hoped, but I don't know that any of us felt sure that Nate would wake up. And now that he is awake, will he be able to say anything? Does he have brain damage? What happened after I left?

"You saw him?" Robin asks.

"I was there when he opened his eyes. He was scared of the breathing tube, and then . . . um . . . well, his heart rate, you know, it was a lot. He . . . he went into crisis, and the doctors had to intervene. I'm in the parking lot waiting for an update from Noah."

"He's dead?" Bria asks.

"No. At least he wasn't when I left," I reply.

*Am I doing a bad job of explaining this? Obviously I'm upset. This is all so overwhelming. It probably is for them too.*

"Should we come? Are you staying? Are you okay?" Robin asks.

"No, we're supposed to wait for word from the family. I just don't know what to do. Noah told me to go home and rest. I'm tired, but it feels wrong to leave."

Bria sighs. "You can't fill anyone else's cup if yours is empty. Noah will update you, and if . . . *when* he's okay and conscious, we can face him together. Finally get answers about what happened and who did this to him. Go home. Your sisters will be waiting."

She's right. I should go home, and when they're ready, when Nate's ready, we can talk.

I have to believe in some kind of higher power. I've waited this long for Nate to come out of his coma. I can wait a few more hours, even a few more days. What's important is that Nate woke up, and I was there when he did. He had some comfort while he was conscious, and that has to mean something, doesn't it?

**I STAY HOME FROM SCHOOL THE NEXT DAY, SACRIFICING** my perfect attendance record. I couldn't sleep Sunday night and have been so nervous that there's no way I can imagine sitting through an AP class.

Mom allows it, mostly because she feels guilty for not being able to tell me anything about how Nate's doing. I know that she's back on his care team after a personal request from the Walkers, but she's been keeping HIPAA compliant, to my complete anxiety.

In reality, I assume there's not much to know. Noah's one text update that told me there wasn't an update. Nate's still alive and in some kind of limbo that they're waiting to see if he can get out of. This feels worse than the limbo we were in before. We had a taste of victory that was snatched away quickly and violently.

I spend the day scrolling through social media, but only of me, Robin, Bria, and Nate, like a narcissist. I think I've watched every single TikTok and Instagram Reel about us, read every tweet and social media post from inside our school community.

The theories are incredible. If these people put a fraction of the effort they put into fleshing out ideas for what happened into, like, solving our school's social-emotional crisis, we would be okay. NWTruther is my best friend. I scour those posts the closest, along with the tagged photos and comments.

NWTruther's posts almost always come at the end of the school day, typically between one of the last two periods and the start of after-school activities. There are some sporadic ones that may have been scheduled posts.

All the comment activity seems to occur between ten and eleven p.m., with the occasional comment during the after-school activity hours. So it stands to reason that whoever is running the account takes part in some after-school activity that limits their free time for most of the evening—and has them actively working with little downtime.

NWTruther is probably either an athlete on the main roster, committed to practices and games, or involved in theater, either as a main character or as part of crew. Newspaper, debate, government, and model UN don't typically go that late, and the newspaper staff is also friends with Noah. What kind of friends would do that to him?

Although... if Noah spilled the beans to some people on the newspaper, and those people are also in other clubs...

I pull up the school website, and my hands begin to shake. I open the pages for theater and all the fall sports. Then I pull up the newspaper staff roster to cross-reference. Noah is the main photographer. Other photographers come in on a part-time basis when needed. We know that Noah was the one photographing the pep rally and probably the game afterward. But there were multiple teams playing that night, and he couldn't be everywhere.

I shoot him a text. Hey, I hope you're hanging in there. The night of Nate's attack, who else was photographing the games? Did they have their own equipment, or returned it to the school?

The newspaper staff is surprisingly small, but there's a lot of overlap with other clubs. Just not the clubs that had me suspicious. A couple of athletes do a column for the paper every once in a while, but nothing consistent. The editor in chief is also on the debate team, and her second-in-command is a part of model UN.

My phone buzzes.

> There are a few cameras that we can check out and bring home for 48 hours. Idk who else was working.

Then a second message. No news yet.

Ugh. I guess the cameras thing is helpful. Maybe. But how could he not remember who was working on such a crucial night?

I narrow my suspects to three people. First, Alain, of yearbook and student government fame, is also on the boys' frisbee team and sometimes contributes to the paper. This is also how I discover that we have a frisbee team. Second, Liv, Robin's and my mutual nemesis, covers spring sports for the paper and has a consulting editor position. And finally, Lily, the yearbook editor who thought tormenting me at a club party would be fun, writes an advice column. I can't imagine anyone I'd like to take advice from less.

Rolling over onto my stomach, I finally return Robin's and Bria's texts from earlier in the morning in our newly minted group chat with my three suspects. Two of the three of them aren't news, given our previous interactions with them, but this is still potentially new information.

So this is what you're doing instead of suffering through Mr. Garson's King Lear?? Bria responds.

Is this healthy 4 u? Robin asks. I'm worried.

Is any of this healthy?? What is health at this point? I haven't slept in like two weeks. I'm subsisting on caffeine and rage, Bria responds.

Robin emphasizes Bria's text but doesn't add anything else.

Liv certainly has motive as a potential past lover of Nate's. She also hates Robin and has turned her wrath on me more than once. She's quit field hockey, though, and her posting habits don't appear to have changed. Though if she's smart, they won't. I was using her name to call Nate, and if she showed up at the hospital, there's no reason they wouldn't have let her in.

She might have communicated with the Walkers, gotten some information.

Alain is a bit of a wild card. He's involved in a lot of activities and, at least according to his Instagram, seems to show up at most parties. He has a diverse group of friends from a variety of clubs. His connection with Nate is tenuous. Maybe they have mutual friends. But Alain doesn't have much of a motive, besides being messy.

Lily is the most confusing to me. She maintains several social media accounts. She has her personal one, one for her three cats, and one for the yearbook. She's posting all the time on all of them, including during the times the NWTruther account has been posting. It just doesn't make sense.

None of them make sense. At least, not perfectly. But they're all I have. Who else could be running the account?

My phone buzzes again. How Bria is able to respond so quickly while in our English class is a bigger mystery than who is behind the account. Mr. Garson is a well-known curmudgeon about modern technology, hell, modern anything. Bria's a special one for sure. She must be working on pure intimidation. He does get a little eye twitch when she raises her hand.

Alain has been exceptionally thirsty lately. Asking me my opinion, wanting me to comment on the record. It'd be dumb to be running the account and trying all that, but . . . he's not the brightest, Bria says.

Robin's three dots appear and then disappear at least four times. She's in study hall, I'm pretty sure, and has relatively free rein to use her phone. She's usually quicker with her responses. God, now I'm analyzing her text habits? I'm down bad. I really am.

> I'll comment later. Gotta check something, Robin texts.

I throw my head forward onto my comforter. She's so infuriating. I want to know what she's up to all the time, what she's thinking. I want to exist in her head.

I want... her.

The TikToks I've watched the most aren't the conspiracy videos. They're of Robin and me. People are maybe shipping us? Which is super weird since we're real people. But there are several videos of us just near each other, even from before everything happened with Nate. Apparently I've always had stars in my eyes for her. And she... oh my goodness. One of the videos has a group photo from a party we both went to. I didn't realize she was in the picture, but she is four people down from me. At first, I thought she was watching Nate, or Nate and me, but no. She's looking at me.

I shake my head. I can't focus on Robin right now, unless she's a suspect in Nate's attack. She is a member of the field hockey team with a connection to the theater, but it's tenuous at best. She's only involved with Janet, who, though weird, probably didn't attack Nate. What would her motive be? Retribution for Bria? Bria can get retribution for herself. But Janet could have made the buttons. Maybe she saw them as an ironic fashion choice or a funny subversive comment on her sister's relationship.

Unfortunately, no one on the boys' basketball team will talk to me, so I can't ask if Janet was hanging around Nate after school.

I'd have to use a proxy to find that out. Which is doubly unfortunate, as I don't really have friends to act as a proxy. My closest connections at Burke are my perceived coconspirators. I've already texted Noah against my better judgment, but he hasn't responded.

The buttons have started appearing on social media too. The people wearing them have started using #prayersupforNate in captions. So I should work backward. Follow the hashtag on Instagram and TikTok and see when the posts began. Maybe then I can figure out when the buttons made their way into the mainstream and narrow down where they could have come from.

This is definitely more productive than AP English. Probably even AP European History. I can study for the test. Hell, I've read half of the texts both classes require for fun. I'm honing my primary source analytical skills. Or is social media a secondary source?

After a good half hour of scrolling, I have two big takeaways. First, the hashtag is only four days old, so this is a relatively new development. Second, the hashtag popped up after we learned that Liv had hooked up with Nate and left the field hockey team. That may be a coincidence, but something tells me we need to take a closer look at her.

Liv hasn't been posting much beyond the occasional cryptic story. She's never worn one of the buttons. She's one of the most popular girls in school. She hasn't been hiding publicly. *She hasn't been hiding* publicly.

I look at her tagged photos. For someone who managed to have a secret tryst with Nate, her social life seems to be on full display via other peoples' posts. She's the connector between several different clubs. People gravitate toward her, at least under the influence of alcohol.

How many photo shoots can one person do by the ping-pong (beer pong) table? And does she own anything other than a red leather miniskirt and brown cowboy boots? It's a uniform that she wore to at least three different events this past weekend. Her father is the CEO of a venture capital company. She's done tours of her closet on her TikTok. Why no outfit change?

I scroll past the last four weekends. I end up in the summer. She's still wearing that same outfit. The only thing that changes is the top.

That outfit has never made it onto her personal grid, just tagged photos.

This is getting weird.

Can you explain Liv's obsession with her one party outfit? I text Robin and Bria.

Being basic, Bria responds.

Something she saw on TikTok. There was some trend over the summer, Robin replies.

Oh great, now I have to figure out what trend would result in a bootleg cowgirl outfit being Liv's go-to. Will it come up if I google *annoying same outfit*?

Bria responds with several question mark emojis. What kind of abomination is this??

Okay, completely unhelpful. New plan. Time to turn to the most online person I know. Well, two of them.

In our "Sisters over Misters over Dicksters" group chat, I pose the question with a couple of screenshots of Liv's tagged photos. I ask my sisters, mostly Mariana and Molly, if they've heard of this trend.

Molly isn't supposed to have access to her phone during the day, given that she's in middle school, but she's Molly. She either told her teachers that it's an accommodation for a nonexistent physical ailment, that it's an electronic emotional support device for chronic anxiety, or that there's a family member in the hospital who could die at any minute.

Mariana is the queen of texting under her desk or discreetly on her smartwatch while still answering questions in class. If she doesn't answer within three minutes, we're supposed to assume she's been kidnapped.

Molly responds first, even though I know she's supposed to be in gym class. Ew no. Who even wears leather? Double ew.

Mila pops in. She's in study hall and is the most attuned to the rhythms of the group chat. Why aren't you participating in handball?

You're not allowed to play handball on your period, Molly replies, as if that's the most natural statement in the world.

You're not on your period . . . Mila replies. And what does handball have to do with it?

She's right. We're tragically all synced, and Mom definitely takes extra night shifts four to five days of every month.

My MALE gym teacher doesn't know that and believed me when I told him there's a rule. Molly inserts a smirking emoji for extra effect.

Oh, Molly. She's too smart for her own good, but it's deeply hilarious. Her gym teacher is clearly an indictment of our reproductive education system, but damn. That's a good one.

Yes, the #fthepaps challenge, Mariana replies. Molly, didn't u use the period excuse last week for dodgeball?

I have a period disorder. Lasts 5eva, Molly replies.

Mila texts me separately in our "Oldest Sisters" text chain. We've really got to rein her in before she gets in trouble.

Probably, but she's just being a kid. It's not like she's lying about anything serious. Molly hasn't brought home a grade below an A-minus in three years. But I guess I haven't brought home anything below an A either, and look where I am.

I'm on social media enough, not a crazy amount, and I've never heard of this challenge. Are there deeper corners of the internet for the people whose phones are basically fifth limbs?

Okay, #fthepaps seems to be some kind of challenge where people channel their inner celebrities and wear the same clothes whenever they're in public so that all the pictures appear to come from the same party and therefore are less valuable in the rumor mill? It's pretty nonsensical to me, but I guess it was all the rage. Most people appear to have stopped, but not Liv.

Hmm... when did Liv start? And does Nate fit into this?

I scroll back through her tagged posts. She wore a pair of

yellow leather pants and a black crop top to a party in May. Her eyes tell me exactly how many sheets to the wind she was.

There she is with Robin and the rest of the field hockey team, including Lily for some reason. Robin looks like a hostage with Liv's arm around her. Did she already know at this point? Ugh, Liv and Lily, a match made in my nightmares. And they're in somewhat matching outfits? Was that on purpose? Are they, like . . . friends? As Molly would say, double ew.

Liv is even in a picture with Janet, shockingly. Janet, who is dressed like she's a cast member on *Little House on the Prairie*. She stares off into the distance like she'd rather be anywhere else.

Noah makes an appearance in the tagged photos too. He looks tense. He's in group shots with Nate, some of the basketball guys, and several of the field hockey girls.

In a few photos, Nate has his arm around Robin. In the corner of one, I spot Janet glaring at them, while Liv laughs on the other side of the photo, holding up a camera.

Damn, whoever has been tagging these photos is really doing the Lord's work. Even if you're on the fringes of a picture with your face blurred, they'll make sure everyone knows you were there. It's helpful, especially given how many photos Liv is tagged in with my other suspects. She's cozied up to Alain in some of them. Like they were a couple at some point.

But in the blurred pictures, she's in the back of the room, looking serious. And even when she's alone, Nate is usually somewhere nearby.

*Is this the night they hooked up? Or one of them? Is that why*

*Alain was so willing to talk to me at the yearbook party and give me a heads-up? He knew what it was like to get screwed by your significant other. He knew what it was like to have Nate Walker fuck with you.*

That gives him one hell of a motive. Though how would he have done it? He's not in drama club and doesn't have access to the props closet. He would've needed something with a hard base, and we still don't know what that was yet.

So if Liv and Nate were hooking up around this time, why would that make her suddenly decide to #fthepaps? What is the connection?

And when did Robin find out? When did the threatening note end up in Liv's locker? I'm sure someone has a TikTok conspiracy on it; I just have to go back into the archives.

My phone rings, and I ignore it. I've got to figure this out.

Whoever's calling is as invested as I am, and the ringing continues.

Finally, I look down. It's Mrs. Walker calling me.

*Oh my God.*

"Hello? Mrs. Walker, I'm so sorry I missed your first call. Is everything okay? Is Nate—"

"H... hi, sweets."

My heart stops. His speech is slow and halting, his throat probably rubbed raw by the breathing tube, but it's Nate. I'm talking to Nate.

I gasp. "Baby. Oh my God. *Nate.* I'm so happy to hear your voice. I've missed you."

"Missed...y...you...too," he replies.

"You were the first person he wanted to call," Mrs. Walker says in the background. "He felt your presence. He heard your voice."

I hold my breath. Nate is awake. He's awake, he remembers me, and he can talk. Nate is awake. He can tell us...oh my God. He can tell us!

"Can he—Nate, can you—"

"Mem...ory...spot...ty" he replies.

"He doesn't remember all of the details about that night," Mrs. Walker says. "That's why he felt so driven to talk to you first."

The implication is clear. She knows about the fight we had, but Nate doesn't. At least, he doesn't remember yet. Will he still want to talk to me when he does?

"That's okay. You're back, and that's all that matters. I'll come right down. Mrs. Walker, can I come?"

"Give it a day," Mrs. Walker says. "The doctors want to keep running tests, and he needs to rest."

"Can I tell...the others?"

Nate groans. "R...Robin? B...ria?"

Mrs. Walker sighs, and I can practically hear the gears turning in her head. She doesn't want me to tell them, but she knows I'm being polite. I'll tell them either way.

"Yes, though they should keep their distance for a bit, please," Mrs. Walker says.

"T...tell th...em. Hi," Nate breathes.

I restrain a laugh. "I will, babe. I will. They'll be happy to hear it. We all...we all are so happy you're getting better."

"We'll see you tomorrow after school?" Mrs. Walker suggests. "Please keep this between the three of you. I don't want a deluge of students at the hospital."

There's a sharp intake of breath, and I hear Mrs. Walker murmuring to Nate.

"L... ove you." It's the clearest thing he's said this whole time.

I burst into tears, and Mrs. Walker hangs up before I can say it back. And now, after everything, I don't know if I can.

## 28

**I SPEND THE NEXT DAY VIBRATING WITH EXCITEMENT. I** haven't really slept and don't feel the need to eat. I'm so wired that I end up at school forty-five minutes early because I don't know what else to do.

Yesterday was a blur after the call from Mrs. Walker. Part of me wanted to keep investigating on social media. Another part of me figured I should probably finish my last supplemental essay for my college applications. After Nate said he loved me, I didn't tell Bria and Robin he was awake and talking, even though I had permission to. There was some piece of me that wanted to keep him to myself. A special little moment just for me.

When I woke up this morning, I realized that was a huge betrayal and I needed to tell them. But a phone call or text could never suffice. It needed to be in person. Robin usually tries to squeeze in a few reps on the leg press before first period, and Bria practically opens the school to pretape the morning announcements before anyone gets here.

I pass the multimedia room first, and there is a light on. I don't hear voices, so I assume Bria is still drafting her remarks. My hand trembles as I knock three times.

"Busy!" Bria says from inside.

"It's Meghan. And it's important."

After a few seconds, the door swings open and Bria stands in front of me, applying mascara. She normally looks annoyed with me, but now she looks *really* pissed.

*Oh shit. Did she find out from someone else?*

"Good to know you're alive," she says. "You went MIA yesterday. Interesting how you're quick to ask questions and slow to answer them."

"I'm sorry. I really am. I was overwhelmed and sick to my stomach, and . . ." I step into the room.

She lets the door close behind me, and the room practically shakes with the impact.

"And? You'd better have some earth-shattering news," Bria replies.

"Nate is awake."

She looks at me like I've lost my mind. "Yeah, girl. We know. You told us that days ago. What is going on with you?"

I sigh. "No, Bria. He's *awake*. His mom called me yesterday, and I talked to him. He told me to tell you hi."

Bria's jaw drops. She grabs her paper with her morning remarks.

I shake my head.

"This is fucking huge. Everyone is going to freak out!"

"And that's exactly why Mrs. Walker asked me not to tell anyone. I got her to make an exception for you and Robin. But no one else. Please. We can see him after school," I reply.

"But—"

"This is not your opportunity to show up Chad or whoever. This is for us, okay? Only the three of us."

She groans, but she's conceded. She slides into her recording chair, her eyes still wide. How is she going to record this morning's announcements without letting it slip, either with her words or her face? She motions for me to start the camera as her acrylics tap against the desk.

Can I count this as a production credit for my college apps?

I press record, and Bria compels her face to smile. She cocks her head to the left like in her campaign videos. Then, like a pro, she delivers her lines. She throws in a joke or two, playfully rolls her eyes at the input of the administration, and very seriously reminds everyone that their votes count, even though she's no longer running. A message to Chad, no doubt.

She very carefully folds her paper, and the smile drops. When I move to turn the camera off, she shakes her head.

"For the first time in a long time, I'm not recording this alone," she says into the lens.

*No, no, no,* I mouth, waving my hands. I do not want to be on camera. I don't even know why she'd want me to be on camera in the first place.

"I've done a lot of things alone at this school. I've weathered more than you all know, including a lot of difficult situations that many of you have caused," she says. "During my tenure as president, I've been on the receiving end of more complaints to the administration than any president in Burke history. At least, according to your social media comments." She chuckles. "And I'm sure many of you are like, *Of course she has. Bria's the bitch.* Keep playing the video. Don't be a coward because I said *bitch*. But these complaints were never about anything I've actually done. In one week alone, there were fourteen complaints about my hair. It changed, and y'all were like . . . 'Oh no.'"

I have to stifle a laugh. White students have always been fascinated by our hair. Whether it's straightened or natural, curly or kinky, in a protective style or relaxed, there are so many questions, so much unwanted touching. So much, *Is that your real hair?* or *Wasn't it different yesterday?* Or the boys who thought it was their place to tell me that they preferred my hair one way or the other.

How often did I change how I looked because I thought it would make some boy like me?

They never really liked me.

Bria takes a deep breath. "A year ago, I committed the ultimate sin. I fell for a guy." She scrunches her nose. "I've cultivated an image that is impenetrable and cold. You think that I don't care, but I do. And I cared about him. I still do. It was stupid of me to believe that he and his girlfriend were on a break. It was even stupider of me to keep it going when I knew that they weren't. But don't we all make mistakes? Why is it that ours—mine, Robin's, and Meghan's—are the worst of all? Why do we get singled out? I know why. You all know why, even if you won't face it."

I try to keep from gasping. Is she really doing this? She's going to release this recording to the entire school in fifteen minutes.

"Being the ice queen was protective. But it hasn't saved me from people, like my own vice president, trying to overthrow me. Or from my own sister running an Instagram account that accused me of attempted murder." Bria's eyes shine with tears.

*Oh my God,* Janet? *Janet is NWTruther? Why on earth would she even do that?*

"You have pitted us Black girls against each other, and I'm done with it. I think I can speak for all of us when I say that *we're* done with it. You were so successful that you convinced my sister that I needed to be taken down a peg for her to succeed." Bria takes another deep breath and swiftly wipes a tear away from the top of her cheek.

*She can't be resigning.* That would be so unlike her, though I'm sure she'd welcome the peace. She can't give in to the people who have been waiting for this.

And Janet. How could Janet do this? There must be some other reason. Sisters fight. Hell, my own sisters think I'm a demon every other day, but they'd never purposely humiliate me or want people to think that I had committed murder. And if I *had* committed murder, they'd cover it up and use the power of social media to make it look like I wasn't even in the country when the crime happened.

"You wanted me to be the villain," Bria continues, "and I played the role for a long time. I don't intend to resign. So come at me. You won't win." She motions for me to stop recording.

I end the video and stare at her. I can't believe she did that. I can't believe she did that for all of us.

"You're brave, Bria. I really admire you," I tell her.

She wipes another tear from her eye. "This past year has really sucked. For you too, I know. I mean, how many attempted murders can you rack up?"

"You always seem so unrepentant. Like you are doing what you want," I reply. "You've been the calmest through this."

"What was I supposed to do? I already looked horrible. So I leaned into it. It's easier to pretend to be what everyone thinks you are instead of your true self. I regret that it made things so bad between Robin and me. We were in Jack and Jill together, the only two kids from this district. We were supposed to be in this together. I wanted to be strong through this, for her."

I hold out my hand and Bria squeezes it. She gives me a small smile.

"Speaking of, should we try and find Robin? I haven't told her yet."

"Sure. Plus, I have a video to drop off and another errand." She opens her backpack to reveal our borrowed headpieces, courtesy of the theater costume closet.

"You're going to wreak absolute havoc before nine a.m.," I tease.

"Would you expect anything less?" she asks.

The thing is, I absolutely wouldn't. I love that she's burning it all down and making everyone confront what they've put us through. I just hope that someone is really listening. I hope that they change and it's better for the next group of Black girls. For the underclassmen.

"I'm glad you stood up for all of us. It has really sucked. And fighting with you and Robin made it ten times worse," I say.

She scoops up her bag and exports the video from the camera to her phone. There's a swoosh as it sends.

My own phone starts dinging like windchimes, which I don't remember programming. I fumble around in my bag. I'm getting a FaceTime.

Bria glances at my phone. "Oh my God!" She swipes to answer the call.

Nate's face fills the screen. Some of the color has returned to his face, and while he still has a nasal cannula for oxygen, he looks ten times better than he did the last time I saw him.

"Nate, babe, hi," I say. "Are you okay?"

"I'm . . . getting there."

His speech is clearer. His voice is still scratchy, but there are fewer pauses. This is my—our—Nate. He's really back.

"Well, hurry it up. Do you know what we've been going through while you've been gone?" Bria replies, stepping into frame.

Nate smiles. "The two of you . . . together . . . That's unexpected."

"Oh, wait until you hear about her and Ro—"

I elbow Bria in the side, and she mouths *ow* at me. Do we really need to drop the news that two of his three girlfriends are not only bisexual, but that they're kissing sometimes? He's still fragile.

Nate's smile fades, and his eyebrows knit together. He's frowning at me, much like the way he did when I brought up the cheating rumors before he was attacked. It almost plunges me back into the anger I was feeling that day.

"You found another guy? Already?" Nate asks.

God, he sounds so hurt. My heart pangs for a few seconds before I remember why we're in this situation and who I'm standing with. I guess Nate and I are not technically broken up, but I'm not going tit for tat with his bad behavior.

"No. Of course not." I glare at Bria. I hold up my left hand, the promise ring glinting in the light. I'm not entirely sure why I'm still wearing it, given the situation. At this point, it seems worse to take it off. Then everyone would know it was a stunt to make myself look more innocent, to make Nate look more committed, while we were under investigation.

"You're . . . wearing it?"

"Of course I am. Unless you don't want me to. It seemed like a fitting good luck charm while we waited for you to wake up."

Bria bites her lip so she won't laugh, and I move to kick her. What am I supposed to say? That I thought it'd be good PR?

The smile spreads across his face again. "I'm glad you didn't . . . listen to me. It's perfect, and so . . . are . . . you," he says. "Sorry, BK."

"No offense taken," Bria replies. "I know where I am on the roster. Always did."

Her eyes tell a different story. She's hurt, and I wish I could take that away.

A couple of weeks ago Nate was my sun, and now I don't know what to do next. I can't break up with him while he's in recovery. Who knows how long he'll stay in the hospital? And then he may need physical therapy, cognitive coaching. He'll have to make up weeks of school assignments and try to get back in shape to play basketball. I'm going to have to stick this out until we leave for college. Then we can break up so we aren't tied down during those formative years.

"I'll keep wearing it, then," I tell him.

"You're coming . . . later?" His voice sounds weaker. He's getting tired. I'm surprised no one has ushered him off the phone yet.

"Right after school." I pause. "We can all come, if you want."

God, I'm so nervous. I'm talking a mile a minute, and Nate's taking a few seconds to process what I'm saying. Why am I tearing up? Am I finally having a breakdown?

Nate is about to respond, but then there's a noise off camera. He looks to the side. His eyes widen.

"What . . . are you doing . . . here?" he whispers.

The phone shakes, and the call ends.

The thing is, I don't know if he ended it or someone else did.

Bria and I exchange a look. Mine is panicked, while hers is vaguely amused.

"Who do you think it was?" I ask.

She shrugs. "Could be anyone." She shows me her phone, which is open to NWTruther's page.

On it is a simple message, black font on a hospital-white background. NATE IS AWAKE!

Bria sighs, and her mouth twitches. As someone who also has sisters, I recognize that face. She wants to throttle Janet but is also trying to figure out what could possess her to do something like this. She can't turn off her love, even when there may not be any trust left.

"How did you find out?" I ask. "About Janet."

She rubs her temple. "I found dozens of the buttons in her backpack. I shouldn't have been looking, but something felt off. Then I asked to borrow her phone for something stupid and found the login."

"Why would she do it?" *Your own sister* is the part that stays silent between us.

Bria's eyes well up. "I don't know. The most insecure parts of me think that it's because of something I did. Because I wasn't a good enough sister or she was mad at me for something I don't remember. But to be honest, I think she enjoyed the drama. She's so rarely the center of attention except onstage, and this was a way to take back the narrative, especially since I've been confiding in her a lot the last two weeks. I gave her *so much* material. I should have known."

Would Janet really be so vindictive? Maybe it was a misdirected attempt at protecting Bria by making it seem like all three of us could be guilty. It's not like the account was bashing only her or targeting her more than the rest of us. Could it be like my sisters taking over my accounts to make me look like a saint?

"I'm sure there's a better reason that we haven't thought of," I say.

"Princess Meghan, always optimistic. Sometimes people are cruel. Don't you know that by now?"

I lay my head on her shoulder for a moment. "I do, but I don't want that for you. I don't want that to be the reason."

She shrugs me off gently but takes my hand. "Let's go find our third."

Students are starting to mill around in the hallway with three words on their lips: *Nate is awake*. It's the talk of the school already. I don't know how Janet even found out. Maybe Bria let it slip over the weekend? This is jubilant. He's *awake* awake. He's functional. He can talk. He can tell us.

*Oh my God, why didn't we ask him what happened while we were on FaceTime?* I suppose it can wait until we're there in person after school. I'm sure the police will speak with him if they haven't already. It will be over. And after everything, I'm going to get the guy whether I still want him or not.

As we walk down the hall, hand in hand, the whispers stop and everyone stares. We're no longer the black widows.

Jess and Andy practically sprint over to us, their faces red. I can't tell if they've been crying or doing a couples' workout.

"Is it true?" Jess's voice moves up several notes on each word. "He's awake? He's okay?"

Bria rolls her eyes, and I almost do the same. These two didn't give a flying fuck about Nate two days ago. Andy was thriving, playing in Nate's position. I use *thriving* loosely, given that Nate averages thirty points a game and Andy has made three shots in as many games.

Bria fields this one. "So you two deface school property, which is on video by the way, according to my security guard friends, and spend weeks, nay, *months* bullying Meghan, and *now* you're acting like we're all friends? Hell no. Back up."

*Hold on, is it really on video? And if so, how did they get away with it? What else is on camera?*

"He's my best friend," Andy says, but he can't make eye contact. "Who are you?"

"She's Bria freaking Kelly, and she's closer to Nate than you have ever been," I snap. "If you were really his best friend, then you would have been supportive and tried to get to know me instead of bullying me behind Nate's back."

Jess looks mortally wounded, and the worst part of me wishes she were. She's such a slimy, two-faced viper. She's sure to show up at the hospital, pretending that she's been my chief source of support in these trying times.

"*Bully* is a strong word," Andy says. "You're bullying us by making these accusations. You know that, right? I can tell Nate everything—"

"Try it," I reply. "I'm the one who has actually been by his side. I've been sitting by his hospital bed, talking to him. Where have you been? Trying to steal his spot on the court and doing a piss-poor job of it."

Jess makes a choking sound, and I'm half convinced she's going to pull a Liv and kick me.

Before she can try, Bria grabs my arm and drags me through the library, gasping with laughter.

"I love spicy Meghan. Why weren't you always like this?" she asks.

We slow down when the librarian glares at us for our fast, loud power walk. But Bria is on a mission. Destination: girls' locker room to find Robin.

My brain wanders. *How long ago did she finish her workout? Is she sweaty? How much can she lift? Could she deadlift me?*

I'm flush.

Bria holds open the door to the locker room, and I go in first. I make my way back to where I know her locker is.

Robin isn't here. I don't even see her gym bag.

Footsteps approach, and my heart skips a beat. But it's not Robin.

Liv Forrest chomps cinnamon gum, and the sound of her chewing practically ricochets off the lockers.

Bria, who is several inches shorter than I am, steps in front of me with her arms out as if she's going to fight off Liv. I'm appreciative, but it's a little comical, knowing what I do about Bria's physical fitness journey from her Instagram.

"Robin isn't here, obviously," Liv says.

"Why are you? Didn't you make a big show of quitting because you were yet another girl hooking up with Nate?" Bria adds, "Maybe the one hooking up with him the night he was attacked?"

Liv holds up her field hockey stick, and I flinch.

"Returning my equipment. Chill, I'm not going to hit you," she says.

"Don't act like it's out of the realm of possibility," I reply. "Your feet and I are well acquainted."

"Yeah, I shouldn't have done that. But you're so smug and self-important. All three of you are."

"Takes one to know one," Bria replies.

"Why aren't you two gathered around Nate's hospital bed, pretending to be dutiful girlfriends?" Liv asks.

She says it with such disdain, as if she isn't the same as us. She did exactly what all of us did, except she knew what she was doing. No. I've got to stop this. It isn't her fault. It's his. We have to stop blaming each other for what Nate did to us.

"Liv, I'm really tired of this. Can we call a truce? Nate screwed all of us over. Let's not fight about it anymore," I say.

She holds out her phone, which is open to Find My Friends.

Oh. It wasn't disdain for us. It was for Robin. Robin, who isn't in the locker room because she's at the hospital.

*Robin is with Nate right now.*

My stomach drops.

"Come on," Bria says. "We have other places to be."

She leads me out of the locker room.

*Was Robin the one who walked into Nate's hospital room while we were FaceTiming with him? Why wouldn't she tell us she was going? What else hasn't she told us?*

Bria reaches into her pocket and pulls out a key. It's attached to a skull keychain that says, *Out, damned spot!*

I wonder if Janet gave it to her or if she took it in retribution.

Bria fumbles with the storage closet lock, which sticks. She groans and motions for me to give it a try.

She pulls the costumes out of her backpack while I try to turn the key. I brace myself and push against the door with my shoulder.

The door squeals as it opens, but only slightly. The bottom is blocked by a disorganized collection of props. How would you ever find anything in here?

Bria ducks beneath my arm and squeezes herself into the closet. She carefully lays the costumes on a shelf before sneezing at the dust surrounding us.

I turn on my phone's flashlight, shining it at the props on the floor. Maybe after one of your students is attacked, you shouldn't have two beat-up looking skeletons lying on the floor three doors down?

Bria scrunches her nose as she picks through some of the items.

I move the light around, not entirely sure what we're looking for. Some kind of blunt object? A bone fragment? A bloody baseball bat?

Bria kneels, as the flashlight glints off of something. She gasps as she holds it up toward me.

A gold ring with a basketball. Nate's family ring. How did it get here?

An announcement comes over the loudspeaker, and we both jump. "Bria Kelly and Meghan Landry, you are excused from classes for the day. Your presence is required at the hospital."

*Oh shit. Here we go. I bet Nate's about to reveal what happened, and the police want all of us there.*

Bria shoves the ring in her pocket and whips out her car keys. "I'll drive. Come on."

We run out to the parking lot, nearly tripping over our own feet. I almost run into Lily, who snaps a picture, no doubt to send to NWTruther.

After today, that account is done. So is the investigation. Fucking finally.

# 29

**THE HOSPITAL PARKING LOT IS FLOODED WITH POLICE** cars and local news media, which the police are trying to hold back. Bria is a pretty good driver, but she looks unsure what to do. It probably doesn't help that her phone has been ringing off the hook, mostly with calls from Janet. She has fifty-seven unread text messages from the last fifteen minutes.

I bet her morning announcements caused quite a stir. An unknown number keeps popping up too, and when Bria lets her voicemails play, they make my stomach drop.

Someone is threatening her, saying they're going to out her behavior to her top colleges, to the administration. The voice is robotic, obviously altered by some program.

The limited vocabulary, vagueness, and repetition strongly suggest Chad, and Bria seethes as she drives us to the back of the lot. I notice that she's chewing on the inside of her cheek.

Whatever is happening, it can't be good, especially not for us. And now we're walking in with Nate's ring, the ring that has been missing since his attack. It looks suspicious, and we probably should have left it where we found it. But we still don't have the weapon that the assailant used.

As Bria turns off the car, a thought occurs to me. In the announcement, Bria and I were the only ones called. How did they know Robin wasn't in the building? Is she still here? Is she why the police have been called?

I take Bria's arm before she opens her car door. "What if Robin—"

"I know," Bria replies. "I know."

I'm more scared now than I've ever been. My gut tells me that something is terribly wrong and we're walking into an ambush. Did Nate name one or all of us? Or is this his way of tying up loose ends, wanting us here for a totally non-nefarious reason?

We both get out of the car. Farther from the building, things are pretty quiet. There appears to be a cadre of adults gathering in the parking lot as well, and I recognize several Burke parents.

Bria inhales sharply. "The Ellisons are here."

My hands reflexively fly to my hair, which I'm hoping hasn't started to frizz. Is Robin with them or still inside?

"Robin lied to me the night of Nate's attack. She told me they were out of town," I say.

"Her mom works late, and her dad travels a lot. She basically has carte blanche to have people over whenever she wants. And you're such a goody-two-shoes that she probably thought you needed parental permission to stay somewhere."

*Or she was setting me up to take the fall. I still don't know exactly what happened that night or where Robin was while I was passed out.*

"Do you recognize anyone else?" I ask.

Her face darkens. "My mom is here. I didn't call her."

"Do you think Janet could have . . . ?"

I think Bria might scream. I don't know why Janet would have called their parents, even if she knew Bria was coming here. This is getting too weird. Who's going to show up next?

Bria shoves my head down, and I wonder if I'm at risk of her snapping my neck.

"What the hell?" I ask as we crouch between cars.

She shushes me. "Samara Sligo is parked over there, standing by her trunk with that stupid camera."

My stomach turns.

Bria's phone starts blowing up again, loudly playing "God Is a Woman." She pokes her head up to make sure that Samara doesn't react before turning the phone to silent. She opens her notifications and actually screams this time.

"Fucking Chad. He went through my actual *trash* like the future serial killer creep that he is, and the only reason he's getting away with it is because his dad's a cop."

I snatch the phone from her, thinking that it can't be that bad. Oh . . . but it is. He's posted at least ten times in the last three minutes. They're photos of crumpled paper covered in Bria's perfectly linear handwriting. They seem to be drafts of everything from campaign speeches to AP exam practice essay questions.

"Where could he have gotten these? Do you write speeches in school?" I ask.

"No, he would literally have had to go through my *trash*. In my *house*. How the hell could he have gotten into my house? I certainly never invited him."

We crouch in silence for a few seconds while Bria seems to calculate how dialed-up her reaction should be.

Most of the notes are musings, pointed ones since they are Bria's, where she comments on the culture at the school. It's a lot of what she said during her video this morning, but much harsher. She called people out by name, then scratched them out. She must have a light pencil grip.

"Bria?" I think I have an idea how Chad got into her house.

She waves me off and keeps reading the posts.

What's really going to get her in trouble are her essays. In a commentary on *A Time to Kill*, she basically defends the idea of murder. Of course, these are practice, and she offers perspective on both sides, but Chad has made sure to highlight the most salacious parts.

*Morally, murder is supposed to be black and white. However, in reality and in Grisham's work, there are shades of gray. In a society where you and your family are treated savagely, as subhuman, is it truly wrong to defend your people against those who seek to subjugate you?*

He has also posted her thoughts on intersectional feminism and a handwritten first-draft analysis of *The Autobiography of Malcolm X*.

Everything she wrote makes sense to me, but he's taken care

to frame it as malicious. As the inner workings of a dark, ambitious person who would be willing to kill for her beliefs. A person who hates men, who hates whiteness. A person who, if betrayed, would kill, especially if the person she was up against was at the intersection of whiteness and masculinity.

He's been waiting to release these for a while, clearly, and Bria's morning announcements gave him a perfect opening.

"Bria, do you think Janet—"

Bria screeches. "She is *dead*. I'm going to kill her."

So she already knows how Chad got her drafts. She hands me her phone.

Janet has texted, B, I'm so, so sorry. I didn't know he'd do this.

Bria toggles back to Instagram, where Chad has answered questions about the authenticity of the documents with a carousel of pictures. Pictures of him and Janet kissing and snuggling in what is apparently the Kelly house.

"Shit," I say.

"This has been going on for months, apparently. They were running the NW Truther account together, but he wanted to take more control. She said no and dumped him. But he already had his reserves ready. At least he's not as stupid as I thought. *She*, however, is such an idiot," Bria says.

"Come on," I reply. "I'm sure she had a good reason, or she simply got caught up. You know, the way we did with our no-good boyfriend?"

It's like she doesn't hear me. Steam is practically coming out her ears. She is anger personified right now.

"Like, can you imagine this kind of disloyalty? From your sister? It's incomprehensible. I would never do something like this." She laughs bitterly. "If what happened to me had happened to her, I'd have killed Nate myself. She only wanted to capitalize on it."

"Let's go in. Let's try and figure out what is happening," I suggest, trying to change the subject back to our other big problem.

"I can't slip past my mom, or Robin's parents, for that matter, so we should split up. Meet outside Nate's room in five?" she says.

I nod, even though I've watched enough horror movies to know that we're never supposed to split up. I don't know how she intends to get into the hospital without going through the front entrance. They've really cracked down on security lately, according to Mom.

Oh my God, *Mom*. She would know what's going on.

I duck between a couple of cars and hit her contact. She answers on the second ring, quite possibly the fastest she's ever picked up the phone while on a double shift.

"Are you okay? What happened?" she asks.

Great, my mom thinks I only call her when something is wrong. Though to be fair, it's the middle of the school day. I shouldn't be calling her unless it's an emergency or I'm sick. And I don't call her when I'm sick. Having a medical professional as a parent means that no one ever buys my sick days, and even when I am sick, she expects that I'll get over it with a few hours of sleep and a dose of DayQuil.

Plus, she's a single mom. She has worked, taken care of us,

and quite literally saved lives on her worst days. I can sit through calculus with a little head cold.

"I'm fine. I got called to the hospital. Robin and Bria are here too, along with a hell of a lot of police. Is Nate ready to talk?" I ask.

She sighs, I think with relief. "Yes, and it's been a zoo. Some of his memories are coming back, so everyone's waiting for him to drop the bomb of who attacked him."

"Oh, thank God. Part of me thought something was wrong," I reply.

She laughs. "Me too. See you soon." She hangs up.

As I approach the front doors, I try to keep my head down. I don't know any of these parents, but I wouldn't be surprised if they knew me. This certainly isn't how I want to meet the Ellisons now that I have feelings for Robin. Hopefully we can have a much chiller introduction when we're all cleared. It's obvious which person is Bria's mother. First of all, there are so few Black people here that I can make some inferences as to Robin's versus Bria's parents. Second of all, Bria's style is a carbon copy of her mother's, while Janet has their mother's exact face. Which I only realize because Janet is standing next to her, biting at her cuticles.

I try to avoid eye contact unsuccessfully.

Janet starts towards me, her mouth opening to say my name. Her mother pulls her back, but it's not clear why. I don't think Mrs. Kelly would recognize me.

I'd better hurry and get inside before anyone actually calls me out. We've been pretty insulated from local media, as the frenzy has been mostly online. But with Nate set to tell the world who attacked him in that closet, renewed attention is a certainty. And with college apps coming due, I can't afford to be in the media.

My phone buzzes, and I try to ignore it. But then, like Bria's, it really starts going. Texts from all three of my sisters, in our chat and separately, flow in. Smug texts from my classmates. An apology text from an unfamiliar number.

I open my notifications and see that NWTruther has posted once again. This time, I'm the only target.

With the prominent hashtag #MadMeghan, a video starts to play of me in tears at a school dance, the spaghetti strap of my dress torn, my shoulder speckled with blood. This isn't from Burke.

It's a video from the night my last boyfriend . . .

Oh my God, it stops right when he falls down the staircase. And it's grainy enough that it's impossible to tell if I pushed him.

Sure, I was going toward him with my hands out in front of me. I came close—tantalizingly close, if I remember the moment correctly.

But I never pushed him. And the video is selectively edited to shield the person who did: my former best friend. She was the one who spread all of those rumors and was standing right behind me. She is about Bria's height and barely ninety-five pounds soaking wet. She's not clear in the video, but she was there.

She pushed him because they were hooking up behind my back and she thought he was leaving me. But he didn't. He never planned to. We were both easy targets. In fact, he deployed a lot of the same tactics he used on me with her, the same manipulation. The love-bombing. But it didn't escalate and get physically abusive, like it did with me.

She knew what he did to me, and she still chose to be with him, and for that I never forgave her. Then she pushed him and let me take the fall.

Now someone wants me to take the fall again, but Nate will prove them wrong. Nate will protect me the way no one did at my last school.

I double back before I reach the doors. Hopefully Bria can be patient, because I'm about to be late.

Janet's eyes widen as I approach her, fire in my eyes and my heart.

"Do you act when you play Lady Macbeth, or have you actually lost your mind?" Before she can answer, I continue, "Making up rumors about your own sister is abhorrent. I hope you have a reason besides being petty. Posting a misleading video about an intimate partner violence survivor to reinforce a false narrative for clicks is even worse. My lawyer will be in contact. Defamation is a fun charge to have on your Juilliard apps, no?"

Mrs. Kelly steps toward me, clearly ready for a fight. For the first time in all of this, I wish my mom were here. This may be her place of business, but I have no doubt she'd cuss out Bria's mother for whatever she wants to say to me.

"I don't know what you're talking about." Janet's voice trembles.

"Yes, you do. I came here with your sister, who I assume is

who you got the video from, and saw the receipts. How dare you." I shoot her the look Bria has given me so many times.

Janet actually trembles. "It was his idea to start the account. I posted at first, but it's his now. Meghan, I am so, so sorry."

"So how are you going to make it up to us? Has anyone sent you anything useful?" I ask.

Mrs. Kelly's jaw twitches the same way Bria's does, but she doesn't respond. That's the difference between the two of them, I guess.

Janet's eyes fill with tears, but she nods. "That fake lawsuit. Alain did it, thinking it was a way to defend you? He thought it would get our account to stop. I think he likes you. But after you rejected him, he kept sending material, along with Lily."

"Like what?" I ask.

"Accusations about you and Noah, mostly. Conspiracy theories that you've been hooking up with him. We didn't post any of it because it wasn't true."

"*None* if it was true, and you know that. What you did was beyond cruel, regardless of whose idea it was. I would be ashamed if you were my sister."

Janet's tears fall, and I almost feel bad for her. But then I think of my sisters and how they've handled this. No matter how annoyed they were with me, they would never hurt me. Even Mila, who I have fought with more than any of them, sprang into action to defend me to everyone after last year's accusations.

I still don't know exactly what she said, but I know that it had something to do with who pushed my ex. She claimed she had seen it with her own eyes, even though she was nowhere near the staircase that night.

That's what sisters do.

I turn and stride into the hospital, ignoring the stares.

The receptionist at the desk is about to wave me through, but she stops. "I'll sign you in, but can you hold on a second?"

This is the same girl who was here before. The one from my previous school. Great.

"Is everything okay?" I try to keep my voice bright.

"Your friend, the tall one who was with you last time, has been pacing the hall, furious," she replies. "She's making some of the other visitors nervous."

Of all people, Robin should know not to make herself look suspicious in front of mixed company. At a hospital full of reporters, no less. What has her so riled up? Did Nate tell her that he wants to get back together with me instead of her?

I look at my phone and find that I've been tagged in another post by NWTruther. This time, it's not of me, thank God.

Ah. This is why Robin is so livid.

Chad is really on his game today. NWTruther has posted several threatening notes that Robin left Liv Forrest, including the one with Nate's name crossed out menacingly.

So NWTruther has taken care of Robin and me, and Chad took care of Bria. Someone wants it to look like we all had motive in Nate's attack, but why? Nate's about to exonerate all three of us. At least, I hope.

When I get to Nate's door, it's slightly ajar. I look around, trying to spot Robin or Bria. Even the hall seems quiet, much less crowded than when I've been here before. Much quieter than I'd expect with Nate about to make his big reveal.

Then the beeping starts and builds with startling intensity. And it's coming from Nate's room.

*Oh my God, the monitor.*

I push open the door and run inside.

Nate is coding, and Bria is standing in front of his bed. Robin is frozen in the doorway of his private bathroom.

*Oh shit*. We all know how this looks.

And then so does my mom, two other nurses, and the lead trauma surgeon. They all dash through the door, pushing us out of the way.

Mom closes her eyes and shakes her head at me. "If I don't do this, both of us are getting arrested." Then she lifts her walkie-talkie and says, "Code blue, room one forty-eight. And get the police in here. Potential homicide."

I guess I was right. Today, this investigation ends for good. But we're not getting exonerated. We're getting framed.

## 30

**IT ALL HAPPENS SO FAST. BEFORE I TRULY REALIZE** what is happening, the police round up the three of us and move us to the nearest empty hospital room. I can hear Nate's heart monitor flatline as we walk. The sound of the boy I loved dying replays in my ears over and over even when the police want to start their interrogation.

Someone shouts about needing more space to separate us. My hearing is going in and out like I'm about to faint.

Nate is dead. This time, Nate Walker is truly dead. And somehow, all three of us ended up in his hospital room at the exact moment his vitals started failing.

*Oh my God. Nate is dead. He's dead.* I'm going to be sick.

I haven't been able to get a word out since walking in on Nate taking his last breaths, and Robin and Bria seem to be frozen, their faces different shades of horrified.

Mom looked sorry that she had to be the one to call the police. I suppose I can't blame her. It would have looked much worse if she hadn't, or if she had let me leave. I did hear her tell the officers that she had just been on the phone with me, that whatever caused him to code had started before I arrived. They don't seem particularly interested in that right now.

I gulp for air. How many times can you be a murder suspect and get away with it?

It's a fantastic story, really. Three scorned lovers, one dead boyfriend. All together when he was dying. God, it's so sordid. It'd make an incredible true-crime documentary.

I have to pull myself together. My body wants to give in to panic, but I can't. Breathing techniques aren't going to help me now. I need to occupy my mind, focus. *Focus, Meghan.* Shit. I have to focus on *something*.

Okay. True-crime documentary, let's go. I can hear the voiceover narrative.

*Let's talk suspects, shall we? Number one: Robin Ellison, the OG. Nate hurt her first. They were the "it" couple at the height of their power, and he ruined it by cheating with at least two different women. One of those women was one of the only other Black girls in the school, and the other was Robin's cocaptain. When Robin found out, it was very public and very humiliating. Then, to add insult to injury, he did it all again behind her back when they were supposed to be repairing their public image. Is there a better revenge motive than that?*

*Number two: Bria Kelly, the Anne Boleyn to Robin's Catherine of Aragon. Bria cultivated a perfect, ambitious HBIC image that resulted in her being elected class president four years in a row. The only thing missing was a political partner, someone to take her to the stratosphere of popularity. She nabbed Nate, only he wasn't really hers to have. And a few weeks into that relationship, Bria's entire reputation was torpedoed, and she became the school slut after being the girl boss. Nate never defended her; he let people think that she was a seductive homewrecker. Wrecking him seems tame in comparison, no?*

*Finally, suspect number three: me, Meghan Landry. The wild card who came to the school under mysterious circumstances and immediately ingratiated herself with the most popular guy in school. Nate publicly humiliated her, then shoved her to the ground in front of witnesses as if he wasn't the one in the wrong. She might have killed her last boyfriend too, making her the black widow everyone thought she was. Sometimes evil puts on a pretty face . . .*

One of the officers waves his hand in front of my face, close enough that he brushes my eyelashes.

I snap out of my true crime reverie. This isn't a docudrama; this is my real life. I'm in a hospital room, being told to sit on a hospital bed so a police officer can ask about me about my boyfriend's death. A death I just witnessed.

"Ms. Landry, you have the right to remain silent. Anything you say can and will be used against you in a court of law. You have the right to a lawyer; if you cannot afford a lawyer, then one will be provided to you—"

I zone out again. I've watched enough *Law and Order: SVU* to know how this is going to go. I've also watched enough TV to know that they aren't supposed to interrogate us without our parents present.

"Your mom is downstairs," I hear Bria whisper to Robin. "Along with mine."

"Samara was here with Noah and their parents when I got here," Robin replies. "They went to the waiting room so Nate and I could talk. Nothing happened between us."

One of the officers slams his hand against the wall, causing all three of us to jump.

"This isn't social hour," he says. "Do you understand how this looks? It'd be in your best interest to tell us what you know." He dangles three pairs of handcuffs from his hands.

"My mother, an attorney, is downstairs," Robin says. "As is Bria's mother, and Meghan's mother is the nurse who called you. It would be in *your* best interest to have them here before we answer questions."

The officers exchange a look, and one of them leaves the room. We sit in silence, while the other officer texts. His phone rings, and he answers it, turning his back to us. He speaks in a low tone that I can't hear.

Robin watches him before leaning in to us. "Samara was here with Noah. Apparently they're dating? Like, for months."

Okay . . . weird, given that she was also hooking up with Robin and basically begging Robin to love her. Was it all an act? And for whose benefit? Especially after she insisted to Robin that she was completely uninterested in men.

"Janet's here, and Chad's now torturing us with the NWTruther account," Bria replies.

The officer glances back at us, still on his call. We all pretend to be staring in different directions until he turns away again.

"And before you say anything, I got a text from Nate's phone asking me to visit," Robin says. "He was alive; we were talking. He basically dumped me again, and I went to the bathroom to fix my mascara before his parents came back. And then you two were there."

"Well, there was an announcement over the loudspeaker at school asking us to come to the hospital for an urgent matter after we FaceTimed with Nate, who declared his undying love for Meghan," Bria replies.

*Undying love* is a bit of an exaggeration. Plus, he didn't have all the information. Once he saw the video of my ex and heard all the rumors about Robin and me, who knows how he would have felt. He loved the idea of me, the image I put out to the world. No one has really cared about the real me until Robin.

Robin reaches out and squeezes my hand. Bria, always subtle, elbows me in the ribs.

"You have anything to add about your hospital entrance? You were late," Bria says.

"I was on the phone with my mom, and she said Nate was ready to talk," I reply. "And I told your sister she sucks."

Bria looks impressed, though I would argue that no one should be allowed to insult your sibling but you.

All three of our mothers burst into the room, trailed by the police officer. Mom's hands are shaking, and her face is pale. Her hair is stuck to her forehead with sweat, and her scrubs are rumpled. This is how she looks after performing CPR.

She tried to save him.

A sob escapes from my mouth, and I clutch my chest.

"Here we go with the waterworks," one of the officers says.

"Her boyfriend just died," Mom says. "And she walked in while he was coding. Maybe you haven't seen someone die, but it's traumatic."

A tall, svelte dark-skinned Black woman with a glorious shaved head reaches out and takes Mom's shoulder. This must be Robin's mother. She's too glamorous and beautiful to be anyone else.

"Technically, he was all of their boyfriend, compounding the trauma," Mrs. Ellison says. "What questions do you have, Officers? You aren't taking them to the station, so we might as well do this here."

Each of us is told to recount our steps so far today. When did we get here? Why are we here? Who told us to come? Was Nate alive when we saw him? What did we say to him? Did any of us have a reason to hold a grudge?

Then, as I suspected they might, the police turn their attention to me. Am I aware a video has been made public of an incident at my prior school? *Yes.* Do I remember what happened that night? *Yes.* Can I tell them exactly how it went down, timing included? *I can try.* Do I make a habit of getting involved with boys who choose other girls over me? *Not intentionally.*

One officer's face looks grim as he looks at Robin, then at me, and my stomach drops. I realize where this is going.

"Rumors have circulated around your school that you and Ms. Ellison have a romantic relationship. Can you elaborate?"

Mrs. Ellison's jaw twitches, but she doesn't seem surprised that Robin would be with a girl. The surprise is reserved for my mother, who is stares at me with raised eyebrows.

Great, now I can add *outed by the police* to my accomplishments. You can't make this stuff up, and even if I could, why would I want to?

"Listen—" Robin begins, trying to answer for me.

The officer holds up his hand, cutting her off. "I asked Ms. Landry."

Mrs. Ellison steps forward to intervene.

I can't let them answer for me. I have to do this myself, even if it's invasive. Otherwise, this narrative is going to turn into one about two greedy bisexuals who wanted to be together and turned against the boy who loved them.

"We kissed once," I say. "In the locker room last week. We're not in a relationship, but yes, there is something romantic between us. It began after Nate's attack. Robin was the person who helped me when I was . . . intoxicated . . . and confronted Nate the night of the attack. He shoved me. You can see it on security video from the school, and she helped me up and took me to her house to sleep it off safely."

"And you were together all night?" the officer asked.

"I was asleep. Nate contacted Robin again, but any interactions they had were when he was still okay, as far as I know," I reply. "We suspect he was hooking up with someone else in the school at the time of his attack."

"When did he give you the ring?" the officer asks, gesturing to my hand.

I look down and wish that I had thrown the ring across the hospital parking lot. I'd almost forgotten that I'm wearing it.

"Nate gave it to me a few weeks ago. It's a promise ring. He didn't want me to wear it at first. When we FaceTimed an hour or so ago, he told me that he was happy I chose to wear it. He gave it to Robin first, but we had it resized."

"Did he give you any other jewelry? Any of you?" the officer asks.

What other jewelry would he have given us? He literally recycled the same promise ring for two of us. It's not like he was frequenting Tiffany's.

Then I remember that his parents referenced Nate's ring. They never found it after the attack.

"No, but Meghan and I found his ring in the props closet of the theater department. His has a basketball to represent him. Incredible," Bria replies, pulling the ring out of her pocket.

Mrs. Kelly groans. Admitting to having Nate's ring, even though she didn't take it from Nate, looks worse.

The officers eye Bria hungrily.

*Oh my God. We walked right into a trap and have something of Nate's from the night he was attacked.*

We're done. We're so screwed.

There's a frantic knock on the door, and Janet rushes in before being invited.

"You can't be here," the officer says, moving to block her.

Mrs. Kelly slides between them. "Janet, you have to wait outside," she says firmly.

Janet shakes her head and holds up her phone. It's the NWTruther page.

God. It's her page too. She's also involved. I keep blocking that out.

Bria looks ready to strangle her, which is not the best vibe given the situation.

Mom puts her arm around me and squeezes my shoulder. She whispers something to me, but I can't hear it over the blood rushing in my ears.

The officers squint at what Janet's showing them, and then I start to put the pieces together.

It's the account's inbox, where people have submitted all sorts of tips. Most of them are probably bullshit. And a lot of them seem to be photos of Robin and me. But there are also photos of other girls accused of being Nate's secret lover.

Most of them don't seem to have any merit, but Janet keeps scrolling until she pulls up a series of photos.

They're all of Samara and Noah or Samara and Robin. Most of them seem to be from the same day, since she's wearing the same outfit in each. Or she's doing Liv's weird TikTok challenge—who knows.

"Who is this?" the officer asks.

"Samara Sligo. She's here too. She has been in a relationship with Noah Walker, Nate's brother, since last year. She also had some sort of entanglement with Robin here," Janet says.

The officer raises his eyebrows at Robin. This interrogation is making Robin look like more of a lothario than Nate.

Shit, now *Samara's* playing into the devious bisexual trope? This just keeps getting worse.

One of the other officers takes the phone and begins looking at the pictures more closely. He appears to be zooming in, and I think I'm getting double vision.

"Samara sent in the photos herself," Janet explains. "Or at least they came from her account. She takes a lot of selfies. But these ones of her and Noah? Several of them are taken in a different bedroom. Not Noah's."

She pauses for a moment, and everyone seems to wonder why she knows what Noah's bedroom looks like.

She sniffs. "We did a project together in eighth grade. Don't be weird. Besides, I've seen Bria's photos with Nate. In that same bedroom."

Well, they could have been taken before Nate's accident, when he was at practice or something. It's weird but not unheard of. Nate's bedroom was pretty tricked out, given that he was the golden child.

Something glints in the corner of the pictures. Samara is dedicated to the mirror selfie pose where you keep one hand partially in your jeans pocket while you stare downward.

What would be glinting?

Bria recognizes it first. "Officers, can you zoom in on her hand in one of the pictures? Any of them."

"You aren't in char—"

"Oh, you'll wish I was at the end of this," she replies

The officer sighs and complies with her request. Samara is wearing a ring in these photos. Noah's star.

But in the selfies with Noah, he's wearing a ring too. It's almost too small to see, but unless he had a second one made...

The police searched Nate's room for that ring, I'm sure, as did the Walkers. They probably went through Nate's locker too, his gym bags. But here Noah is, wearing Nate's ring.

He never took off that ring, not even to shower. Not even on the court. He was wearing it the night he was attacked. I remember it from when he pushed me. He wouldn't have taken it off even if he was hooking up with someone.

But somehow, it's in these pictures, and then it was in the props closet.

My heart practically stops beating.

Samara was dating Noah and has been teaming up with Chad. Chad was dating Janet, who has a key to the props closet. The key we just used. One of the three of them must have left the ring there to hide it, but we found it.

Why would they leave the ring in the props closet *now*? My heart starts thudding against my chest.

Who else would have a key to the closet? Did one of them attack Nate?

I clear my throat.

Mrs. Ellison motions for me to be quiet.

Why wouldn't Noah tell me about Samara? We spent hours and hours together at the hospital. He even asked me for dating advice. Hell, he gave me a lot of unsolicited feedback about my own dating life. But he never mentioned Samara... Why?

He had both rings too, and Samara knew about it. Samara,

who has been working with Chad to oust Bria from her position. Samara, who started hooking up with Robin right after Nate's attack...

What if Samara was hooking up with Nate in the closet that night, and Noah caught them? Or Samara attacked Nate, and Noah helped her cover it up because he cares about her?

Robin smacks herself on the forehead, and the officers turn to her, looking ready to swoop in. Like she's the dangerous one here.

"Oh my God," she says. "I'm an absolute idiot."

"Don't say that," I say, assuming that she's talking about having trusted Samara. Samara was infatuated with her too. She played us all. I wouldn't have thought she and Noah were friends until I saw them together at that party. But this? Did she get close to Robin to frame her?

"You wanted to know who else would have had after-hours access to the newspaper. Who else was photographing games the night of the game. Samara. While Noah was at the basketball game, she was taking photos of girls' tennis. I remember because the courts are next to our practice field, and she had the flash on. It was annoying as hell, and I don't think any of those photos were even developed," Robin says.

"Apparently, she's bad enough with the settings that she completely messed up the camera. The newspaper put in for a replacement. I got to approve the budget item. Do you know how much those things cost?" Bria replies.

Mom's eyes widen. She motions for my attention and mouths, *Tapered base.*

*Well, shit. That's the weapon.*

Mrs. Ellison must be a lip reader. "Officers, I think we need to move to another location. I'd also like to call in two of my law partners so each of the girls has legal representation."

*Now* she wants us to have individual lawyers? We've just proven the person who set this all in motion is literally just outside the door. With Noah. Samara had access to Nate today too.

Oh my God. Noah is going to feel so terrible. This could break him. His brother is dead, and his girlfriend did it.

Two officers lead the Walkers in. Mrs. Walker is sobbing, while Mr. Walker seems stoic, glaring at everyone.

Noah just seems uneasy, gripping the strap of his camera. He makes eye contact with me.

I mouth *I'm sorry* at him without fully understanding why. I'm sorry about the loss of Nate, for sure. I'm sorry for what we're about to do. I'm sorry he got drawn in by a dangerous and violent partner. I know what that's like. I always thought we were alike. I never wanted it to be like this.

Noah turns away.

"Noah Walker, hand me the camera and any items in your pockets."

*Wait... This isn't right. Why are they going after Noah? Is someone watching Samara?* Panic rises in my chest. An innocent Black kid can't take the fall for this.

Mr. Walker steps toward the officer. "What is this about? Do we need a lawyer?"

I examine Noah. His camera is new. This must be the budget

item Bria referred to. But what about the scratched one he was using at the pep rally?

Mrs. Ellison holds up her hand. "Nathaniel, respectfully, he needs to be compliant."

Noah closes his eyes. One by one, he turns out his pockets. A couple of five-dollar bills fall out, along with three pennies. At least four receipts, probably for his mocha obsession, float to the floor.

*Way to be unhelpfully helpful, Noah.* Nathaniel Sr. will be mad about Noah's sugar intake, but a mocha a day does not a criminal make. Thank God.

Noah's overstuffed, cracked faux-leather wallet makes an unflattering splat when it hits the linoleum.

I hold back a laugh. I've been begging him to get a new wallet since the first time he bought me a Snickers from the vending machine while we waited out one of Nate's practices. Maybe now he'll buy a new one. Or I could get him one for Christmas. That's a nice idea. Maybe we should invite the Walkers to our place for the holidays. I assume they won't be up for a big Thanksgiving celebration next month, but they might not want to be alone either.

Noah hands his phone to Nathaniel Sr. The screen lights up with a photo of Noah and Samara. That must be new. I've never seen it. I swear I saw his phone at the hospital over the weekend.

Then, finally, Noah flips out the last pocket near the knee of his tragically green cargo pants.

A cracked lens cap clatters to the ground, and Noah bursts into tears.

"I'm so sorry," he says, looking at his father. "I didn't mean to. I shouldn't have..." His body heaves.

Nathaniel Sr. takes a shaky step away from Noah, looking disgusted. His hand hovers over his mouth.

Then a voice speaks up from the corner. "Noah, dear, *shut up*." Mrs. Walker takes Noah by the arm and speaks forcefully through her tears. "He's not going to say another word until our lawyer gets here."

The police start scrambling, but for once, not for us girls.

## 31

**SOMEHOW A WEEK LATER, WE END UP BACK WHERE WE** started. I'm sitting in the basketball stands with Robin and Bria, hoping our jeans don't stick to the metal when all is said and done. Noah was arrested at the hospital, and the Walkers are trying to decide whether to contribute to the case against him. At least, Mr. Walker is. Mrs. Walker has already defended him publicly and privately.

I lean my head against Robin's shoulder as Principal Turner walks onto the court, looking shaky. The past week has been hard for all of us. Nate's funeral is this weekend and will be private, so the school wanted to do a memorial as well.

Bria squeezes both of our hands. Principal Turner introduces the boys' basketball coach, who holds up Nate's jersey.

Noah has tried to call me from his juvenile detention facility a few times. I answered one call just to hear what he had to say. Part of me still wonders how we didn't see it. That all of our suspects were wrong. That the three of us were always innocent. Everything was so muddy.

We thought that whoever attacked Nate must have done it out of romantic jealousy. We missed the most classic story in the book, about a jealous brother whose rage built over time. Nathaniel Sr. was about to announce his congressional campaign, and he'd chosen Nate to be a prominent fixture in the rollout. He was going to star in the campaign ads, even make public appearances. Noah wasn't even asked to take promotional photos. He was relegated to the periphery like he had been so many times.

Samara was an unwitting bystander. She and Noah had something going on for five months, sort of, when she realized she loved spending time with him, but not spending *time* with him physically. As a parting gesture, she ran into Nate outside the locker room after the game. She asked him to talk to Nathaniel Sr. about including Noah in the campaign. Noah, returning from shooting the basketball game, found the two of them together and assumed there was something going on between them. He stormed off, and Samara followed him, explaining what she was actually doing with Nate.

When Noah went back to confront Nate, he was calling Robin to tell her about Samara's request. The brothers argued, and Nate got in Noah's face. He taunted him about being the star, about being the favorite.

That was when Noah hit him with the camera.

Noah sobbed as he explained all of this on the phone. He said he regretted what he'd done, that he wished he could go back in time.

I want to believe him, but I've known too many boys who make false apologies like that.

The police found more remnants of the old camera hidden in Noah's backpack, and Mom was right. There wasn't any blood, but there were skin cells and hair from Nate's head.

Noah kept the evidence. And that's what makes me the uneasiest.

The NWTruther account has been shut down and its contents deleted. Chad was suspended for two days for harassing Bria, and the administration is considering barring him from seeking future school office. *Considering* is the key word, since they are not likely to follow through.

Chad has taken a seat two rows behind us, glaring at the back of Bria's head.

Janet dumped him the day Nate died, and she has been lying low. She's tucked into one of the upper corners of the bleachers, her head buried in the *Macbeth* script she's already memorized. Her excuse, according to her public Instagram apology, was that she thought the NWTruther account would be funny at first, and then she used it as a tool to keep the heat off Bria. That's why the account seemed to target me more than Robin and Bria. I was a slam-dunk suspect. Her declaration had to be public despite the fact that she and Bria are under the same roof. Bria has imposed strict boundaries, so she sees Janet as little as possible. Their parents, while not in favor, haven't done much to deter her.

The basketball coach raises the jersey higher. His voice cracks as he starts his speech. He wipes a tear from the corner of his eye.

"Nate Walker came into my office the day after he graduated from eighth grade," he recounts. "He was already on my radar, given his reputation, but I could never have imagined the way he would impact me in that meeting. He was just starting to hit his growth spurt. He was gangly, and his voice cracked on every other word. But he looked at me with that intense gaze that we all knew so well, and he told me that he was going to be my starting point guard in the fall. Now, if you were around in those days, you know that we already had an award-winning point guard who was going into his senior year. There was no way in hell that this freshman, no matter how good he was, was going to start over a senior who had won state." He chuckles.

I wonder how well I really knew Nate. I've never heard this version of the story. Nate starting as point guard as a freshman was the stuff of school legend, but I'd always assumed there wasn't any real competition.

Robin sniffles. "We were texting all the way up to that meeting," she whispers. "He was so freaking scared. But he pulled it together; he always did."

Coach continues. "We all know what happened next. We just missed out on state that year but took it the next one. Nate Walker wasn't only a first-class athlete. He was a leader. His teammates had a deep respect for him, and they pushed themselves to be better based on Nate's example. Nate was under pressure at all times. He had his father's legacy to live up to. He had to keep his grades up. He was trying to figure out his identity and how he wanted to present himself publicly."

Robin, Bria, and I are the elephants in the room. Everyone knows that we were part of that public presentation, but no one wants to address it.

Andy and Jess sit in the row in front of us, and they keep turning their heads to look back at us. I've never seen so many fake tears in my life. Truly, I hope they join the drama club.

"Nate was a complicated young man," Coach says. "He was damn near perfect as a basketball player, but he was imperfect as a person. We know that he hurt people. We know that he *was* hurt. Something he told me a couple of days before he was attacked sticks with me. He said, 'I feel torn between two worlds, between who people want me to be and who I really am. I feel like I'm constantly pretending, and the only place I can really relax is on the court.

"Nate was a shining star to so many, and he burned so bright that we only got to have him for a short time. That is the worst sadness. No one else will ever wear this jersey number at Burke. Nate may have been number nine, but he was number one in our hearts. Thank you, Nate."

He drapes the jersey over the podium and walks off to the side.

Robin wipes a tear from my cheek. "I know," she whispers.

And she does. So does Bria. We all know this weird, throbbing sadness that has been sitting heavy on us for these last few days.

Several of the basketball players line up to speak and pay their respects to Nate. It doesn't surprise me that the three of us weren't asked to say anything. I half expected Bria to give remarks as class president, but nope. Principal Turner didn't have the balls to say it to our faces, but I've heard that he thought we'd bring negative attention. As if any of these people speaking in platitudes knew Nate better than we did.

It's okay though. We've been stared at enough since returning to school. One, because everyone wants to see how we're reacting to Nate's death, and two, because everyone wants to know what really happened. How did it all go down?

Out of respect for the Walkers, we haven't been answering any questions, despite the media's and our classmates' intense interest. They were bold enough when they just thought Nate was cheating. Lily, now tasked with designing Nate's memorial section of the yearbook, has been particularly brazen. She finally wants my input and even has Alain, who she's on-again with, trying to convince me to help. Alain, who thought maybe I would make out with him if he saved me from our classmates' accusations with a fake lawsuit against the school. Needless to say, I haven't felt so inclined.

Liv is three seats down from us, and she stares straight ahead. She rejoined the field hockey team yesterday, in time for playoffs. Robin welcomed her with open arms and, with a little encouragement and help from Bria, released a carefully crafted Notes app apology about her previous threats. Things are still tense, but they can be on the field together without concern for anyone's safety.

My phone buzzes with yet another alert. This one isn't for a yearbook party, thankfully. The three of us are going to the Walker house to talk about giving a eulogy for Nate, together. Mrs. Walker will be visiting Noah; this offer is courtesy of Nathaniel Sr.

I think he's going to ask us about Noah too. I've talked it out with Mom, who was finally able to tell me more about Nate's condition, when he was injured, and how he died as details made their way into newspapers.

Nate's death was a direct result of the previous trauma *most likely*. He died of a brain aneurysm, which was probably caused by the head trauma, though that's less common. As it turns out, Nate had an arrhythmia, and he was taking off-label blood thinners under the table because his parents didn't know. That could also be the reason for the aneurysm, but we won't ever know exactly.

That hurts. We want there to be a clear answer. Some connection that makes complete sense. But there's not. It's still messy. Bria remembers times when Nate had trouble catching his breath. Robin remembers him getting headaches and double vision. I saw him have unexplained nosebleeds. All symptoms of the arrhythmia or the medication, but also normal enough that they could have nothing to do with his health condition. Maybe we're misremembering.

I still don't remember where I was the night that Nate was attacked. Noah never said anything about seeing me at the school, but I felt something in his eyes.

Robin interrupts my thoughts. "Come on, let's get over to the Walkers.'"

"Thank God," Bria replies. "If I have to listen to another

basketball bro call Nate a *real man*, I'm going to need you to whack me with your field hockey stick until I forget everything."

I elbow her. "You can't make head trauma jokes. We're at a memorial."

Bria shrugs. "Dark humor helps me cope. You know this. We're *friends*."

The three of us stand up, and it seems like the crowd shifts with us.

It took months, and some of the worst days of my life, but I've finally accomplished what I wanted to do at Burke: I've made real friends. They're here healing alongside me.

I've found the friends who will hold me up when it seems like everyone is against me. I've found the friends who always have an extra scrunchie to lend. I've found the friends who will help me bury the past.

They already have, and we're taking our secrets to the grave, together.

# Acknowledgments

Thank you to everyone who took a chance on this story of revenge, love, and figuring out how to operate as a Black girl in a society that often wants us to make ourselves smaller. I hope that you enjoyed the (mis)adventures of Meghan, Robin, and Bria and that we can all support more stories of young Black people across genres.

To my agent, Dorian Maffei, we started our work together in the YA space, and what a time it has been! The journey has been unconventional at points, but you've been by my side and advocating for these characters every step of the way. Twitter is wild, but it brought us together, and for that I will always be grateful. You are a dream agent; thank you so, so much for everything.

To my editor, Annette Pollert-Morgan, you saw something in that first manuscript and went out of your way to figure out how we could form a partnership with this project. You gave great feedback while leaving as much room as possible for the vision

I had, and it has resulted in a book I could not be more proud of. Thank you for believing in me and in these characters.

To the team at Sourcebooks Fire: Aimee Alker, Alison Cherry, and Thea Voutiritsas for these incredible and detailed copyedits, Jenny Lopez for editorial support and answering so many of my questions, Rebecca Atkinson for publicity pushes, and all of the other people behind the scenes who have helped bring this book to life.

To my friends, thank you for all of your excitement around my books. Thank you for allowing me to be my sometimes messy and chaotic self with you all and for supporting the chaos queens I write about.

Mom, Dad, and Adrienne, thank you so much for your continued support and love and for your boots-on-the-ground marketing for all of my books. I could not have accomplished what I have without you, and I am so lucky that the universe chose you all to be my family. Your encouragement and enthusiasm mean the world to me, and I love you all so much.

Sean, you are with me every day, giving me the strength to keep working toward my goals and giving me the space and comfort to rest when I need to. You're my favorite person to bounce ideas off of and laugh with, and I love the life we have built together. I love you, I like you, and I appreciate you.

Finally, to Riley, you can't read this yet, but I love you so much, and I am so excited to watch you grow and learn and become your own person. I hope you enjoy this book someday (but no pressure!), and I hope that you're able to make all of your dreams come true. Mom loves you, and everything I do from now on is for you.

# About the Author

Alex Travis was born in New York and made her way to Northern Virginia to begin her daytime career as a full-time school psychologist. She has a BA in psychology from the University of Pennsylvania and a Ph.D. in school psychology from the University of Maryland. Alex wrote her first book at the age of eleven and has been losing herself in fictional worlds of her own creation since then. Alex makes her home in Virginia with her husband, an outrageous collection of Funkos, and too many books to count.

# sourcebooks fire

**Home of the hottest trends in YA!**

Visit us online and
sign up for our newsletter at
**FIREreads.com**

..................................................

Follow
**@sourcebooksfire**
online